MOM BALL

A SWEET, SMALL TOWN ROMANTIC COMEDY

KACI LANE

Copyright © 2024 by Kaci Lane

All rights reserved.

This is a work of fiction. Names, characters, organizations, places, events and incidents are either products of the author's imagination or are used fictitiously. Any resemblance to actual persons, living or dead, or actual events is purely coincidental.

No part of this work may be reproduced, or stored in a retrieval system, or transmitted in any form by any means without written permission from the author.

For Blake and Lane — my favorite baseball players, past and present.

Also to Mark Paul (the baseball guy, not the guy from "Saved by the Bell").
I don't consider you my target audience, but I'm part of yours.

NOTE FROM THE AUTHOR

Since this is a work of fiction, some dates and details may not match the logical timeline or rules for real life.

I wanted the story to reflect a professional baseball player's life as accurately as possible, but still take some liberties to create the best love story for my characters. Luckily, with fiction, we can have the best of both worlds. I hope you enjoy *Mom Ball*.

Kaci

MOM BALL

CHAPTER 1

Brooke

I sip sweet tea and snuggle against my lawn chair. Daisy comes into the sunroom with my cousin Erica slogging behind her.

"You're up, Aniston."

Aniston leaps toward Daisy like a kid in a sack race. We laugh, and she frowns.

"What? It's been a while since I've gotten a massage."

Morgan snorts. "You mean Easton doesn't massage you?"

"Sometimes, but he doesn't hold a candle to Daisy's magic." Aniston pats Daisy's shoulder. "Pun intended."

Daisy laughs, and I roll my eyes. However, I agree that her homemade candles take a relaxing massage to the next level.

"Come on." Daisy exits and waves Aniston toward her.

I lean back, content with the home spa day I planned since none of us have time for a real spa day. Not that I've had one in years, but that's beside the point. We're all busy with work and kids—Erica's kid being the orchard's new website—and Aniston has additional obligations as president of the PTSO.

I take a big gulp of my drink and try to ignore the constant question looming in the back of my mind. The one that would likely have come up during the recent daddy-daughter dance had my child been a girl. The one that's bound to come up sooner than later with my son.

Who's my daddy?

Thanks to my loving family and a comfortable life at the apple orchard, Timothy hasn't asked that dreaded question . . . yet. But I know it's coming one day.

"Hey, where are those cucumbers I sliced for our eyes?" Erica asks as she lathers on some of the facial cream I brought.

Morgan leans up. "Wait, those weren't snacks?"

Erica glances at me. I shrug at her, then laugh.

"It's okay, Morgan," I say.

"Oops." She laughs. "Since they were on that tray with the lemon slices, I thought it was some kind of dieting charcuterie board."

Erica shakes her head. "No, the lemon slices were for our drinks."

Morgan raises her chin, then twists her lips. "Oops again."

"It's okay." Erica gives her a forced smile.

I bite back a laugh. My cousin is such a Southern belle and Morgan is, well, Morgan. They're cordial, but they couldn't be more different. The only thing they have in common besides me is that Erica sometimes shops at the Pig and Morgan works there.

Morgan sits back and sucks her Diet Coke until the straw slurps against the ice. I close my eyes and soak in the sun shining through the glass room. I wiggle my nose when the heat itches my skin. I don't want to scratch it and mess up my skin cream.

"This is nice. Us chilling while the kids play in the pasture."

I jerk my head toward Morgan. "Pasture? I thought they were in the house with my mom."

"The girls are. The boys went to play ball."

"Timothy is playing ball?" I wrinkle my forehead. It feels like it's breaking beneath the hardened cream.

"Yeah. He's plenty old enough to play with them. My kids came out of the womb hitting stuff." Morgan leans to one side and pulls a lemon out from under her. "I say whatever keeps them off drugs."

"Don't you have like a seven-year-old?" Erica asks.

"Yeah, but better to learn young." Morgan sucks on the lemon slice.

Erica snarls before leaning back and closing her eyes. I stare outside, my stomach knotting as I try and recall the cow rotation.

The county owns that field, which connects to our land. They alternate between running a golf course and keeping cattle on it. There's a good chance our kids will either get hit by a golf ball or worse—a bull.

I spring to my feet and tighten the sash on my robe. Morgan and Erica stare at me like I'm crazy.

"What's gotten into you?" Erica asks.

"I'm going to check on the kids. The cows may be out, and if not, there will be crazy people driving golf carts and hitting balls."

Morgan tugs my robe. "Land the helicopter, Brooke, they're fine. Ethan's in charge."

"That's what I'm afraid of." I jerk loose from her grip and head toward the door.

My flip-flops clap against the concrete on my way through the patio to the garage. Daddy keeps a four-wheeler ready to go by the house. I can maneuver it inside the pasture easier than my Corolla.

I straddle the seat and tuck my robe beneath my thighs so it won't blow open. All I need is to flash a random Apple

Cartian on my way to rescue Timothy. With one hand on the gas and the other securing my robe, I fly down the drive in third gear.

Stray hairs escape my topknot and stick to the cream on my face. I unsuccessfully attempt to blow a strand out of my eye, afraid to let go of my robe. I turn toward the gate to the pasture on two wheels, then park.

Grass hits my bare legs as I jog to the gate. Of course it's locked. I gird my loins and climb the metal rails, then hoist my short legs over the top. I step down a few rungs and hop to the ground. Thanks to all my years as a cheerleader, I manage to land without breaking anything. Except for maybe my dollar store flip-flops. To be fair, they were living on borrowed time.

I move best I can in the near knee-high grass, which is another indication it's cow time.

"Timothy!" I yell his name as I stagger up a slight hill.

When I come to a clearing, I spot the brains behind this outing—Ethan. And I use the word "brains" loosely. He's your typical young teenager, obsessed with sports, outdoors, and Aniston's niece, though he'd never admit the latter.

"Ethan!"

He comes toward me, a bat in hand.

"Miss Brooke?" He stares like I'm a swamp monster.

But with four-wheeler hair and cleansing clay on my face, it's probably an accurate assessment.

"Do you know where Tim—"

"Mama?" Timothy bounces toward me before I can finish his name.

I rush toward him and hug him close, kissing his cheek. He laughs and pulls back. "Why are you sticky?" He rubs a smidge of cream from his cheek.

"I was worried the bulls were in here. Y'all don't need to come out here without asking first."

"I told my mom we were coming," Ethan offers.

I slant my eyes his way. "That doesn't count for Timothy."

"Yes, ma'am. Sorry." He nods toward the road. "We can go back. Andrew is already outside the fence getting the ball."

"You shouldn't send your little brother in the road by himself."

"I didn't, I sent Carter too."

I press my lips together and fight the urge to scold Ethan. Sending Aniston's nephew, who's maybe a year older than Andrew, isn't much better, if not worse.

"Let's go." I hook my arm around Timothy's shoulder.

The three of us walk toward the gate. Both boys climb the fence effortlessly, then wait as I take my time on each rung to avoid a wardrobe malfunction. I'm facing the field, stepping down, when I hear Andrew chattering wildly to the other boys.

"He got our ball, and he said he'd show me how to pitch."

"Cool, could you help me with my curve?" Ethan asks.

"Sure. You look like you've got a strong arm, young man."

I freeze on the bottom rail. That voice travels from my ears to my toes, making my entire body shake. I'd know it anywhere. It's the same voice that promised me the world years earlier. The voice I haven't heard in person since our last night together. The night I gained the child who would become my world.

Nate

"Are you stuck?" One of the boys turns back to the fence.

A woman in a bathrobe wiggles her foot but doesn't answer.

I cross the gravel road and stand a few feet behind her. "Need help, ma'am?"

She bends at the waist, poking her butt toward me. I blink as she dislodges a flip-flop from the fence.

Not knowing what to say, I take a half step closer in case she falls. She straightens and spins around, then jumps when she notices me.

"Brooke?"

My heart speeds up and the blood drains from my face. I'm likely as pale as she is, wearing some kind of paint on her face. Even with that, I'd recognize her anywhere.

"You know my mom?"

I jerk my head to the kid who asked if she was stuck. "That's your mother?"

A million questions race through my mind as I turn back to Brooke in slow motion. Most importantly, why wouldn't anyone mention to me that my ex-girlfriend has a kid?

Does she also have a husband? Does she still live here, or is she visiting family?

Granted, I never asked Mom about Brooke after she ghosted me in college. Still, you'd think her name might come up in conversation. I have a bad habit of glazing over when she spills useless Apple Cart gossip. However, Brooke's name would've caught—and held—my attention.

"Hi." Her voice is low and strained.

"Hey," I manage to say. "Let's get you out of the weeds."

Without thinking, I take her hand. Her fingers curl, but start to loosen as I lead her across the tall grass. By the time we reach my side of the road, her grip is relaxed in mine.

The smallness and soft touch of her hand against my larger calloused one sends a rush of warmth through my body. It's way too familiar and brings up emotions I'm not ready to battle.

I drop her hand like a bad habit.

A habit I'd love to pick back up.

It's hard to tell with all that paste on her face, but I think she's blushing.

"Thanks," she half whispers. She dips her head, then turns to her son.

Her son. I'm still in shock that nobody told me. That's possibly the first secret ever kept in this county.

"Ready to go back home?" she asks.

The boy stares at me a few seconds. "This man said he would help us with baseball."

"I'm sure this man is busy."

"It's Nate." I mean to clarify that to the kids, but it comes out a little sarcastically toward Brooke. Having the love of your life refer to you as "this man" is about as low of a blow as it gets.

Well, she *was* the love of my life. But I haven't exactly tried to fall in love again. Obviously, she's moved on, so I best let it go.

"I'm sure Nate is busy." Brooke's throat catches on my name like it hurts her to say it.

"Dude! I knew you looked familiar. You're Nate the Great, aren't you?" The older boy comes uncomfortably close and studies my face.

All the boys stare at me like I'm on exhibit at the zoo.

"Who's Nate the Great?" Brooke's son asks.

One of the younger boys pops him on the arm.

"He plays for the Braves," the other answers.

The older boy sticks out his hand. "Ethan Archer, nice to meet you."

"You as well." I shake his hand and smile. "And who else do we have here?"

"That's Andrew." He points to the smallest kid. "That's Carter." He points to the slightly larger kid. "And Timothy." He nods toward Brooke's son.

I commit the boys' names to memory. In particular Timothy's. Was he named after his dad?

"Can we do ball with him, Mama?" he asks.

"I'm sure Mr. Nate is busy." She presses her lips tightly.

I glory a split second in the fact that she said my name effortlessly this time.

"I was about to cut the grass, but it can wait."

Brooke cocks her head toward the pasture.

"Not that, over here. I bought this house."

Her eyes widen to the point that some of her face goop cracks. A piece of her hair sticks to it.

I lift my hand to push it away from her face, then freeze. Instead, I readjust my cap to make it look as if I never intended to touch her. Holding her hand was hard enough. I might not can control myself if I get near her face.

"Timothy, it's *play* ball, not *do* ball." Ethan rolls his eyes, then he smirks at me. "Kids, huh?"

I narrow my eyes, and his face straightens. Andrew and Carter are over my stardom and now preoccupied with poking a worm in the road. I watch them a second more, then focus on Brooke. "If it's fine with you, I'd be happy to help your boys with ball sometime."

"I only have the one boy," she answers quickly.

I laugh nervously. An odd sense of relief covers me. Instead of hiding a slew of kids from me, Brooke only has one. And possibly a husband or ex-husband.

I try not to focus on the ex part. She chose to end our relationship when she was in college. If she is single, I doubt a chance meeting in a pasture almost nine years later would magically change her mind.

"Okay. If everyone's parents are all right with it, I'd be glad to help."

"My mom won't care," Ethan says. "Unless you charge a bunch."

I laugh. "It's on the house."

He smiles.

"Can we, Mama?" Timothy clasps his hands together under his chin.

Brooke folds her arms and lets out a deep breath. He gives her a pleading face.

"Sometime." She scans the other boys. "We're all busy today, and I want to tell your moms first."

I study the other three boys, trying to decide if any of them go together. I may have unknowingly committed to helping four families with ball.

All in a desperate attempt to see my ex again.

A shot of guilt hits my chest. I check Brooke's ring finger as she uncrosses her arms. Nothing. She looks like she just got out of the shower, and there's a good chance that's why she's not wearing any jewelry. Still, I choose to believe she's single.

And I try to block the idea of her in the shower from my brain.

It isn't working.

"Timothy, do you want to ride with me?" Brooke asks.

"If I can drive."

She nods. "Go get the four-wheeler."

Timothy looks both ways down the road before crossing it.

"Come on, y'all." Ethan taps the other two on the shoulder with his bat.

They stand and watch the worm wiggle away. Ethan turns around after they walk a few feet. "Bye, Nate the Great."

I wave and try to remember the last time someone called me that in an adoring way. Not since before my injury, or at best since my surgery. Nowadays, I feel more like Nate the Late.

Brooke stares at me, and I realize we're alone. There are so many things I want to ask and say, but I refrain. Good thing too, since Timothy drives up.

"It was good seeing you," she says with a sad smile.

Was it? I want to believe that, but her body language leans toward just being polite.

"You too." I mean it.

She takes extra caution holding her robe together as she climbs on the four-wheeler behind Timothy. One of her flip-flops is busted on the side and slips off.

I pick it up and hold it out. My hand lingers for a second when she takes the shoe. She wedges it between her and Timothy, then tucks her robe beneath her thighs.

I step back and pretend I didn't just gawk at her legs.

"Bye, Mr. Nate." Timothy waves and grins.

"Bye, nice to meet you."

"Bye." Brooke's voice is almost a whisper.

I lift the corners of my mouth and watch them drive away. Everything in me wants to run them down and ask them to spend the afternoon with me.

But what would Brooke say to that? Or worse, possibly her husband?

"Y'all come back," I yell behind them.

They keep driving, and I swipe a hand down my face. Really? Could I have said anything more impersonal and hillbilly?

Looks like I've lost my game in more ways than baseball.

CHAPTER 2

Brooke

If someone had asked what I least expected to happen today, seeing Nate would be right up there with winning the lottery. And that's considering the fact that I've never played the lottery.

I clutch my broken flip-flop like my life depends on it as I try and process the reality that my ex-boyfriend moved a literal country mile down the road.

Plenty of people have gossiped about Jonah and Carolina flipping the Vanderburke Mansion. The most probable story I've heard to date is that Samuel who runs the bank bought it. There's been little activity other than a Sold sign on the lawn late last summer, and the Nash couple in and out a few times with some furniture. I assumed someone out of town bought it.

Never in my wildest dreams would I have imagined Nate living there. Isn't he supposed to be in Atlanta to do ball, as Timothy would put it?

My heart beats harder as I consider my son.

I've never mentioned Nate to him or him to Nate. Actually, I've mentioned nothing to Nate since college.

We talked as normal a few times after he visited me at my dorm. Once I found out I was pregnant, I made a lame excuse about us needing to focus on our careers and quit answering his calls and texts.

Real mature, I know.

But I was eighteen and pregnant from one incident. It took all the courage I had to tell my parents and move back so they could help me. All the whispers around town didn't help, especially since they all assumed it was a one-night stand.

It was—just with my long-time boyfriend.

Did I make a mistake not telling him? Maybe. But I couldn't live with myself if I allowed a baby to ruin his ball career. Between loving parents and a well-off family, I had all the support I needed.

Or so I thought.

Seeing him today stirred up a bunch of emotions I haven't felt in years.

Timothy brings the four-wheeler to a screeching halt in front of the house, jerking me out of my thoughts. The other boys walk up as we dismount.

Timothy talks with them, but their voices are muffled, as I'm still in a trance. I slog toward the sunroom, holding the broken flip-flop in my hand.

Morgan is the first to notice me when I enter the room. "What happened? You look like you've seen a ghost."

My limbs tingle. She's older than me and doesn't know much about my high school relationship. However, the others would well remember Nate and me together—especially Erica.

When I came home pregnant and enrolled in Apple Cart Community College instead of Bama, none of my friends or family pressured me with questions. Not even Erica.

At the time, I was thankful. In hindsight, it makes today harder. How could I possibly start to explain my ghost of boyfriends past?

Even worse, admit that Nate is my baby-daddy Bruno. The one topic everyone has steered clear of mentioning to me.

"I'm fine. The boys are fine." I plop down on a lawn chair and toss the broken shoe on the ground.

"What happened there?" Morgan picks it up.

"I popped the strap climbing the fence."

She laughs. "What I'd pay to see that." She slaps the flip-flop against her leg. "Ouch. You mind if I keep this for a backup paddle?"

"Be my guest." I lie back and close my eyes.

Morgan has been known to wield any type of non-lethal weapon at her kids. Purse straps, fly flaps, wooden spoons, and flip-flops. Andrew is the usual recipient, but all have had their share of heinie pops.

I'm thankful Timothy hasn't given me any problems so far.

"Mama, guess who we met?"

My eyes pop open to Ethan's voice.

"I told you to stay outside during our spa day."

"But we met Nate the Great."

"Nathan Miller?" Erica leans up, a cloth falling from her eyes.

"Yes, he's our new neighbor," I say.

Erica cuts her eyes toward me in a questioning stare.

"Y'all all know him?" Carter's eyes widen.

"He grew up here and went to our school," Erica offers.

Thank God, she went with that and not the whole "dated Brooke" explanation. I half smile at her with gratitude.

"He said he could help us with ball." Ethan raises his hands in excitement. "For free!"

Morgan smiles. "Well, now that does make Nate great."

"He's going to help all of us, even Timothy."

Erica raises an eyebrow at me.

"Maybe. Timothy's never even played ball," I say.

"So he needs help the most," Ethan counters.

I sigh.

"Well, I guess that was your ghost, huh, Brooke?" Aniston's voice carries coyly across the room.

We all turn to the doorway. "How long have you been there?" I ask.

"Long enough to know you need a massage," Daisy says, peeking around her.

"That's one thing I agree with." I stand and turn to Ethan. "The baseball is TBD."

He nods and lowers his head.

Aniston hands me a warm towel as I pass her. "Wash your face before falling asleep in there. Remember what happened to me when I misused skin cream?"

I laugh. "Don't we all."

Aniston was red for a week after getting her face too heated while wearing her sister's skin cream. She had to recruit Adrianne to do her makeup so she could attend a banquet with Easton and not look like a tomato.

I wipe my face and toss the dirty towel at Aniston. She scoffs. I follow Daisy toward the massage table without looking back. Serves her right.

Maybe Daisy can work some kind of miracle on me. My body keeps alternating between tensing up and loosening like Jell-O. And I had none of this stress before today.

Sadly, Nate still has an effect on me.

Nate

In the few days since I've moved back to Apple Cart, not much has changed. There's an extra Dollar General, and the Pig got a facelift. Today I can add one more difference to the list.

Apple Cart County Baptist added a drum set. I guess the elders opposed to anything besides keyboard and string music have all died in the time I've been gone.

A younger guy plays the drums, but the same women sit at the piano and organ. I don't recognize the guitar player, but he's older as well.

The drums are a nice touch, making "I'll Fly Away" a little less of a snooze fest. Mom pats her knee and sings along. I didn't inherit her love of hymnals.

My eyes scan the crowd as I hide a yawn.

Like a beacon from heaven, Brooke's brown hair shines under the fluorescent lights. It's down and curled rather than in a messy bun. Her face is smooth with her usual natural makeup look, instead of the painted goop.

Mom clears her throat loudly.

"What?" I whisper just as loudly.

She pinches my ear like I'm a kid.

"Ouch."

"It's not polite to stare in church. Pay attention to the choir."

I would, if Brooke were in the choir.

Against my wishes, I mind Mom and face the front of the church. I make it a few more songs before my eyes wander.

Timothy turns around and waves at me.

I give as tiny a wave as possible with my big hand. Brooke stays facing forward, but I pretend she sees me out of the corner of her eye. Her family is closer to the front, but on the other side. Just far enough for me to not see her without turning my head.

Mom hits a high note on the last chord of the last song. I flinch at the unexpected pitch. While I'm irritated, I make a note to ask her about not telling me Brooke has a kid, and possibly a husband.

There's no man on their pew besides her dad.

I force myself to face forward again. The guy could be working or sick or something. I'll need to check her ring finger again. She's at church, wearing makeup and earrings. If she has a wedding band, she'll have it on.

The pastor reads a list of announcements while the choir and band exit the stage. Not much interests me except the part about having a golf benefit once the cows are sold from the county pasture.

Golf is a sport I've learned to like over the years. Charity events like to invite athletes from other sports to play in tournaments, and it's a nice change of pace from killing the ball all the time.

That event is sandwiched between baby showers and planning the Easter program.

Without warning, he goes into prayer. I bow my head and wait for the "amen." Then I conveniently lift my head in the direction of Brooke.

The sermon is a blur as I zone in and out of paying attention. My focus is on Brooke and tossing around scenarios of what she's been up to since we broke up.

I can't leave today without talking to her. If things start to go sour, I'll claim I came over to talk about helping Timothy with ball.

Once the final "amen" is said, I spring to my feet.

An older couple stands between me and the end of the pew. I don't want to hurry them or smoosh them between pews trying to get out. Mom is turned around talking to someone on the other side of me. My only option is patience.

The good news is I can easily see over the couple's heads.

I follow Brooke with my eyes as they take their time shuffling to the end of the pew. She stands and picks up her things.

I'm finally free and on my way across the sanctuary when a hand hits my chest.

"Well, if it isn't Nathaniel Miller."

Mrs. Ethel stares up at me. She hasn't changed much at all, except that she's now using a walker. One of those fancy ones that has a little seat and a pocket on the front.

She slides her hand down my chest, and I squirm when it reaches my belt. Old people are funny. Once they reach a certain age, they think they can act however, wherever.

I take a step back and clear my throat. She moves her hand and uses it to wag a finger at me. Better than the alternative.

"Did you buy that mansion Jonah and Carolina fixed up to sell?"

"Yes, ma'am, I did."

She turns to the two older ladies behind her. It's nice to see her entourage is still in good health. "Told y'all it was true."

She reaches toward me, and I curl my shoulders in cautiously. Luckily, she swats her hand instead of touching me. "I knew you would come home to Apple Cart one day." She smiles. "You're our hometown hero."

"Well, I don't know about that . . ." I crane my neck to find Brooke.

Paul comes up and wraps his arm around Ms. Dot. "Dot, we best hurry if we want to beat the Methodists to Mary's."

"Okay, dear." She follows Paul.

Dear? That's new to me. I remember Mom mentioning her husband passed recently, but she didn't say anything about Paul.

The other women follow them out, and I make my escape down the aisle. A few more people greet me on the way. I'm polite, but keep trailing forward.

When I finally reach the front of the church, I see Brooke climb in a car and drive off.

I stand on the porch and sigh. Why did I let her get away?

Today and before.

My feet weigh more than I can bench press—even before my injury. I stand plastered to the brick tiles until a hand rests on my shoulder. I turn to Mom, relieved it isn't another handsy granny.

"Sorry, son. I get to talking a lot on Sundays."

I press my lips together to not laugh. She's always been social, and so have I. Too bad I couldn't be social with Brooke.

"Why don't you follow me home. I put a roast in this morning."

"Sounds awesome."

We walk across the gravel parking lot toward her car. "Have you given any more thought to moving in with me?" I ask.

"Oh, I couldn't impose."

"Mom, it's a huge house. I intended on you moving in when I bought it."

She frowns. "I don't know. I've lived in the same place ever since we came to Apple Cart."

"But you'd only be moving a few miles out of town."

"I'll think about it." She gives me a forced smile.

I open her door for her. Once inside, she pauses. "You are coming for lunch, right?"

Instead of saying yes right away, I lean over the door. "On one condition."

"I have tea."

I laugh. "Not that. Tell me why you never mentioned Brooke had a kid?"

"Brooke Marshall?"

I put on my most sarcastic stare.

"It happened so long ago, and you never mentioned her to me after the breakup. I assumed you wouldn't want to know or even care."

My stomach bottoms out, and I push back from her door. I nod until the shock wears off. "Okay. See you in a few minutes."

I shut Mom's door and stare at my feet on the way to my truck. Not interested? In Brooke?

When have I ever acted uninterested in Brooke?

I might go for long periods of time without thinking of her. But she always pops back in my brain the moment I try to get serious with another woman. No matter the person, I compare her to Brooke. And Brooke always wins.

Kind of stupid considering we broke up at eighteen.

At the time, I didn't want to appear weak to anyone. Not even my own mother. It made more sense to focus on baseball and use the pain of our breakup to push me forward. Anytime Mom visited or called, I talked about ball or working or my roommates. Never about missing Brooke.

In hindsight, she may have thought the breakup was mutual.

It wasn't.

And if I've learned anything this weekend, it's that Brooke still makes me crazy like she did in high school.

CHAPTER 3

Brooke

The only downside to working a normal shift is that I have no excuse not to go through the car line. Granted, it has run better with Aniston in charge.

I pull up to the hospital and grab my almost empty coffee cup. One perk to working at the hospital is we never run out of coffee or Band-Aids.

I may or may not have taken advantage of the latter when Timothy was into making fishing lures.

He's gone through several fads and had many interests. For some reason, I never anticipated him wanting to play baseball. It makes sense for him with a lot of friends playing. Plus, it's in his blood.

I squeeze my cup as I enter through the side door. So far, carrying this secret has served me well. Now that Nate's back in town, it makes me nervous. I've seen him two days in a row, and both times Timothy was with me.

I go through the motions of securing my purse and lunch in the locker room. Armed with my mug and phone, I march down the hall in search of more coffee.

Voices come from the break room, which isn't usual any time of day. What is unusual is one sounds exactly like Nate. Maybe it's my imagination.

Nope.

I poke my head in the doorway and leave just as quickly. Nate sits at a table, arms folded, across from a physical therapist.

Interesting.

I've dealt with enough in the past to appreciate people staying out of others' business, and I've never been particularly nosy. However, I'm drawn to the door like a moth to a flame. I stand close as I can to the opening without being spotted.

They're discussing the hospital layout, which is strange.

"I think every hospital needs a designated physical therapy environment," Nate says.

Oscar agrees and gives a laundry list of what he goes through every time he comes to our hospital. He currently floats around at different rural hospitals on different days.

"I don't know where I'd be without physical therapy," Nate continues.

I lean closer, wanting to learn more. There's so much of his story I don't know. Sure, he's been in the news and on TV throughout the years. But I don't care to know about his baseball career. I care to know about him.

Nate scoots his chair like he's about to stand. I jerk back against the wall in a panic. When I do, my coffee mug hits the ground and bounces. Thankfully, it's now empty. Unfortunately, it's big and metal and sounds like Daddy working on the industrial-size apple slicer.

I watch it roll a few feet, then jump forward like it's a

grenade I have to grab. Once it's in my possession, I hightail toward the end of the hallway without looking back.

Forget getting a refill. I pass another coffee counter and don't stop until I'm at the nurse's station. Easton, or Dr. West, stands at a filing cabinet. I have to remember where I am before I address him since I see him outside of work a lot now that he's engaged to Aniston.

"Brooke, you're late."

I lift my brows and check my Apple watch. "Actually, I'm right on time."

"I meant for you." He laughs. "You're always beating me to work."

I nod and laugh.

"Here's the first X-ray of the day. Reception just brought it back."

He hands me a folder on the counter beside him. I pick it up and roll my eyes at Bessy McCain's name. She calls herself a holistic doctor, but still comes in on occasion. Then she complains if Dr. West prescribes medicine that isn't natural herbs. Oh, and she never wears shoes.

"Good start to the day, huh?" he says.

"Makes the car line look like a cakewalk."

He laughs.

I take the chart and make my way to the front waiting area. Bessy's bare feet welcome me when I open the door. I can't help but stare at them as I call her name. They dangle above the floor, as she's vertically challenged. Yet another reason she should wear shoes.

She hops down from her chair and scurries toward me. That tile floor has to be cold. The hospital is always cold.

I tug my jacket tighter around my chest and force my eyes toward her face. "Morning, Mrs. McCain."

She nods.

I lead her down the hallway, thankful we don't have to

pass the break room. It's bad enough that I drive by Nate's house every time I leave the orchard. Now I see him at church and at work?

What's next? Will he show up at the hair salon?

I sigh and open the door to the X-ray room. "Okay, Mrs. McCain." I allow her to enter, then close the door behind us. "Your chart says you have something going on with your heel."

Imagine that. Someone who never wears shoes is having trouble with her foot.

"Yeah, I have this spot on it that's a hurtin' and my essential oils ain't cuttin' it."

"Let's have you sit on the table and prop your leg up."

I should've suggested something different, but for an older woman with a frumpy build, Bessy is very flexible. She swings her leg high and wide, flashing me in the process.

And shoes are not the only essential she leaves out of her wardrobe.

I blink like ten times to try and erase the image from my brain. We see a lot in the medical field, but it's not common to see *that* area when X-raying a foot.

Of course, she's wearing one of those snap-button house dresses we refer to as muumuus in the South. It's free flowing and not much different from our hospital gowns. Except it does close all the way.

Thank God.

Her dress flattens out when her leg is lowered. Relieved at that, I turn her foot and prepare the machine to take images.

I hurry behind the window and instruct her how to turn after every few photos. She does surprisingly well, and I get some detailed scans of what I'm guessing is a shard of glass.

"Mrs. Bessy, the doctor will have to make a conclusion on what exactly it is, but it appears something is lodged in your heel."

"Well, I declare."

"If you don't mind waiting, I'll get Dr. West."

"Take your time, dear. According to the *Farmer's Almanac*, it's not a good day to do anything but go to the doctor."

"All right, then."

I text Dr. West that Bessy's X-rays are ready for him, and he asks me to take her to one of the exam rooms. This would probably be a good time to warn him she's not wearing panties, but I can't imagine typing that in a text.

"He wants me to take you to room three. I can get a wheelchair for you if it's more comfortable."

"You're sweet."

I unfold the wheelchair we keep in the corner of the room and help her onto it. My eyes are glued to a spot on the wall above her head in case she tries to show off any acrobatic skills getting in the chair.

Out of impulse, I pull a blanket from the closet. "Here. Your legs may be cold." I drape it over her lap. Cold or not, I don't want her flashing anyone on the ride down the hall.

"Just one second." I file the X-rays in her chart to show Dr. West. Then I tuck them under my arm and wheel her to room three. "He will be here as soon as he finishes up with his other patient."

She half smiles, and I exit before anything else gets odd.

I close the door and shove her files in the pocket on the wall. Unless Easton needs more images, I can move on with my day.

I turn and bump into something hard. "Oomph." Hard as in a muscular chest.

My eyes trail a tight athletic shirt to a neatly trimmed beard. It's Nate. *Again!* I jump back, banging my head against the door.

"Are you okay?" He reaches for my head, and I flinch.

"Yeah, uh, weird morning. That's all." More like weird week, thanks to him moving back.

His big hand cups the back of my head. It's warm and kind, and I try not to enjoy his gentle touch. After what feels like both a short second and a lifetime, he removes his hand, brushing my hair slightly to the side.

I suck in a breath and think of an exit strategy. Which is hard when something his size is blocking my path and the only alternative is retreating to a room with a backwoods witch doctor who doesn't wear shoes . . . or panties.

"You're wearing scrubs, so I guess you're not a patient."

"Nope." I cross my arms, hoping he will back up at least enough so I can't smell his cologne.

"I thought you were in college for teaching."

"That was before—" I stop myself. Now's not the time to let the cat out of the bag on him being Timothy's father. "When I got pregnant with Timothy, I moved back here and went to the radiology school."

He lifts his chin. "But you always wanted to be a kindergarten teacher."

"It was easier to be with my parents and finish college sooner. Besides, I've raised my own kindergartener." I laugh nervously.

"That you have." He smiles. "What grade is he in now?"

"Second."

"Cool." He scratches the back of his head and fumbles with his cap.

A telltale sign he's a little nervous. At least it's not just me.

"I'll let you get to work. I need to head out anyway."

"Good seeing you." I clamp my mouth shut.

Is it though? Maybe it felt good to see him, but it's not exactly good for me to see him.

"You too. See you around our road." He gently touches my arm for a beat, then turns and walks away.

I grip the spot still warm from his touch and demand my heart to quit beating so fast.

Having a kid on my own and keeping his dad a secret has

taken a toll on my dating life. As in made it nonexistent. Plenty of people have tried to fix me up, and a few promising guys have asked me out. But I never made it on a date with any of them.

Not because they weren't interested, but because I wasn't. None of them measured up to what I had in mind for my husband and Timothy's dad. I assumed it was because I'm super picky and protective of Timothy.

Now I know it's because they weren't Nate.

Nate

Running into Brooke set my stomach in knots. I expect to see her on our road, or even at church, but not the hospital.

Part of me is a little disappointed she didn't get to be a teacher. I'm sure she's great at the radiology thing, but I know how much she wanted to teach kindergarten. Maybe she could give me advice on backup careers in case my shoulder never heals.

I shake my head. That's not something I want to consider. At least not in my twenties. I'd planned on playing until my mid-thirties, then maybe opening a training facility or something. I'm still too young to feel this old.

Mary's Diner comes into view, and my stomach growls. Maybe it's from the Brooke thing, but food never hurts. I pull in the parking lot. It's late morning, which means she's probably still serving breakfast. Mary's is the kind of place where you can order anything and know it will be good.

The door drags across the welcome mat. It's just loud enough for every head to turn when I enter. Paul and Dot sit in a corner booth, and a couple of guys in camouflage sit at a table. I nod to all and continue toward the front.

Everything is the same. Checkered tablecloths, framed photos of Apple Cart back in the day, and my high school jersey hanging on the wall behind the counter.

I sigh and think back to my glory days playing high school ball. I'd assumed the best would be when I made it to the big leagues. It's great, no doubt. But playing for your school with your buddies is far more fun.

"Hey, sugar." Mrs. Mary smiles widely, showing the gap in her front teeth. "I was wondering when you'd come by."

"Where you want me to sit?"

"Anywhere you like." She wipes her hands down the front of her apron. "You caught us between breakfast and lunch rush."

"Thanks." I take a seat in the corner booth where Brooke and I often sat. We'd share a bigger table across the room when friends ate with us.

Second to my mom, Mary has fed me more than anyone. Mom would help her prepare for catering events at times when money was tighter— really it was always tight. Mary would send her home with a plate for me when they finished.

I've barely settled in my seat when she brings a big glass of sweet tea. "Here's a menu, but let me make a suggestion."

"Absolutely."

"We still have breakfast food and we're starting to grill steaks for lunch. How's scrambled eggs with steak and hash browns sound?"

"Delicious." I take a long drink of my tea.

She gathers the menu and smiles before hurrying to the back.

I slump down and push my side of the booth farther from the table. I grew two inches since high school, and the change is noticeable sitting here.

A black-and-white photo of the original high school stares

at me. It burned down long before Mom and I moved here. I went to the school built sometime in the eighties.

It's rumored that a former principal set the school on fire to get an upgrade. People say she was mad that the athletics facilities got a new gym. The weird thing is we still called that gym the "new gym" when I was in school.

Mary returns with my food, humming a cheerful tune. She's never in a bad mood, at least that I've seen. She can be stern and serious, but never unhappy. With any luck, eating her food will transfer some of that upbeat attitude to me.

"This looks delicious."

"It is." She laughs and slides into the seat across from me.

I stab some of the scrambled eggs with my fork. She catches my hand midair. "Boy, you forgot your prayer."

I smirk and lower my fork. I thank God for the food and the visit with Mary and say a quick "amen." This time she doesn't intercept the eggs when I reach toward my mouth.

"How long you plan on staying in town?"

I swallow and consider my answer. Mary never asks a casual question. She usually has a deeper question buried beneath it somewhere.

"You know I bought the Vanderburke Mansion."

"I do."

Of course she does. Mary knows all in Apple Cart, even before the rest of us.

"I'll live here in the off-season and whenever I'm not needed with the team. I'm trying to get Mom to move there too."

"That would be nice."

I chew a big bite of steak and nod.

"Great location. Across from the golf course, just a stone's throw from the Marshall family orchard." Mary's eyes twinkle as she draws out the last part of that sentence.

I stare at my plate, not caring for her insinuation. She has a bit of a reputation as a matchmaker. Brooke being my ex will only add to her meddling.

When I bought the place, I didn't know she still lived down the road. Would I still have bought it had I known?

I don't want to answer that.

"You know, I always pictured you being a good coach and mentor to young men."

"That is kinda my current retirement plan."

Mary straightens the condiments in the corner of the table, then looks at me. "You don't have to wait until retirement to start helping out." She gives me that all-knowing look.

"Funny you say that, since a kid asked me the other day about pitching lessons."

"Oh really, who?"

"Ethan Archer." I don't dare add that Brooke's son was with him. That would be like tossing kindling on the fire.

"He's a good ballplayer. There's several kids in this town who have talent and drive, but no father figure to help them. So sad." She shakes her head.

The question of Brooke's relationship status comes to mind. I know Mary knows, but I don't dare ask. That would prove my interest in her.

Mary's lips curve into a grin. "I best get back to the kitchen. One of the church small groups comes in for an early lunch on Wednesdays." She stands and winks before hurrying away.

I chug my tea and sigh.

It would be in my best interest—and Brooke's—to assume she's involved with someone. Even if she's not. She broke up with me long ago and hasn't bothered to contact me since. If that's not a clear message, I don't know what is. For all I know, she hurried out of church on purpose.

If she wants me to help Timothy, I will gladly. I'll treat him like I would any other boy eager to learn ball.

Lord knows I've had plenty of single moms sign their kids

up for pitching lessons with ulterior motives. I call them cleat diggers. Cleat chasers and gold diggers rolled into one.

Only difference is the mom is Brooke, total opposite of cleat diggers. She ended our relationship when my career started to take off, and her family has plenty of their own money.

This time I'm the one who might have an ulterior motive.

CHAPTER 4

Brooke

It's been two days since I've run into Nate, so I'm probably due for a sighting.

Ah, speak of the devil.

I turn my head toward his place in time to spot him walking across the property like a well-groomed yeti.

I snap my head so fast my neck pops. "Ouch." I palm the back of it and continue down the gravel road, hoping he didn't see me see him.

At least today is Friday.

Mama had to pick up Timothy from school because they needed me to stay late. A few guys in their twenties decided to get drunk and play demolition derby with Jeeps in a mud pit.

They were rushed in as I was clocking out for the day. Easton and I found a broken arm and a fractured ankle among lots of bumps and bruises. Thank God they fared better than the Jeeps. Idiots are lucky to be alive.

Poor Timothy. I know I'm overprotective, but I see a lot at work. Plus, he's really my responsibility. In reality, I've always had my parents to help with him. But that doesn't make me want to protect him any less.

I pull up to their house. Timothy and I share the carriage house on the other side of the backyard. We lived in the big house until he was three, and he still has a bedroom and lots of toys there.

The front windows reflect the last bit of sunlight peeking through the trees. I blink at them as I climb the front porch. We're all counting down the days until the time changes.

I open the storm door with a slight creak, then the heavy wooden door. As soon as I enter my parents' house, I instantly relax. Something about growing up here and their unconditional love always calms me.

Even if I were to marry someday, I wouldn't dream of moving us too far from the orchard.

I follow Timothy's and Mama's voices to the kitchen. She's standing over the stove, stirring a pot big enough to feed an army.

On closer inspection, I see sugar and apples. Cinnamon apples, an even better comfort after a long day.

I kiss Timothy on top of his head and scrunch my nose.

"Hey, Mama." He grins.

"Why is your hair so sticky?"

"He helped me make applesauce." Mama winks.

I laugh. "At least he smells decent."

Timothy jumps down from the counter and grabs his backpack from the corner of the room. He rushes toward me, pulling out a paper.

"Whoa." He slams into me and bounces back. "Careful, buddy." I cup his shoulder and steady him.

He flaps the paper in front of me. Mama laughs from the stove. "He's been waiting two hours to show you that."

"Okay." I take the paper and hold it away from my nose

so I can actually see the words: *Apple Cart Armadillos Little League Sign-Ups*. That's an awful long way to spell purgatory.

"Can I do it? Tomorrow is the only day to sign up."

I drop the paper on the kitchen island and stare blankly at my son. He's handsome and smart and quick witted, but he's never been accused of being athletic.

His dad is an MLB pitcher. Shut up, brain!

I shake my head. "Where did you get this?"

"The teacher had some for anyone interested to take home."

"And you got one?"

He nods enthusiastically. I make eye contact with Mama over his head. She gives me a guilty stare.

"What?"

"I may have told him we'd sign him up tomorrow."

I scoff. "Without talking to me first? Shouldn't this be my decision?"

For better or worse, my dad and the older of my younger brothers come in the screen door from the sunroom.

"Bushels are loaded for tomorrow's pickups." Daddy kisses my mom quickly, then turns to the sink and washes his hands.

"Cinnamon apples are coming along too," she says.

"I can stay and help with those," Austin offers. He hurries toward the pot.

Mama swats at his hand with a rag. "Not until you wash your hands."

"We all know he just wants to eat some," I say, crossing my arms.

He takes the towel Mama used on him and pops my hip with it. I shriek. Timothy laughs.

"That's not funny," I say. "He hurt your mama."

Timothy straightens, and Austin sits at the island. "What's this?" He holds up the paper.

I moan and lean against the tile countertop.

"Are you playing, bud?"

"I want to."

Austin looks at me.

"It may be too dangerous."

My brother snarls. "Are you kidding? We used to play baseball in the hay loft with tree limbs and apples all the time and look how we turned out."

"Exactly."

Daddy grabs the towel to wipe his hands and stares at Austin. "All this time and I never could figure out how smooshed apples got in the barn. I even blamed the county's cows once."

I laugh. Austin smirks. Daddy shakes his head and sits at the table. "If the boy wants to play, I'll get him some gear."

I stare at the ceiling. "Seriously, y'all. Nothing has been decided. He's never even tried a sport before."

"Best try while he's young rather than wait. It only gets more dangerous the older he gets."

"Thanks, Daddy, that's so reassuring."

"I'm serious, Brooke. Ain't nothing wrong with my boy playing ball. Your brothers played sports, you cheered, and we enjoyed watching all the games."

"I'll help him," Austin says.

"Aren't you supposed to be planning your wedding?" Mama asks.

Daddy, Austin, and I exchange a look. Mama's current obsession is Austin and Haven's wedding later this year. She can't understand why everyone isn't as excited about every single detail—especially the groom.

"By planning, you mean saying 'yes, darlin'' to whatever Haven shows me?"

"The man is wise beyond his years," Daddy comments.

"No offense, Austin, but didn't you quit ball when you were on JV?" I ask.

"I had to help here. If I played ball, it wouldn't give me any time to fish and date all the cute girls."

I roll my eyes.

"Priorities." He winks at Timothy.

Yeah, he's probably not the best role model.

"Thanks, Uncle A, but I already got a helper."

"That's right, Ethan was helping you the other day," I comment.

"Not him, Mama, the real baseball man. The Nate the Great guy."

Mama drops her massive spoon and it clanks against the pan on the way down. Apple goo oozes down the side of the stove to the floor. All the adults stare at me with wide eyes.

"Yes, Mr. Nate did offer to help the day we ran into him by the pasture." I say it loudly in a clipped voice to get everyone off my back.

As usual, nobody cared to make mention that Nate moved close enough to hit the broad side of our barn with a baseball.

When you live in a small town that makes gossip an Olympic sport, it's nice to have a family who doesn't air your dirty laundry. I especially appreciated it at nineteen when I came home one weekend with a load of dirty laundry that included a few pregnancy pants.

They never pushed me for answers, just loved me and offered to help.

But in some cases, a little heads up would be nice. Like when your ex, who they all loved and wanted you to marry, buys the mansion at the end of your property.

Austin walks to the sink and wets some paper towels to help Mama clean the mess. I look at Timothy, whose eyes are wider than a Pixar puppy.

I squat so we're eye to eye. It doesn't take much, since he's getting taller by the minute. "Timothy, if you really want to play baseball, like for you, not because your friends are playing, we can sign up."

His cheeks raise into a wide smile that quickly fades. I frown.

"Can Mr. Nate the Great help me too?"

I sigh and straighten. "We'll see." I force a smile, then catch Mama's and Austin's reactions across the kitchen.

They both give me a pitying face. I appreciate the gesture, but it only increases the guilt of my ultimate secret. One that I think they might be on to.

I pat Timothy on the shoulder. "One thing at a time, sweetie. We'll start with signing up."

His big smile returns, and my anxiety lowers the slightest bit.

I take a seat at the island and whisper to myself, "One thing a time."

The last thing I want to do on Saturday morning is sign my son up to play baseball.

Yet here I am.

It's true, you really will do anything to make your children happy. Timothy's face is evidence of that.

He hangs on to the back door of the car like a dog approaching the park. As soon as I stop, he jumps out and runs toward the crowd.

There's a line of kids and adults in front of a folding table at the entrance to the ballpark. Morgan sits behind the table and waves like a madwoman when she spots us. We both wave in a much milder manner.

"I think Miss Morgan is glad we're here."

"Yep."

It's odd coming here for any reason other than to watch her sons. I never thought I'd see Timothy inside the chain-link fence, but there's a first time for everything.

Jeffrey stands behind the table, hands on his hips, dressed head to toe in Atlanta Braves gear. I laugh to myself and dig my phone out of my pocket to take a picture for Nate.

Then I remember that I don't have that kind of close relationship with Nate anymore, and I don't even have his number. About a month after the breakup, I deleted him from my phone so I couldn't call him in a moment of weakness.

"What are you doing, Mama?" Timothy nods at my phone in midair.

"Checking my face." I click the button to turn the camera view to a selfie.

"Is it in case Mr. Nate the Great is here?"

I sigh and shove my phone back in my jeans pocket. "Timothy, that's not his real name, and why should I care how he sees me?"

"You seemed a little embarrassed when he saw you on the four-wheeler."

"Well." I roll my eyes. "That had nothing to do with him. I'd be embarrassed for anyone to see me like that."

He gives me a look that communicates how well he knows me and how mature he is beyond his years. The one person I can't fake out is Timothy. I cup his face and widen my eyes. He narrows his, then smiles when I make a silly face.

The line moves and we're now third. A man in full camouflage with the sleeves cut off his shirt crowds the table. Morgan's head jerks to the side.

Uh-oh. He better watch out.

"Sir, you can't make payments on registration fees."

His biceps flex, making the rattlesnake tattoo on his arm dance. He turns his head and spits a wad of tobacco in the dirt. It lands awfully close to Morgan's sandaled foot. She moves her legs back and snarls.

"Lady, I just got a twenty-four-month lease on a new Hype Fire bat." He raises one hand, then slaps it on the table, causing Morgan to flinch.

"Well, sir, we don't lease registration fees here at Armadillo Little League."

He stomps away, letting out a string of words I'm certain Timothy will question me about later. I hold my breath and wonder what we've gotten ourselves into.

Morgan flips her hair over her shoulder and shakes her head at me. I bite back a laugh as she rolls her eyes.

"How are y'all doing this morning?" she asks the couple in front of us in her most pleasant Southern belle voice.

I bite my bottom lip to keep from laughing. Morgan is my spirit animal when it comes to dealing with difficult people. Sadly, I tend to smile and act as if bullies don't bother me, then go home and cry about it.

This couple is normal from what I can tell. They turn in their forms, sign, pay, and go on their way. Timothy steps up to the table, beaming. I lay out our IDs and reach for my checkbook.

"I'm so excited you'll be playing ball this year, Timothy," Morgan says.

"Me too!" His eye catches a bat nearby. "Smith said he'll buy me a bat and glove."

When Timothy was born, my parents were big on wanting original grandparent names. They somehow landed on Granny and Smith while harvesting Granny Smith apples. Mama makes sure to explain that to everyone, since her name alone is least original of all.

"Yeah, good for you not having to lease them." Morgan winks at me.

I laugh at her sarcastic tone. She continues helping me fill out the paperwork and I write a check.

"Oh, we need an extra phone number and your license number on this check."

"Okay." I wrinkle my brow.

Morgan must read my confusion, because she leans closer

and whispers, "You'd be surprised at the people who try and scam us out of a hundred bucks."

"After the snake-arm guy, I don't think so," I whisper back.

She laughs so hard she snorts, making me laugh too.

"That's all, guys." Morgan stacks our paper on top of more in a folder.

"When do we practice?" Timothy asks.

"Slow your roll, slugger. We haven't even announced teams yet. It will happen soon enough . . . believe me." Her final two words ooze with exhaustion.

"See you soon," I say.

She nods, then turns her hospitality on for the next person. Funny how she's never this courteous when checking people out at the Pig. And to think that's her actual paying job.

We leave Morgan to work her magic and pass Jeffrey, who's standing high and mighty in front of a field. His two sons are nearby dressed in jerseys with more accessories than I wore in my pageant days. But to their credit, I don't see any fake eyelashes or nails.

I watch one pitch to the other. A lump forms in my throat as I imagine a ball coming that hard at my son's head. Yes, he will be wearing a helmet to bat, but that still makes me antsy.

"Mama, look, it's Mr. Nate the—" Timothy pauses, before spouting out, "the Great."

My eyes follow his across the parking lot toward the batting cages. Nate stands in the sunlight, a T-shirt taut across his chest, his forearms muscular and glistening with sweat.

Ugh. I sound like the deprived single mom in a Nicholas Sparks novel. In particular, the one where she took care of dogs and the movie version included Zac Efron.

"He looks busy," I say. Then I use that as an excuse to watch him dig dirt with a shovel a few more seconds.

Before I can snap out of my admiration trance, Timothy jets off in that direction.

I have two choices. I can go to the parking lot and hope he comes to the car after a quick hello, or I can run after him.

In true helicopter-mom fashion, I choose the latter. My ponytail bounces as I clutch my sling bag to keep it from banging against my chest. By the time I reach Timothy, Nate is leaning on his shovel, smiling.

His whole arm is glistening in the sun, and there are a few wet marks on his shirt, outlining his chest muscles. I clinch my teeth and silently scold myself for picturing him shirtless. Besides, we're nearing thirty. He can't look the same as he did at eighteen.

Maybe he looks better.

I grunt, and both guys stop talking and stare at me. I clear my throat and hope my face is flushed from running to cover my blushing. "Sorry, my throat is dry."

"Here." Nate lifts a water bottle in front of my face.

"That's nice, Mr. Nate, but Mama shouldn't share your germs."

"You're right, son, thanks." I dip my head as Nate lowers the drink.

Poor kid has no idea he's made up of half Mr. Nate's germs. For everyone's sanity, I'll keep that to myself and pretend he has cooties.

Unfortunately, I raise my head at the exact moment Nate decides to raise the end of his shirt and use it to wipe his forehead. I clamp my eyes shut.

"I was telling Timothy that—" he says, then pauses. "Are you sure you're okay?"

My eyes pop open to him staring at me. The good news is his shirt is back on his body. The bad news is I caught enough of a glimpse to confirm he looks even better now.

"Of course," I say nervously.

"Okay. I was saying that I need to finish flattening this area in front of the cages.

"Don't they make machines to do that kind of work?" My question is more rhetorical, as I know they do.

"Yeah, but I'm trying to stay in shape when I'm not on the field."

Mission accomplished.

"So you decided to manually dig a ditch?"

He laughs. "I'll probably regret that later."

I smile, and he smiles back. My nerves tingle. This is too familiar and awkward all at once.

"Timothy, let's go home and let Mr. Nate finish his work."

"What I was getting at, Brooke . . ."

Whatever he says next sounds like Charlie Brown's teacher. Hearing him say my name creates a lump in my throat.

"Is that good, Mama?"

"Hmm?" I turn to Timothy tugging at my shirt.

"Can Mr. Nate work with me tomorrow afternoon?"

My mouth parts to give an excuse, but I honestly have none. "If that's all right with Nate."

They both laugh.

"What?" I look at Timothy, then Nate, then back at Timothy.

"He just suggested it, Mama."

"Oh yeah. I need to go home and drink water or something."

They laugh again.

"I'll see y'all tomorrow, then. Just come by sometime after lunch."

"Yes, sir." Timothy extends a hand toward Nate.

He removes a work glove and shakes Timothy's hand. "Firm shake, I like it."

Timothy smiles. I nod and give Nate a smile that I hope doesn't look forced or cheesy, or forcefully cheesy. Then I escape to the comfort of my Corolla.

CHAPTER 5

Brooke

I'm really glad Nate wasn't at church this morning.

That's a horrible thing for me to think. I want everyone to go to church, really. It's just ironic that with so many Baptist churches in our county, he has to attend mine.

Well, his mom is a member there and he did go there growing up. So yes, it's my personal problem.

"I think that one's good, sweetie." Mama steps beside me and takes the dish from my hand. The same Pyrex I've been scrubbing for so long that my hands are now wrinkled from the running water. She turns off the sink and starts drying the dish. "You seem stressed."

I shake my head.

"You didn't say much during lunch, and you didn't eat much either."

"I wasn't that hungry." Not totally true, since I could go for a snack about now.

"Does it bother you that Timothy is going to work with Nate today?"

I pause from rubbing my wrinkled hands together.

"Timothy told me," she confesses.

I roll my eyes.

"What's it going to hurt? He's the best person to help him with ball. What's more convenient than a pro baseball player we all know and love living at the end of the driveway?"

"Love?"

Mama touches my elbow gently. "I didn't mean it that way." She sighs. "Like." Her voice is sarcastic and drawn out.

I smirk.

"Seriously, I think it's good for him. Your daddy never played sports, and your brothers haven't in ages." She leans closer and whispers, "They weren't the best either."

She leans back against the counter and I laugh. "I guess you make a good point. I want Timothy to do well at anything he decides to do."

She smiles. "And that's why you're a good mother."

"I hope." I turn my hands over and make fists. Their current condition is a good way to fight against touching Nate.

Timothy runs in, letting the screen door slam behind him. His breath is heavy when he stops.

"What have you been doing?" I ask.

"Conditioning." He stretches one arm across his chest and twists.

"Excuse me?"

"You know, running. Getting ready to practice." He does a few more random stretches, then opens the refrigerator.

I raise an eyebrow at Mama. She winks, and we both try not to laugh.

"I'm going to run home for the car."

Timothy gives me a thumbs-up with a bottle of Gatorade sucked to his mouth.

We walked over for lunch after changing out of our church clothes. It would be easy to ride the four-wheeler, but I don't want my hair knotted.

On second thought, I'd best check my overall appearance.

I go in the carriage house and hurry to the bathroom. My lipstick is gone and my foundation could use a touchup. I quickly redo everything but my eyes and pull my hair into a high ponytail. Then I take it back down. I wore a ponytail yesterday.

Groaning, I drop my head on the counter. It shouldn't matter if I wear back-to-back ponytails. This isn't *Mean Girls*.

Am I subconsciously hoping Nate will touch my hair?

I shudder and raise my head. Then I inspect my face once more to make sure I didn't mess up my forehead.

Timothy is waiting on the front porch when I get to Mama's house. He runs to the car before I can fully stop. "What took you so long?"

I frown. "Nothing?"

"Did you have to poop?"

"Timothy!"

"Well, did you?" He hops in and slams the door.

"No."

"I didn't think so. You didn't eat much at lunch."

"Why does everyone keep saying that?"

He buckles his seat belt, making me proud. I wasn't going to insist since we're maybe a mile at best from our destination, but it's nice to know I taught him safety. I buckle mine too.

"You're wearing lipstick."

"As I do every day."

"But you only put it on in the morning."

I put the car in drive and stare ahead. I refuse to be interrogated by a second grader. He takes the hint and doesn't say another word until we turn into Nate's drive.

Timothy opens the door and jumps out with my brother's

old glove and a ball. That's all we could find short notice, but I assured him Nate would have baseball stuff.

Nate comes from the backyard, smiling. "I was fighting off a nap. I thought y'all weren't coming."

"Mama had to put on makeup." Timothy smirks at me.

"Um, I put on Chapstick." Not a total lie, since my lipstick is tinted Chapstick.

"It looks nice," Nate comments.

My cheeks heat up and I turn my head.

"Let's get started." He claps his hands together, bringing me back to attention.

We follow him down the slope to the backyard, past several blackberry bushes. An old metal building comes into view when we get to the clearing. He leads us to it and lifts the rolling door effortlessly.

My mouth drops as I scan a room of baseball equipment, complete with a pitching machine and batting cage. In addition to that is free weights, an exercise bike, and a TV.

"Wow."

"Jonah had the house in great shape, but this was an old shop. I slowly had it renovated after buying."

"Who did it?"

"A moving company brought my own equipment, and Jonah helped with facilitating it all. He knew a really nice guy who turfed the church soccer field and Evalene Mayberry's carport."

I lift my chin, curious as to how Jonah had a hand in this and I didn't hear about it. His wife and business partner, Carolina, isn't exactly Fort Knox when it comes to keeping things hush.

Metal clanks, and I crane my neck. Timothy's head pops up behind a counter.

"Timothy, stop snooping, son."

"Sorry, Mama. He has a kitchen too."

I turn to Nate. "Really?"

"A mini fridge full of sweet tea and Mountain Dew, plus a microwave." He shrugs. "The previous owner had a wet bar, so I decided to leave it partially intact."

I laugh.

"The sink has come in handy when I need to clean my balls."

I choke and cough loudly. *He means baseballs.*

"Want some water?"

I nod. He goes toward Timothy and returns with a bottle of water. A new bottle, without his germs.

I chug it like I'm stuck in the Sahara.

"Better?" Nate asks.

The bottle is half empty when I lower it and nod.

"Good. Make yourself at home. I'll get Timothy started."

He leaves my side, and I survey the area. There's a well-worn couch near the TV. I sit on it and turn so I can watch where he's taking Timothy.

They start at a wall filled with bats. Timothy's face lights up when Nate pulls down several smaller ones for him to try. Not that I would recognize any of them, but I'm sure they're Nate's from over the years.

His mom never had a lot of money, but she spared no expense when it came to helping supply him with baseball equipment. He might not have had the flashiest or newest supplies, but he always had what he needed. Even when she didn't.

I always admired and respected her sacrifices for him. Little did I know I'd one day be a single mom to a son.

They settle on a bat and go to the cage. Nate adjusts a tee and sits on a bucket nearby. He explains some things to Timothy, then stands and helps him position the bat.

Out of nowhere, my eyes start to water. I stand and exit through the smaller door on the opposite end of the building. It's all I can take seeing them together like father and son.

All the whys and ifs that plagued me for years hit me like

a head-on collision. If I had to put myself through a CT scan right now, I'd find plenty of internal damage.

Nate

Maybe it's because I'm not used to younger kids, but Timothy is impressive to have never played ball.

He has great hand-eye coordination and picks up on everything I teach him quickly. His form is already good, and he's showing a lot of potential.

I need to find Brooke. I bet she'd like to see how well he's doing.

"Hey, you want to show your mom what you learned?"

He nods enthusiastically.

I stand from sitting on a bucket and scan the shop. There's no sign of Brooke, and I don't hear anyone.

"Let's find her." I lift the batting cage net, and Timothy follows me outside. The sun is lowering and it's cooling down.

"You think she ran home to cook dinner or something?"

Timothy shakes his head. "Mama never leaves me for too long, especially not with a stranger."

"I'm not a stranger."

He wavers his head. "Technically, no, but how well do we really know you?"

I laugh. He's a sharp kid, and funny.

"Your mom and I actually go way back."

"Didn't you grow up here?"

"I did. And we used to go—" I clamp my mouth shut and clear my throat. "To school together."

He smiles. "What was Mama like back then?"

"Nice, fun, beautiful."

He smiles wider. "She's still nice and beautiful, but I don't know about the fun."

"Really?"

"Yeah, she worries a lot."

I speed up toward the front of the house, relieved to find Brooke sitting in her car. If I keep talking, Timothy might figure out pretty quickly we were more than classmates.

He sees her at the same time and runs toward the car. I follow him, matching my steps to his with my long legs.

"Mama!" He opens her door.

She jumps and catches her breath.

"Were you going to leave me?"

Brooke shakes her head and starts to cry. She pulls him in her lap and hugs him close. "Never. You know better than that."

He pulls back, and I take a step away.

"You know I would tell you if I went somewhere, even to the house for a minute." She glances at me, then back at him. "But if I did go, you can trust Mr. Nate. He's a good man and not a stranger."

Timothy nods his head, then smiles up at me.

Now I want to cry.

"Uh, he's looking good in there. I thought you might want to see."

"Thanks." She smiles and dabs at her eyes. "I just needed some air."

"Then why did you get in the car with the windows up?" Timothy asks.

Brooke climbs out and sighs. I pull Timothy to the side so she can shut the door.

I've never been a parent, but I totally get needing some time alone. Before and after games, when my shoulder flares up, and many times right after our breakup.

The three of us walk in silence downhill toward the shop. I notice our shadows side by side. A weird emotion creeps up.

If I had to describe it, I'd say jealousy mixed with regret.

What if I had fought for Brooke when she broke up with me? Drove to see her instead of just calling and texting all the time?

I might could be her husband and Timothy's dad.

Even worse, what if I'd left when I'd planned on it the last day I was with her? I'd surprised her at college and stayed the night in her dorm. Nothing happened—that night.

It was the next afternoon when I should've already been back in Atlanta. Instead, I'd lingered around because she didn't want me to leave.

She'd wanted everything as badly as me.

However, being the guy, I should've backed down. That's on me. Nothing was the same after that day, and our relationship lasted only another month.

It was the last time I saw her in person until she was hanging on the fence in her bathrobe.

We enter shaded territory, and I'm no longer haunted by our shadows in perfect sync. I shake off the idea that this could be my family as soon as my feet cross the threshold of my personal training facility.

Brooke and Timothy are here for one reason. Baseball. Nothing more, nothing less.

I offered to help him, and they took me up on it. He's doing a great job, and I want to see him succeed, as I would any young kid with a passion for the game.

"Come on, Timothy." I lift the net for him and bend under it. Brooke stares at me from the other side like she's done hundreds of times before when I played. She remembers it too. I can tell by her eyes.

I give her a half smile before forcing my focus on Timothy and the batting tee.

The. ONLY. Reason. I'm. With. Them.

Focus.

"All right, King of Swing, you ready?"

"King of Swing?" Timothy laughs.

"Yeah, every good baller needs a nickname."

He laughs and so does Brooke. The air lightens a little and I can feel the tension leaving me slowly. I put a ball on the tee and resume my spot on the bucket.

Then I make a silent pact with myself to stay there. No getting close to Brooke in any way. No more wondering if there's a dad in Timothy's life. Even though I suspect whoever his dad is, he has at least some natural athletic ability.

I'll be the bucket man and nothing else, even if it kills me.

CHAPTER 6

Brooke

"I want to thank all y'all for coming tonight." Jeffrey twists a large bedazzled ring around his finger while he talks.

I can't get a good look at it, but my gut feeling is he didn't get it from college. It complements his jersey and baseball pants, which are more suited for a player than a grown man running a parent information meeting.

"Me and Coach Bubba have a predicament with the eight-and-under boys this year." He scans the small crowd spread across the gym bleachers.

Jeffrey turns to a man sitting nearby who's dressed in gym shorts and a fishing shirt with a few too many buttons undone. I assume he's Coach Bubba.

"We have enough for a solid team, but not two."

"What are you implying, Coach?" Morgan shouts from the bleachers.

I drop my head as every eye turns our way. You'd think by now I'd know better than to sit with her at a school function.

"All I'm saying is we can't have a team with fifteen kids. Wouldn't give everyone fair playing time."

Morgan opens her mouth, but Jeffrey holds up his hand to stop her. She grunts, and I swear a small stream of smoke comes from her nostrils.

"We have several on the wait list right now." He makes a grabbing motion toward Bubba.

Bubba unfolds his arms and reaches for a sheet of paper on the table in front of him. Jeffrey takes it and clears his throat. "These people signed up last and are on a wait list. Timothy Marshall."

"That son of a . . ." Morgan whispers.

I elbow her. "It's okay. I wasn't exactly sold on this anyway."

She grunts louder.

"Jack Daniels and Charlie Daniels." He turns to Bubba. "Are those real kids?"

"They're absolutely real kids," Maribelle calls loudly behind us.

Morgan pats her knee. "We got this, girl."

She smiles at Morgan.

I pull my legs into my chest. It will only be by God's good grace if we make it out of here without a bunch of mad mamas attacking Jeffrey.

"And an Angel and Precious. Last name on both says . . . Pending?" Jeffrey flips the page over as if he will find an answer.

"Custody crap," Tami says from the corner of the gym.

I hadn't noticed her until now. She must've come in late, because she's hard to miss. Sadly, she's as close to a celebrity as our town has thanks to her TikTok following.

Well, unless you count Nate with baseball.

I twist my mouth. I'd almost made it a full day without thinking of him.

"Why don't you put your girls in softball, Tami?" Jeffrey asks.

"Why don't you put your tongue back in your mouth, Jeffrey?" She widens her eyes and lunges forward, almost dropping the baby on her hip.

Jeffrey clears his throat and turns toward us. In his defense, Tami isn't wearing much and often advertises that she's on the prowl for a new baby daddy—in more ways than one.

"Anyway, that's where we're at in making a team."

Maribelle raises her hand.

"Yes?" Jeffrey points to her.

"What can we do to get our babies off the wait list? I mean, my kids need something to do while my husband is working. Besides destroy our house." She follows her comment with a long sigh.

"Get more people to sign up by Friday."

"Then those new people and the wait-list kids will be a team?" I ask.

Jeffrey opens his mouth, but Bubba beats him to answering. "According to section A, item twenty in the rule book, we would then hold a draft."

Jeffrey glares at Bubba, who pulls a tiny booklet from his shirt pocket and waves it to make a point.

"That's right, Bubba. Jeffrey can't stack a park-league team this year," Morgan coos loud enough for Maribelle and me to hear.

"So we need like five or six kids by Friday?" Maribelle asks to clarify.

"Yes, and it's already Tuesday. So I get it if that's too much to ask." Jeffrey's voice is filled with fake pity.

"Nah. If I can get a thousand followers every new post, I can come up with a few kids to play ball." Tami straightens against the door frame, giving Jeffrey a smug expression.

"You can't do anything illegal to get kids, Tami."

"Neither can you, Jeffrey." She snaps her head, again almost dropping the baby.

I don't know what happened between those two, and I'm good with that.

"So if I register more kids in this age group by Friday, say when school ends, we can draft teams?" Morgan asks.

"Correct." Jeffrey has a begrudging tone, which makes her smile.

"Heck, we'll have plenty by then," Tami chimes in.

Jeffrey grits his teeth and cuts his eyes toward her before turning back to the bleachers. "If there's no other questions, that's all I have. Thanks for coming out tonight."

He disappears somewhere in the back of the gym, leaving Bubba to fold up the table and chairs. He's probably on the run from Tami, since she has it out for him. Or Morgan, or Maribelle. The man sure knows how to turn women against him.

As we're exiting the gym, Morgan pulls me and Maribelle to the side. "We need a game plan to get more players. I want y'all to think of everyone who might want their kids to play ball."

"What if we don't like them?" Maribelle frowns.

"Then we hope Jeffrey drafts their kid. If y'all want your kids playing baseball here this year, we need warm bodies who identify as kids under eight."

"I'm really fine with Timothy not playing this year. I think he's not—"

My eyes cross and focus on Morgan's fingers pinching my mouth shut. "That boy's gonna play, and I'll get him on Andrew's team."

I try and ask how can she guarantee that, but it sounds more like gibberish.

"Trust me, Brooke." She lets go of my mouth. "See y'all soon. Text me names."

Morgan disappears into the night toward her van. I wiggle

my lips to try and rid them of that post-dental-work feeling Morgan induced.

"I guess we better get to it." Maribelle gives me a tired smile.

"I hope it works out." I give my best fake smile in return. "Good night."

"You too." Maribelle crosses the parking lot.

I shove my hands in my scrubs pockets and try to think positively. I wasn't sold on the idea of Timothy playing in the first place. Maybe this whole wait list thing is a blessing in disguise.

Headlights turn left and right as people leave. Soon I'm standing alone, except for Jeffrey in the distance checking his tires. Probably for slashes.

That's my cue to leave.

Nate

The trailer beeps as Jeffrey navigates around the blackberry and blueberry bushes on my property.

I shake my head. Why in the world did I agree to this?

Mom steps beside me and smiles wider than the offensive bumper sticker on Jeffrey's truck. That's why I agreed to this.

"This is so nice. We're going to be neighbors," she says.

"Again, Mom, you could've just moved into my house. You literally wouldn't have to see me unless you wanted to." I thought she'd jump at the chance of moving away from the mobile-home park.

"Of course I want to see you." She pats my cheek. "I just didn't want to give up my own home."

"So you had no problem moving, as long as you could take your actual home?"

"You finally get it."

Shows how much I know about women.

She laughs and walks carefully down the steep hill on the side of the house. I hurry and catch up to her in case Jeffrey isn't paying attention.

He doesn't strike me as the most careful driver. On top of that, I don't think he sets up many trailers in backyards. Or maybe he does. This is Apple Cart County. Not a lot of zoning and property restrictions in a place that shares a golf course with cows.

Mom takes a seat in one of my back patio chairs and watches Jeffrey like it's free entertainment. In a way it is, except that I'm paying him to move her trailer.

"So you really love this old house that much?" I still don't get the appeal in a nineties-model mobile home with plastic shutters. I've been after her to upgrade it for years.

"More what's in it."

"Mom, we could've moved your stuff."

She wavers her head. "I know, but you already have an oven."

"The oven?" I widen my eyes. "That's what you didn't want to leave?"

"Well, yeah. It took me some time to learn how long to cook everything in it to perfection."

I can't really argue with that.

Jeffrey's truck backfires, and we stare across the yard. Luckily, Mom's home is still in one piece.

He parks it in a nice little clearing, far enough away from my baseball shop to give her some privacy.

Once I'm sure it's safe, we start toward the truck. A bigger guy and Jeffrey are securing it in place when we get to them.

"What about my porch?" Mom asks.

"I'll build you a new porch."

"That one was perfect for my wind chimes." Her face falls.

"Mom, I tried, but the trailer park said it was there before us so it had to stay." I put my arm around her shoulder.

"You mean modular-home neighborhood." Jeffrey enunciates every word like he's teaching me a new language. In a way, he is.

"Huh?"

"Our business is rebranding."

"Oh, okay, then."

The guy beside him pulls a rag from his back pocket and wipes sweat from every piece of skin showing.

"Would you guys like some water?" I ask.

"Absolutely," the man answers.

"Give me a minute." I hurry to the shop and grab two bottles of water from the refrigerator in my kitchen area. I don't want to leave them alone with my mother for too long. Not that I think they would do anything to hurt her in a predatory way, but they might accidentally run over her.

They both thank me for the water. I notice "Bubba" sewn on the pocket of the other guy's shirt. Makes sense. He looks like a Bubba.

"Thanks, Jeffrey," I tell him.

"You're welcome." He chugs some water, then turns to Mom. "Ma'am, we tried to tie down the furniture best we could, but ran out of ratchet straps when we got to the spare bedroom. My apologies if anything is in shambles."

"That's okay. As long as the oven still works."

I sigh. I'm beginning to think Mom loves that oven more than me.

"I know you paid me already, Nate, but I want to ask a favor."

Dear God, please don't let him ask that I put in a word for his kids.

I don't know Jeffrey well, but I've already heard he's one of those guys who thinks his kids are going pro. Even though they're still playing coach-pitch and rocking baby teeth.

He disappears into his truck. I kick the ground awkwardly, afraid of what he'll bring out.

"Is he okay?" Mom asks.

"I don't know. He was with Misty for a while, so that might've gotten to him."

"No, that man." She nods toward the clearing.

I follow her gaze to Bubba lying on the ground with his cap over his eyes.

"I think he will be."

Jeffrey returns with a shirt in his hand.

"If you don't mind, Nate, I'd like you to sign this jersey for me." He whips open the jersey. It looks vintage. I haven't seen anyone with that style since I was a kid, and I certainly didn't wear it. I'm already skeptical when he shows me the back.

"Uh, that's not even my number." I raise my brows as I notice "Jones." "And it's got Chipper's name."

"Yeah." Jeffrey tosses it over his shoulder. "I know, but I promised a signed Braves jersey for my kids' travel-ball raffle."

"I could get you one with my name and number if you give me a few days."

"No offense, son, but Chipper's way more famous than you." He pats my shoulder.

"Well, thanks for moving my mom's home. Be careful backing out." I turn to go back in the house.

"Wait, so you ain't gonna sign it?"

I sigh and turn around. Jeffrey is holding a Sharpie he somehow pulled out of thin air. Or maybe his butt. Who knows with this weirdo.

Shaking off the butt hypothesis, I grab the pen and scribble my name right beside Chipper's. That should show him.

"Thanks."

"Mm-hmm." I force a pleasant face. "Mom, let's go inside so they can get out safely, then we can come work on your place."

"Sounds good." She smiles at Jeffrey. "Thank you."

"You're welcome, ma'am."

Jeffrey heads to his truck. He stops by Bubba and kicks him in the side. Mom and I both wince as Bubba moans and comes to life.

"Bless his heart," she mumbles to me.

"Looks like they've done this before."

Mom shakes her head. "I'm adding them to my prayer list."

"Please do."

CHAPTER 7

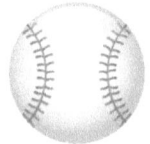

Brooke

My phone vibrates for the fourth time. I silenced it after two calls, but Morgan won't stop. I would turn it off completely, but then I might miss something from a doctor or nurse.

I finish the X-ray on a kid's ankle, trying my best to ignore whatever Morgan wants. Actually, I'm almost certain I know what she wants, which is more reason to avoid my phone.

Unlike her and Maribelle, I have contacted zero people this week concerning baseball. Unless you count taking Timothy to Nate's house for one more practice.

Yet another reason I'm not excited about him playing ball.

I help the little boy back in the wheelchair so his mother can roll him to a room. "They have room two ready for you. I'll let the doctor know the X-rays are done."

"Thank you," the mother says.

I open the door and lead them in the direction of the patient room. The boy is about the same size as Timothy. I don't dare ask how he hurt his ankle, because I'm afraid the mom will say baseball.

When I leave the room, I'm extra cautious turning around. I have been ever since the day Nate surprised me in the hallway.

I wait until I'm back in the X-ray room to text Easton that I have images ready for him and a patient in room two. That's when I notice a ton of texts from Morgan. None of them say anything other than "Call me." Most of them in all caps.

I roll my eyes and call her.

"Brooke! Where have you been?"

"I'm at work. Aren't you?"

"Yeah."

"What is it?" I sit in the desk chair behind the imaging wall. Best get comfortable. Morgan likes to have lengthy conversations.

"I found enough kids to go in the draft."

"Huh. I thought you said we needed one more."

"That coupon won't work."

"What?" I hold my breath, hoping this isn't some sketchy BOGO coupon for ball players they found on TikTok.

"Sorry, talking to the person I'm checking out."

I pinch the bridge of my nose and listen to her have a conversation with someone concerning a fifty-cent coupon for washing detergent. Morgan is lucky everyone at the Piggly Wiggly knows her so well, or else she might be without a job.

"Anyways, Aniston said Carter is ready to play again."

"Really?"

"I know, isn't that great?"

"Yeah." I fight the temptation to think it isn't. Selfishly, I want an excuse for Timothy not to play. However, Carter hasn't played baseball since his parents died. If he's wanting to play again, that's a good thing. "Okay, I'll let you go."

"Wait!" Morgan screams in the phone.

I hold it back and rub my ear.

"There's one more catch."

Of course there is. I bite my bottom lip and wait for the news.

"A coach for the second team has to be present for the draft to happen."

"Can't Coach Bubba do that?"

"No. He can't be a head coach."

"Why not?"

"He's not a parent."

"Okay . . ."

My stomach swirls. I don't like where this is going.

"Here's the deal. I can represent the coach spot at the draft."

"What!" Now it's my turn to yell in the phone.

"Hear me out. Once we get a team, we'll see who's got good dads and make them the coaches."

"I don't know, Morgan. What if you get stuck coaching?"

"You think they'll let me be a head coach?" She snort-laughs.

"If they wouldn't, then what makes you think they'll let you do the draft?"

"Because I'm bringing someone more respectable with me."

"Who?"

I can almost hear her smile over the phone. "No, no, no."

"Yes, for Timothy. You have to. Just tonight, okay?"

I sigh and ball my hand into a tight fist. Good thing I'm on the phone, or I'd be tempted to punch her.

Against my better judgment, I pull up to the elementary school gym a few minutes before six. Morgan, who's usually late, is waiting for me by her van, a huge grin plastered across her face.

"You won, I'm here." I sigh as her grin grows.

At least I had a little time off work to pick up Timothy and get him settled doing homework at my parents' house. Morgan must have just left work, because she's still wearing her red shirt with the Pig head on the back.

She struts to the gym entrance and opens the door for me. I walk in cautiously like I'm entering a hostage situation. There's a lone table set up in the center of the gym and only the middle row of fluorescent lights is on. Hostage situation is an eerily accurate metaphor.

Footsteps come from the side, and we both turn our heads to Jeffrey across the gym. He flips on the rest of the lights.

"Ladies, welcome. The men will be here shortly." He motions to the table with chairs around it. "Have a seat at the table."

I give Morgan a cautious glare, then follow her to the table. It's so quiet, we can hear the lights warming. The chair squeaks on the floor when I pull it back.

Morgan reclines in the chair beside me and pulls out her phone. She's content with scrolling Facebook, then complains when there isn't enough cell service for her to comment on a post.

We sit in silence for about two more minutes. Mainly because I don't care to know any more than I have to about the draft. I'm here for moral support only.

Footsteps and low talking come from the door. I turn to five men, Jeffrey and Bubba included, walking our way. I lean toward Morgan as they get closer. "How many extra kids did you add?"

She bites her bottom lip and stares at the lights, then back at me. She shrugs.

"I know of like five, but Tami said she put something on TikTok about it."

I drop my head to the table.

"Ladies."

I raise my head to the men joining us at the table. Other than Jeffrey and Bubba, I only recognize one more. He blushes and looks away when I make eye contact. I would too. My only memory of him was when I worked the emergency room and he came in for a rash. It was poison ivy on places the sun doesn't shine.

Let's just say I bet he'll look twice before he poops in the woods again.

"All right." Jeffrey sits down last and slaps a few papers on the table. "Looks like we're all here. Let's get this show on the road."

"How many kids did we end up with?" Morgan asks.

"Twenty."

She nods at each guy, then raises one brow.

"My team is blessed with a lot of assistant coaches this year." Jeffrey turns the papers toward her. "So I took the liberty of marking off the coaches' kids since they're frozen."

Morgan's eyes bug. "You can't do that."

"Rules are rules." He taps the paper. "See here, I froze Andrew for you."

"So you get six kids automatically, and I get one. What kind of draft is this?"

Bubba pulls the same small book from his shirt pocket as before. "According to section B, item eighty in the rule book, any parent willing to give up their time is guaranteed to coach their own kid."

"But y'all get six? Why can't I get six travel-ball boys?"

"Now let's don't go mixing tea with lemonade. Travel ball has nothing to do with park-ball drafting." Jeffrey leans toward Morgan. "If you had assistant coaches, we'd freeze their kids for you too."

Morgan grabs my arm and pulls me closer to her. My chair screeches on the floor. "I have Brooke."

"Wait—"

She pinches my arm to shut me up. I obey because my arm is throbbing and she kind of scares me.

"Fine. Bubba, mark the Marshall kid off too."

Bubba pulls a pen out of his pocket and puts a check next to Timothy's name. I puff my cheeks and pray I don't throw up. This is getting way out of hand.

"See, we got half the kids squared away. The rest shouldn't take long." Jeffrey shakes his arm and stares at a large gold wristwatch. "I may even make the second half of that cornhole tournament in Moonshine County."

I let out the breath I've been holding and slump down in my chair. Morgan owes me big time for this. Way more than her usual almost-expired free snacks from the Pig.

Nate

I tap my thumb against my knee and stare at the wall in the doctor's office.

Now that Mom is safely squared away in her home—in my backyard—I can focus on my shoulder. Though I'm not sure if that's a good thing. Therapy will be rough after a few weeks of nothing more than yard work and soft tosses to a second grader.

"Nathaniel Miller," a nasally voice calls.

I turn to a young woman, who I assume is a new intern because I've never seen her here before. I try to ignore the twitch my shoulder gives when I push my hands off my knees to stand.

When I walk toward her, she smiles. "Nate the Great, right?"

Her eyes are starstruck and she's still calling me "great." Yeah, she's for sure new around here.

"If you say so."

She's wearing a lanyard with the name "Shelby" on the tag. She's also wearing scrubs.

Brooke works in scrubs. I bet she'd be hot in some Braves scrubs. Maybe I could score her a pair?

I shake that thought before it gets out of hand and follow Shelby to a larger room with medical tables with all kinds of torture devices.

"Have a seat and relax."

I try not to laugh. They always tell me to relax, then wire my arm like a car battery.

Shelby turns the dial on the machine, and my arm tingles like I fell in an ant bed. "Good, or too much?"

"It's fine," I lie, knowing I need it and that my arm will adjust to it soon.

"Okay, let me know if it gets too much."

She turns and walks across the room. I wait until she's busy helping someone else before I close my eyes and try to relax.

Every tingle in my arm reminds me of a memory.

Pitching last season. Throwing out my shoulder. Having surgery. Prepping to pitch this season. Digging a ditch at the park. Soft-tossing balls to Timothy. Moving Mom's china cabinet—with the china in it.

Yeah, that last one was probably the nail in the coffin that caused my current discomfort.

When my arm is all but numb, the machine cuts off. I open my eyes to Shelby peeling the sticky patches from my skin. A few arm hairs come off with one and I wince.

"Sorry." She rubs my arm.

I look away. There's no way I'm allowing a tiny girl to sense my pain.

"Dr. Trenton will be over in a minute."

"Thanks."

She offers a closed-lip smile, then moves on to someone on a table across the room. I watch the other guy flirt shamelessly as she tapes up his calf. Reminds me a lot of my buddy, Ace. He flirts with anything female and breathing. He'd most definitely flirt with a cute young woman.

Some of my teammates joke that I'm playing mysterious to make women want me more.

Truth is I spent the first part of my career with Brooke, then getting over Brooke. After that I focused more on ball and didn't date unless I knew the woman well enough to make sure she didn't have an ulterior motive. And the last few weeks I've moved into my Seeing Brooke Again Era, which brings up all kinds of emotions I don't want to deal with.

I lean my head against the wall and squirm against the rubber padding on the table where I'm seated. I should be in Florida for spring training, but I'm here working with a team-approved specialist, still recovering from an injury. It's becoming more of a recurring injury. One that's made me think about retiring sooner than later.

I'm not even thirty, but pro athletes age in dog years.

Speaking of aging, Dr. Trenton is goals. The man is a retired Navy Seal who could pass for much younger if not for eye wrinkles and gray hair. He's the only person I know who can make scrubs intimidating.

He marches my way, a faded bald-eagle tattoo partially showing under his short sleeve. He extends his hand without a verbal greeting. The bird's wing turns on a flex when he squeezes my hand and gives it a firm shake.

I grit my teeth to play off the tension caused by him squeezing my already sensitive hand. Dang ant bed machine.

"Did that hurt?"

I narrow my eyes, trying to decide if he's referring to the machine or the handshake.

"That's what I thought." He pulls a pen from his scrubs pocket and jots down a note.

"It wouldn't bother me if I hadn't been on the tingling machine first."

He jots down something more. I lean forward, attempting to peek at the notes. But he's also fast and slaps the folder shut.

"Nate, I'm going to work your shoulder through some different exercises than before. What's concerning me most is that the pain is now crawling down your arm."

Well, yeah, when you clip shockwaves to me.

Instead of answering, I do as I'm told when he stands behind me and pulls on my shoulder. Going through the motions of rotating my arm has never hurt so much. I'm blaming the china cabinet. Why does she even need that thing? We eat off her Pioneer Woman collection from Walmart.

But it's Mom's, so I moved it without question. Anything for her and . . .

My thoughts almost drifted to include Brooke.

They are the two women I'd do anything to protect. Anything to help. The only two women I've ever loved.

Crap. That's why I can't have an actual relationship with anyone. It has less to do with me thinking everyone is a cleat digger and more to do with them not being Brooke.

The doc presses his thumbs into my shoulder blade, causing me to jolt to attention.

"Let's stand and work the bands a little." I follow him toward the corner of the room. "Have you done anything recently to upset the injury?"

"I might've moved around some furniture last week."

He shakes his head and hands me a resistance band. "Start stretching."

No sooner than I pull the band outward, his fingers are needling in my shoulder again. He touches the tender skin of my surgery scar, and I cringe. I scrunch my face and concentrate on the exercise.

After a dozen or so reps, he circles in front of me and instructs me to stand straighter. "You need to stay away from any unnecessary lifting."

"What about working out?"

His head wavers. "I need to have a discussion with your strength and conditioning coach for final say, but I'd go easy on the weight for any shoulder exercises."

I sigh. It's such a catch-22. I can't pitch if my arm is weak, but I can't build up strength if it will hurt my arm further.

"Look, I know this is frustrating. Nobody likes to think of ending a career."

"What are you saying?" My voice is shaky, and now all my nerves tingle, not just the ones in my left arm.

"What I'm saying is if there's any chance of you making it on this season's roster, you've got to take better care of yourself."

I hang my head in defeat. I finally started a few games last year in the majors, only to end the season with a bum shoulder. Now this?

Buying a home in Apple Cart was my retirement plan, but I didn't plan on retiring so soon. Nothing in me wants last season to be my last.

"I'll help all I can, but you've got to take care of that arm and shoulder." He crosses his arms and gives me a stern face. "You're recovering from a major surgery. Things aren't the same as before."

I study the eagle on his arm, staring at me as well. I lift my eyes and nod slowly.

"You're a bright, talented young man. Follow doctor's orders and you can still have a few seasons. Or heck, I hear the Savannah Bananas are always looking for new entertainers."

I frown. As much as I enjoy watching Banana Ball, starring in a sideshow isn't the way I pictured going out.

CHAPTER 8

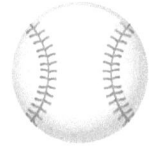

Brooke

"Moooooo."

I crane my neck to make sure the cows are still at a good distance. Thanks to Jeffrey, we couldn't get a field to practice on this week. Unless we settled for starting at nine p.m.

Our property is covered with apple trees and farm equipment, and Morgan lives in town on half an acre. Even the church soccer field was already claimed for a preteen laser tag party. That leaves the good old community pasture.

Aniston gets out of her van with Carter. She sips her energy drink as she leans closer to me. "You know, I have a pasture without cows."

"Yeah, but it's not as big. Plus, you have a pool and a pond to distract everyone and you live farther out of town."

She shrugs. "Just sayin' . . ."

"I appreciate it." I smile at her, then focus on the other parents and kids coming toward the gate.

Ethan holds it open for them to enter. Georgia squeals

when her heel sticks in a cow pie. She tiptoes toward the edge of the field and rubs her foot against a tall patch of grass. When it's almost off, she looks at Aniston pitifully. "I am so sorry I made you shovel manure last year."

Aniston snorts and smiles. "Welcome to the dark side."

Georgia perks up a little at her approval. It's probably to her benefit she stepped in poop, since she and her son are dressed like they're attending the US Open, or maybe playing in it.

Tami's girls are picking weeds that resemble flowers, and Maribelle's kids are running circles around her.

"Is that kid wearing a cape?"

"Appears so." Aniston laughs.

Oh shoot, I said that out loud.

The last few people enter and Ethan closes the gate.

"Thank y'all for coming, and for being flexible with our, uh, venue." Morgan cuts side-eye at me.

She told me before everyone arrived that she'd have it out with Jeffrey later. I can't decide if I want to be there for that. I witnessed enough of his craziness during Toy Bowl when I helped coach cheerleaders.

That, I signed up to do.

"We'll get an idea of where all your kids are in ball." Morgan scans the group.

So do I, and I don't like what I see.

"I brought all my kids' supplies in case some of y'all don't have gear yet." Morgan nods to Ethan. "That's my oldest. I'll make him throw to them and stuff."

Everyone looks back at us with blank stares. Except for Georgia, who raises her hand.

"Yes, Georgia?" Morgan sighs.

I nudge her, and she clears her throat.

Morgan doesn't care for Georgia since she caused Aniston so much trouble last year after she moved back to take care of her niece and nephew. After lots of fights—verbal, then culminating in physically fighting in a bouncy house—they finally called a truce. However, Morgan isn't as forgiving as the rest of us.

Maybe if my husband left me and our four kids, I'd find it hard to forgive too. Of course, I'd first need a husband for that to happen.

"I bought Herrington a bat and glove."

"Lemme see." Morgan motions her over.

Georgia grabs a golf bag and drags it toward us. I assume this means she didn't buy a bat bag. "Here." She hands Morgan a bat, then a glove.

"Uh, sorry to tell you, but this is a T-ball bat and a first baseman's mitt."

Georgia's eyes widen.

"Don't peel off any stickers and you can return them."

Georgia blinks. "But I had them personalized." She flips the bat to show initials engraved on the end. A matching monogram is embroidered on the thumb of the glove.

Morgan offers her best non-verbal "bless her heart" face. "Maybe try eBay?"

Georgia nods, then packs it all back into the golf bag.

"Okay." Morgan slaps her hands together. "We can discuss equipment and uniforms and such in our group chat. For now, let's practice."

I stand aside as she instructs the parents where to set up their lawn chairs. Another cow moos in the distance while Ethan gathers the kids to work on basics.

I walk toward the moo to make sure there isn't a bull around. At least the grass hasn't grown so high that we can't find the cow patties. Give it a few more months and we'll be practicing in a jungle.

"Brooke?"

That voice.

I take a deep breath and turn my head to Nate crossing the road from his property. It's been a week since I last saw him, which is either way too long or too short. I can't decide, and I don't want to.

"Hey. What are y'all doing out here?" he asks.

"It was either this or practice at nine, according to Jeffrey's field schedule." I roll my eyes.

"That's ridiculous. Y'all can't do anything with cows and poop all around. Come across the road to my place."

"I—"

"I'll go tell them."

I'm trying to respond when he jumps the fence and jogs toward the parents. I watch for a few seconds, then follow him.

By the time I make it to everyone, they're folding chairs. Morgan whistles, and Ethan's head whips around like a dog's. "Bring it in, we're going to Mr. Nate's house."

The kids cheer, and Tami gives Nate a look that momentarily makes me jealous. Then I realize Nate is *not* mine . . . and it's Tami.

Ethan gets the gate, and we funnel to the other side. Paul and Ms. Dot zoom by in a golf cart. Maribelle jerks her twins back before they get run over. Paul honks, and Dot yells out, "Sorry," as they speed toward the orchard.

Chances are he plans on trying to pick apples that don't yet exist. Ever since my mom said he could come pick apples anytime, he's taken full advantage.

I'm so focused on the kids and the golf cart that I don't notice Nate's hand on my back until he slides it away. My stomach tingles. He was likely holding me back from death by Paul's drive-by.

Yeah, that's it. Nothing more.

We look both ways and cross the road, dragging chairs and equipment behind. Nate jogs ahead and points past his house. "I have a makeshift training center in my shop and a nice level lot in the back."

Without hesitation, the kids hurry behind him and race to

the shop. One kid falls down and gets tangled in his clothes. Unsurprisingly, it's the boy wearing some type of cloak.

I help him up, and his mom thanks me.

"You're welcome."

After he catches up with the others, she sighs. "Hi, I'm Agatha."

I shake her hand. "Nice to meet you. I'm Brooke, Timothy's mom."

"This is Reece's first sport ever. He has so many allergies that I've always homeschooled him and kept him from team involvement."

I nod.

"Our allergist suggested I start integrating him into society to get used to germs. I thought an outdoor sport might be a good start."

"So is the cape something to do with his allergies?"

She laughs. "Oh no. That's our compromise. He wanted to play Quidditch."

I think that's a *Harry Potter* thing, but I'm not certain. I decide not to ask.

Aniston slaps a hand on my shoulder and smirks. "Looks like your man came through for us."

"He's not . . ." I shake my head.

She winks, and my face heats up. Then she rushes inside before I can protest.

I'm the last one inside, except for Georgia. She had some trouble rolling the golf bag down the hill. I wait on her to be polite and help her drag it over the threshold.

Timothy waves at me from the batting cage. I wave back and scan the area. Even though there are ten different families in here now, I still have jitters since I'm in Nate territory.

Families.

That word alone makes me more nervous. Technically my family is here too, but neither of them know they're family.

Within five minutes, Nate has the boys at three different

stations. Ethan is running one and Morgan another, while he mans the third.

For the first time, I appreciate him as a baseball coach. Until today, I've looked at him as a baseball player. As someone who wanted to be a teacher for most of my life, I can sense he has a real knack for it.

The kids rotate through the stations. I make it a point to talk to all the parents and welcome everyone. I'm still much more suited for the role of cheerleader than anything to do with baseball.

An hour later, I'm helping Georgia pick up balls scattered across the floor. I mindlessly reach for one in the corner and a hand falls on mine. My eyes lift to Nate. He grins, and I drop my gaze to our hands.

I curl my fingers around the ball. His hand slips away when I lift mine. "Here," I say.

"Thanks." He takes the ball, causing our hands to touch again.

This time I'm sure it's intentional because he takes his dear time removing his hand. I clear my throat and stand. "Thanks for . . ." I gesture around at everyone.

"You're welcome." He smirks at Morgan talking to the parents, then narrows his eyes. "What's up with the kid in the cape?"

"His mom mentioned something like Quidditch."

"Ah, *Harry Potter*."

I laugh. "I forgot you're a fan."

"Only of the books and movies. Not the sport or wardrobe." He nods toward the boy. "But I can work with that now that I know."

Some of the people exit the building, including Morgan. She must have officially ended practice. I attempt to leave, but my feet won't budge. Nate isn't leaving either.

"So I can pay you for this."

He lifts one brow.

"For using your facilities."

He laughs. My face warms. When there's awkward silence, I tend to try and say something helpful or kind.

"Y'all can use this place anytime."

"I know you said Timothy could come, but a whole team and all these parents is another level."

He tosses the ball and catches it, then looks at me. "Seriously, I enjoyed tonight."

"You did?"

"Yeah. It's fun to teach baseball, especially when so many kids are brand new to the sport. It's like I get to introduce them to something I love."

My throat catches when he uses the word "love." It's a word I've heard him say countless times—mostly to me, about me.

I sway uncomfortably, as if doing so will loosen my cemented stance and allow me to walk away.

"When do y'all practice again?"

"That would be a question for Morgan."

"Well, let me know when you find out. As long as I'm in town, y'all are welcome to come over."

"Thanks."

"Mama," Timothy calls.

I turn to him jogging toward us. Nobody else is left in the building, which kicks my temperature up another notch.

"Miss Morgan said we're done and that she's going to skin Jeffrey's hide before next practice, whatever that means."

Nate chuckles. "That might not be necessary, buddy."

Timothy grins. Nate reaches out and rustles his hair, and I choke back a tear.

"I told your mom to let me know about practice from now on. I'll be happy to help whenever I'm here."

"Really?"

"Yep. I'll walk y'all to your car."

My legs finally agree to work, and the three of us make it

to my car parked in the ditch by the pasture. Nate opens my door for me, bringing on some nostalgia I don't need to deal with right now. Timothy hops in the other side, oblivious to anything between his mom and Nate the Great.

"Seriously, Brooke. Call or text me about your practice schedule." He smiles at me, then Timothy.

Timothy smiles back, and I swallow.

"Thanks, Nate." I smile and close the door. "For everything," I add under my breath as I glance toward our son.

Nate

Brooke and Timothy drive into the setting sun.

I stand at the edge of the road and watch until their car is no longer in view. Then I walk down the hill to turn off all the lights in the shop. Or should I say training facility.

Luckily there is enough space between Mom's trailer and the building for us to practice some fly balls next time.

I enter the shop and shake my head. What am I doing? Morgan is the coach, and I all but took over. Not that she seemed to mind. She literally stepped aside and told me to do what I thought was best.

It's not like I don't enjoy helping these kids. It's that doing so means I'm around Brooke even more. And that may not be best considering I still have feelings for her.

However, I did get a good look at her hand today. She had on regular clothes and makeup, even earrings, but no rings. I'll make sure to check next time I'm at church to confirm it.

I stack the buckets of balls to the side and grab a resistance band. Before finding everyone in the pasture, I was on my way to work out my own arm and shoulder. I hit off a tee this morning and ran a few miles. Then I made myself take it easy on yard work.

The more I'm here in so-called recovery mode, the more I contemplate coaching. I've helped with lots of high school camps over the years, at first for extra money and then for fun. It's nice to do that on a smaller scale, where I can really get to know the kids.

I loop the band around a pole to execute a different exercise and close my eyes as I pull it tightly. My shoulder has been better today, but it still stings at times. If I hadn't stopped weed eating when I did, I'd likely have it on ice by now.

As I work through the mundane routine of stretching my shoulder a million different ways, my mind drifts to Brooke and Timothy.

Even if she's single, he still has a dad. He might not live here though, since nobody's mentioned him and I haven't seen him with Timothy. Once they start having ball games, I should know if he's in his life.

What dad wouldn't want to watch his son play baseball for the first time?

Mine.

I let loose of the band and it pops against the wall. My father is always a sore subject. In high school, I tried to find him online through any means possible—Google, Facebook, inmate searches for the local county jails. Nothing.

It's like the man no longer exists. For all I know, he may not. But the one thing I didn't do was ask Mom.

She worked herself to the bone for the two of us and supported me in every way possible. For the most part, she was all I needed. But I'm still human, and as I got older and watched my friends with their dads, I got a little FOMO.

I'd hate to know Timothy is going through the same pain

as me. At least he has a grandpa and uncles nearby. He also has me down the road.

As long as I can keep from hitting on his mom.

I sigh and rotate my shoulder. When I'm done with all my therapy requirements, I cross the room to the kitchen area. I may not be in pain, but a little ice never hurt.

Instead of going in my house, I plop down on the nearby couch with my Ziploc bag of ice and the TV remote. I have a sudden desire to watch some *Harry Potter*.

CHAPTER 9

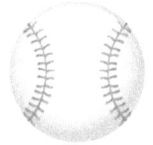

Brooke

Monday was one of those days that proved it's impossible to predict anything.

We had a man come in with his thumb hanging by a thread because he decided to go noodling for catfish. Another guy tried to talk me into making his lung X-ray look like he didn't smoke so he could get a cheaper life insurance premium. Then there were the usual patients coming in with broken bones from falling out of tree stands or trying out the new trampoline park between here and Tuscaloosa, which I'm pretty sure isn't up to code.

Thank God my parents were able to pick up Timothy from school and that Apple Cart never has traffic. Worst case scenario, I get behind a tractor on the way home.

I hurry to the parking lot and start home before anyone asks me to work overtime. That's the biggest downside to working at a hospital. It's always open.

Aside from the one traffic light in town, I make it home without any interruptions.

Timothy isn't in the house or our yard, so I walk to Mama's. She's standing on the front porch sweeping.

"Hey, is Timothy in the house?"

"No, he went for a walk."

"Where?"

She nods toward the driveway we share. "Up the road. I told him to be careful and not get in the pasture."

I frown. "Then why didn't I see him?"

"Maybe you weren't looking on the side of the road?"

I shake my head. Mama would've had a hissy fit if she couldn't find us. One generation has really relaxed her parenting.

"I'm going to borrow the four-wheeler."

The so-called emergency four-wheeler sits in its place at the edge of the house. I jump on it and back into the yard.

A few weeks ago I did this same thing to find Timothy. Except that time I knew he was in the pasture and I was wearing an exfoliating mask and my bathrobe. Makeup and scrubs are a better combination, but it does nothing to calm my nerves.

If he got in the pasture again without permission, I'll ground him until his next birthday.

I ride slow enough to look and listen in case Timothy isn't close to the road. I call his name a few times and get no answer.

I'm all but panicked when I hear a faint dinging sound by Nate's property. It calls me in like a siren to a ship. Out of instinct, I turn down his drive and follow the sound to Nate's baseball shop. The dings get louder as I park the four-wheeler and walk toward the metal building.

I open the small door to Nate tossing balls to Timothy. Despite wanting to wring his neck for running off here when he told Mama he was talking a walk, I stand in awe with my jaw dropped as he hits every ball thrown to him.

A few seconds later, Nate turns his head toward the door. I step back, hoping he won't see me, but I'm not quick enough.

"Hey, Brooke. Come in, he's a natural."

I enter and close the door behind me, a little embarrassed that I opened it without knocking.

"Timothy, why didn't you ask to come here?"

"You were at work."

"Why didn't you ask Granny or Smith?" I cross my arms and walk toward them.

He shrugs.

Nate stands when I get within a few feet of them. "I'm sorry. I had no idea y'all didn't know he was here."

"Sorry." Timothy hangs his head.

I unfold my arms. "It's okay, but we were worried. We need to know where you are, and Mr. Nate might have been busy."

I glance at Nate. He smiles. "I told him I'd help him anytime I'm home, didn't I, buddy?"

Timothy smiles and nods.

"I appreciate it, but we never want to impose or be a burden."

"Brooke, you and Timothy are never a burden."

My heartbeat speeds to an unhealthy level. I can't answer that without revealing how I truly feel about him and more. Especially since my gut instinct is to ask him to marry us.

After the shock of those words coming from his mouth wears off, I manage to respond in a more conventional way. "Well, thanks for helping him again." I turn to Timothy. "We need to get home for you to eat and shower."

Nate pats him on the back. "You did good tonight, bud."

"Thanks, Mr. Nate."

"Call me Nate, since we're friends." He jerks his gaze toward me. "If that's okay with your mom, of course."

"It's fine." I smile, but my stomach pinches. I've worked so hard to keep things professional between Nate and me that I haven't tried to keep them professional between Nate and Timothy. I guess it's fine if they're friends.

That is, until Nate is gone all the time playing ball.

"Come on, Timothy." I wrap my arm around his shoulder and help guide him toward the door.

Nate follows us. I don't turn to see, but I'm fully aware of his presence. His big body looming over me and his signature scent drifting in the air. You'd think he'd have switched to more sophisticated deodorant by now.

We continue out the door and toward Nate's house, where I parked.

"You came on the four-wheeler?" he asks.

"Yeah." My voice is hesitant. Something in me doesn't like him saying "the four-wheeler," as if implying he remembers that particular four-wheeler.

Either he's thinking of me driving off in my bathrobe, which isn't good, or he's thinking of when we rode it through the apple trees in our younger years. Also not good.

Knowing he remembers it conjures up my memories of us on it together. Back when we were together.

That was a simpler time when nobody was worried about adulthood or where we'd end up. And I sure as heck wasn't worried about half-a-dozen plastic sticks on my dorm room desk that had every indicator from double lines to pink pluses that a baby was growing inside of me.

"You can drive, Timothy."

"Yes!" He smiles and hops on.

I knew that would encourage him to leave.

I climb on behind him and ignore how his hair matches his daddy's and how Nate used to drive this thing. Nate takes a step toward us, and I nudge Timothy to drive ahead.

"Bye, Nate," I say swiftly before he can continue a conversation.

Then we drive toward the apple trees and away from the forbidden fruit.

Nate

Morgan called me this morning about practice. I'd have much preferred Brooke call me, but we're not there yet.

At least after Morgan's rant about Jeffrey screwing her over again and then attempting to butter my ego about how much I helped, I got to ask something.

"Is Brooke involved with someone?"

She laughed until she was out of breath, then assured me that was a big NO.

That was all it took for me to agree to run practice here, however she wanted. Now I'm setting up stations and eagerly awaiting Brooke's arrival.

I should say the team's arrival, but who am I kidding?

I hear cars outside and open the large rolling door. I told Morgan everyone could park in my backyard instead of by the road.

A few days after we moved Mom's trailer to the back of the property, I had a pathway graveled from the front of my house to hers. As much trouble as Jeffrey had moving the trailer down the hill, I knew I needed to do something.

The first person to get out is the woman who carries a golf bag. Her son follows with the bag. Next is the woman with twins and the kid who kept picking his nose.

I make it a point to learn some names tonight. If I'm going to continue helping these kids, I can't call them Quidditch and Booger Boy.

Brooke's car crawls down the new drive, and everything else disappears from my sight. I'm laser focused on her as if I'm staring at the batter from the pitcher's mound. The crowd and noise around me no longer exist.

She parks and climbs out, and I savor the sight of her bare left ring finger.

"Charlie, cut it out!"

That noise breaks through my wall of focus. I turn to the woman with twins yelling toward the edge of my shop. One of her kids is peeing on an ant bed by the doorway.

I bite back a laugh and walk away.

It doesn't take long for Morgan to find me. "Hey, Nate. I told the parents what kind of bats were legal for this age, so maybe they won't show up with random crap today." She cranes her neck, then looks back at me with a snarl. "Except for Reece wearing that stupid cape."

"I have a plan to hopefully get him out of that." I give Morgan a reassuring smile and commit the name Reece to memory.

"Oh, and Brooke's looking nice tonight, huh?" Morgan elbows my bad arm and I let out a little grunt.

"I asked about her status to see if Timothy had a dad around."

"We all know that's an entirely different deal." She winks. "Your secret's safe with me."

I open my mouth to refute her theory—even though it's dead right—when someone taps my shoulder. I turn to the woman who goes with Quid—uh, Reece—standing behind me.

"I appreciate you letting our kids practice here. Reece is allergic to outside."

My eyes widen, and Morgan snorts.

"Ma'am, I plan on taking them outside for some drills in a bit," I say. "If you'd like to go out and watch to monitor him, you're welcome to."

"Thanks. How thoughtful." She smiles and walks away.

Morgan shakes her head. "You handled that better than I could've."

"What would you have done?"

"Told him to suck it up, buttercup, but don't suck the buttercups."

I laugh. "And earlier you said you weren't a natural coach."

"What's the plan for tonight?" Brooke's voice calls from behind me.

I stop laughing with Morgan and look at her. "Uh, I'm going to do some stations again, then have everyone group up at the end."

"Let me know what I can do for you."

Morgan snorts, and I grit my teeth at her. She cowers and her face pales. I'm not one to scare women, on purpose at least, but Morgan is the exception.

I should've never asked her about Brooke.

"Can y'all get everyone's attention so we can start?" I ask.

"Yeah," Brooke says.

She turns toward the parents and kids coming in. Before she can speak, Morgan sticks her fingers in her mouth and lets out a shrill of a whistle. I shake my finger in the ear closest to her. Brooke laughs.

Adults and kids alike stop and stare our way. That's one upside to her crazy ways.

"If everyone can gather here in the middle, I'll explain what we're doing tonight," I say.

I scan the crowd for the kids I want to practice hitting first. My eyes land on my mom holding a Tupperware dish. "Mom? What are you doing out here?"

"I thought the kids could use a snack." She opens the lid.

"We haven't even started yet."

My warning is too late, as the twins crowd the bowl and fight over the same cookie. Their mom jerks them back.

I could end this snack interruption in a millisecond by telling Mom that one of them peed right before sticking his hand in the bowl. For the greater good, I keep that to myself.

Every kid gets a cookie except Reece. I assume his allergies include foods too. Once everyone is settled with a cookie in hand, I get back to business.

"Okay, thank you, Ms. Miller, for the snack. I'll explain everything while y'all eat."

I use Ethan to help with ground balls, then put Morgan to the side with a hitting stick. She seems strong enough to handle that with a group this young.

"When I call your name, go to Ethan." I call four names from the list Morgan texted me, and commit each one to memory when I watch which kid joins the group. I do the same for the next two groups.

"Brooke, could you help me run the pitching machine while I teach them technique?"

"Sure." She follows me to cage.

I lift the net for us to go under and notice Mom standing with her bowl. She's smiling widely.

"Thanks, Mom. We're good on cookies for now." That's my subtle hint asking her to leave and let us get to work.

"I was just going to say how nice it is to see you together again."

"We're not—" Brooke and I answer in unison.

We face each other, and I'm tempted to say "jinx," but act my age. I'm more focused on the "not" being part of both our answers.

"Nate's kind enough to help us get this team going. He's being a good friend."

Mom nods, looking a little sad. When we don't give her any more grains of gossip, she turns and heads for the door.

"Okay, Timothy, you're up first." I hand him a bat and have him stand at the plate.

"Hey, Mama?" he calls while I'm adjusting the pitching machine.

"Yeah?" Brooke asks.

"Why did Ms. Miller say it was good to see you and Nate together again?"

I take a deep breath. Kids ask a lot of questions, and I'd been prepared to answer them all day. But the questions I rehearsed concerned baseball, not my past love life.

"We grew up together and went to the same school." Brooke half smiles at Timothy.

He nods. "Oh yeah."

She turns to me and bites her bottom lip. I swallow. That should not make me want to kiss her, but it does. However, I need to focus on helping these kids and not helping myself win back Brooke.

Just because we grew up together doesn't mean we're destined to grow old together.

CHAPTER 10

Brooke

After Anne's slight interrogation, I could really use a cookie. Too bad she took off as soon as we shut down her idea.

I can't say whether she would want me to be with her son after I broke his heart once. Still, Anne has never been anything but sweet and supportive of me and Timothy. Even though she has no clue he's her grandson.

Nate turns off the pitching machine, and I start collecting the rubbery balls we used for it. He points to the ground where Reece dropped his cape.

"Don't forget your cloak, bud."

Reece ducks back under the net and grabs the cape, then hurries toward the center of the floor with everyone else. I smile at Nate. "That was pretty impressive how you got him to take off the cape."

"Thanks." He grins. "It might backfire on me later when he figures out there are no Quidditch games to save it for."

I laugh. "Whatever works. When you're a parent, you do

what's best for the present and worry about the repercussions when they come."

"I'll take your word for it." He grabs the bucket I filled with balls and holds the net up for me.

"Thanks." I duck under it and wait on him.

"For what it's worth, you've done a great job with Timothy."

"Thanks." My voice is almost a whisper. The guilt of knowing he doesn't know Timothy belongs to him is almost too much. Speaking of later repercussions, I'm afraid the day he finds out will be brutal.

Luckily, Nate leaves me to round up the rest of the kids. I hang back and watch while Reece hands his cape to his mom. She almost tears up and mouths a "thank you" to Nate. Now I almost tear up.

He would make a great dad. Not that I ever had any doubt. My only hesitation was making him a dad before he needed to be.

Morgan stands in the center of the parents while the kids follow Nate and Ethan outside. By the time I reach the group, only Georgia and Aniston remain. Everyone else is out the door.

Georgia's arms are folded and she narrows her eyes on me. Aniston wears a mischievous smirk, and I'm a little scared to know what's going on.

"Georgia here would like to buy Timothy's number?" Aniston taps the top of Georgia's high ponytail.

"Wait, what?"

Georgia bats her eyes. "It's nothing personal, just that sixteen is a special number to our family."

"Yeah, I think Timothy only chose sixteen because it's Nate's number," I say.

A sad little laugh-cry comes from Georgia's clenched jaw.

"Ladies." Aniston moves between us and hooks an arm around our shoulders. "Step into my office. Let's negotiate."

She walks us to the kitchen area and stops at the edge of the counter. Georgia takes a seat on a bar stool, and I watch Aniston grab a napkin and a pen from near the sink.

"Okay." She returns to her spot at the end of the counter, between us. "Both boys want number sixteen, but right now Timothy's got it, correct?"

Georgia nods slowly.

"Let's see, he is a coach's son, so technically he should have first pick." Aniston glances at me and lifts the corner of her mouth.

I want to protest that I'm not officially a coach. I'm simply the person keeping Jeffrey from killing Morgan. However, I'm more eager to see how this plays out.

"I met my husband for the first time when I was sixteen, on the sixteenth of March, at the sixteenth hole of a golf tournament." Georgia beams.

I don't have to respond, because Aniston does it for me. "Then we have Timothy, who has no father figure to look up to and nobody to help him with ball until a kind pro athlete moves down the road and offers him a positive role model."

Aniston did a great job of painting my son's point of view like a sad Hallmark story. Georgia squirms in her seat. So much of this is messed up that I can't begin to comprehend it all.

"So the question to be answered is what is this number sixteen worth to the both of you." Aniston points the pen at me, then Georgia. "Georgia, write down your price." She sets the pen on the napkin and slides it toward her.

Georgia twists her mouth and scribbles something on the napkin. She slides it toward me.

Aniston intercepts it. "I think you can do better than that."

Georgia grabs the napkin and adds a zero. She drops the pen beside it and pushes it across the bar. "That's my final offer."

Aniston studies the napkin as my stomach flips. Our eyes meet, and her lips curve into a devious smile.

"What do you think, Brooke?" She taps the edge of the napkin as she shows it to me. "For this price, could you possibly break the news to your son that he won't get to wear his role model's number for his inaugural ball season?"

I sigh. "You know, he will be disappointed, but I think this price shows how much it means to Georgia's family."

Georgia's large white teeth shine like Chiclets. I nod, and she gives me a huge hug. "Thank you so much, Brooke. You are just precious!"

When she moves back, I let out a breath. Georgia jumps from her stool excitedly. "I'm going to write you a check." She holds up a finger. "Let me get my wallet from the golf bag."

Aniston watches her hurry toward the opposite end of the room. I pick up the napkin and widen my eyes to make sure I'm reading it correctly. "I would've given it to her for nothing," I whisper.

"Good thing you got a friend like me, then, huh?"

I shrug. "It appears so."

Georgia returns, fanning a check in my face. I take it and stare at the number. It has the same zeros as the napkin. Not that I care, but she has a reputation of not doing things by the book.

"I'll go tell Morgan the good news." Georgia grins.

"Tell me what?" Morgan sticks her head in the doorway before Georgia makes it there.

"Timothy and Herrington are trading numbers."

"Are they now?" Morgan cocks her head at me.

"Yes, Georgia was kind enough to *buy* it from me."

Morgan lifts her chin.

"Can you make note of that on your little sheet, Morgan, so nobody gets confused?" Georgia bats her eyelashes.

"Yes, Georgia, I'll get right on that. Soon as I pick up a batch of pies from the orchard and get my kids in bed."

"I really prefer you do it now, since you sometimes forget and all." Georgia adds a fake little laugh.

"Why don't you do it if you're so worried. My papers are in the corner." Morgan points to the edge of the room.

Georgia hurries that way, and Morgan takes her time coming to us. "Practice ended better than expected. I can take Timothy with me to your mama's house if you want."

"If it's over, I'll be heading home too."

"I volunteered you to help Nate pick up and lock up."

"Gee, thanks."

She lifts her hands. "Thank him. It was either you or Maribelle, and I think he's a little worried about leaving Charlie with free range to pee on his blueberry bushes." She rolls her eyes. "Not that mine are much more civilized, but that kid's like a puppy with an overactive bladder."

"Sure, you can take Timothy. Tell him to shower at Granny's to save time."

She salutes me, then pauses her hand midair when she notices the check. "Dang, girl. This is better than child support! I would've sold my kid's name for this many zeros."

Aniston laughs. "Better pocket that before it gets out of hand, Brooke."

I fold the check in my back pocket. "I'll start cleaning up and be home as soon as possible."

"No rush." Morgan smiles and walks toward the door with Aniston. Georgia meets them with a clipboard in hand.

I straighten up the equipment we used tonight and collect empty water and Gatorade bottles. I'm pouring half-drank Prime down the sink when Nate comes in holding his shoulder. He grits his teeth and rotates his arm a few times, then stops when he notices me.

"You okay?" I ask.

"Yeah."

"Are you sure? Because you always made that same face when your arm hurt."

He sits at the bar and sighs.

"Ice?"

He nods. "Don't say anything. Only Mom and people to do with the team know I'm in pain."

"Like constantly?"

He wavers his head. "I injured my shoulder last season and had surgery over the holidays."

I blink. There's a box of Ziploc bags conveniently beside the ice maker. I can't help but think he's iced it recently.

He nods. "I'm technically on injured leave now. That's why I'm here instead of Florida for spring training."

I finish filling a bag with ice and stand beside him. My hand draws to his shoulder like a magnet. I curve the bag to fit around his upper back and shoulder blade. He sighs, then leans his head back.

Due to our height difference, his face is incredibly close to mine. Like I can smell his orange gum distance.

I flinch, causing the bag to slide. I lean to center it on his shoulder, putting our faces even closer.

His breath is warm and slow and calculated. I count the seconds between each exhale until it all becomes too much. After a few breaths, he turns his head ever so slightly so that nothing more than Georgia's napkin could slide between us.

I'm convinced he's going to kiss me.

I want him to kiss me, but he can't. Not now, not yet. There's so much unspoken between us. So much tension hanging that I need to fill with real words, not nonverbal communication.

My lips part, but only for words. "I should go home and get Timothy ready for bed."

He bites his bottom lip and sits up straighter on the bar stool. Then he puts his hand on the ice pack next to mine. It's warm, and the contrast between his hand and the ice sends shivers down my spine.

I let go and take a step back. "See you later."

"Yeah." His voice is husky.

Maybe it's the pain he's in, or something more. I don't stay to find out. I hurry toward my car without looking back. If I so much as stare at Nate one more second, I'll close the gap on the last nine years.

Not tonight.

It's our first game. Okay, technically practice game, but I'm still just as nervous. I pull up to the field and take a deep breath.

Morgan turns in on two wheels and comes to a screeching halt beside me. She hops out and tosses a handful of Cheetos in her mouth. I watch her jerk open the back van door and several baseballs tumble out.

All four of her kids follow, the last being Sofia. She's the most dramatic, rolling her eyes so far that I can't see the pupils.

"Go on, don't get hurt," Morgan instructs them as Timothy and I exit our car. "Boys, take this stuff to the cages."

She opens the back of the van and a bat rolls to the ground. Ethan and Andrew unload a wagon and a bucket of balls. Then Ethan collects the balls from the ground and adds to the bucket. Morgan licks Cheetos crust from her thumb and smiles at me. "First practice game. Pretty exciting, huh?"

I shake my head.

"Yeah!" Timothy pumps his fist high.

"That's what I'm talking about." Morgan high-fives him. "Now scoot to the cages." She pats his behind.

"Is it normal to be this nervous?" I ball my hands in fists.

Morgan crunches more Cheetos and shrugs. "I mean, this is your kid's first game ever. Ethan had a game last night, and my oldest two have played ball for years." She holds up the bag and pours crumbs in her mouth. Then she stares at me while chewing the last bite. "Give it time. You won't care after a few years."

I raise an eyebrow. I'm not sure this is the attitude a coach needs to have. Regardless, I follow her to the batting cages. All the kids except for Tami's daughters are there, and Ethan is helping them hit off a tee.

Morgan enters from the other side and calls Reece to her. "Come on, I need to practice pitching." She winds up her arm and pops her neck.

I turn to Aniston and Easton standing beside me. "Maybe you should pitch to them, Easton."

He laughs. "I'm afraid it might look like I'm casting a fishing rod."

I sigh.

"It will be fine." Aniston glances around at the parents and smirks. "Morgan's got to be better than most of these dads."

I follow her gaze to Georgia's husband, Carlton. He's wearing a sweater vest and organizing Herrington's equipment in the golf bag.

"Ethan can't pitch?"

"According to Bubba and his blasted rule book, it has to be an actual parent or guardian," Aniston tells me.

I nod.

"Trust me, I checked," she adds in a whisper.

Every kid goes through a round with Ethan on the tee, then Morgan pitching. Except for Angel and Precious, who show up as we're finishing.

Tami looks confused. "I thought this game started at ten."

"Remember we posted to come thirty minutes early to warm up?" I remind her.

"I thought that was optional," she answers.

I shake my head.

"My bad. I was up, but making new content."

Easton's eyes widen at the word "content." I'm certain he's remembering the time she came in with a sprained ankle from shooting one of her TikToks. For some reason, she hung herself over a mailbox and her heel caught on the curve when she tried to get down. She fell in the ditch and couldn't walk. Someone handing out church tracts door to door found her an hour later and gave her a ride to the emergency room.

Ethan exits the net with the balls, and Morgan follows. "All right, to the field!" She points like a pirate discovering an island.

I fall in line behind Herrington's family and notice that the golf bag is monogrammed with the number sixteen. Georgia is wearing #16 earrings too.

They really must love that number.

"Hey, Morgan, I flipped earlier, and y'all got the visitors' side," Jeffrey quips.

"You flipped without me?" She narrows her eyes at him.

"I would say we could flip again . . ." He nods toward the home dugout, which is about eighty times nicer than the visitors'. "But all my boys have already settled in."

"Have they now?" Morgan pulls a scorebook from her bag. "Easton and Aniston, I trust the two of you are smart enough to figure this out."

"I can do you one better." Easton lifts his phone to his chest. "I downloaded GameChanger."

Morgan snorts. "Good luck with that in this dead-zone service area."

He taps his phone and frowns when the app spins. Aniston takes the book and pencil from Morgan and gives her a closed-lip smile.

"Brooke, I need you on first base. We can't steal bases or anything cool like that at this age, so your only job is to make sure they run through the bag."

"Got it." But do I? The only baseball I ever paid attention to was Nate's games starting in late middle school. I literally remember nothing from my brothers playing other than candy from the concession stand.

"Maribelle, you can keep the batting order." Morgan pats her pockets and comes up short. After glancing around the ground, she reaches in her shirt and pulls out a slip of paper. "My bad. Forgot I stuck it in Grandma's secret pouch." She winks.

Maribelle pinches the edge of the paper with her index finger and thumb like she's holding a snotty tissue. She winces and takes it to the dugout.

"Let's get our bats, boys," Morgan says.

I give Aniston a silent plea for help. She rubs my back. "You got this. Remember, they run through the bag."

I nod, then head to my post on first base. Jeffrey's entourage of coaches stares at me from their ivory tower. It has a concrete floor and little shiny hooks to hold their bags. We get dirt and a wooden bench that's seen its better days.

Morgan adjusts a cap on her head and pulls her hair through the back. She gets in some kind of squatty stance and smiles at Jack. I don't even try and understand her process with the batting order, since Jack is a loose cannon.

Somehow the stars align and God smiles on us, because Jack hits the first ball she throws. I watch him like a hawk as he barrels toward my base.

Unfortunately, Jeffrey's team scoops the ball and gets it to the first baseman way before Jack. He's out.

Carter is up next and watches every ball. He mopes off the field, dragging his bat.

Poor kid is probably shell-shocked since he hasn't played a game without his parents. I study the snakelike pattern in the dirt where his bat left a mark and take a deep breath. Aniston comforts him in the dugout.

Timothy is up next. I choke back a tear and pray he does okay. He swings and misses, then stands and watches three balls.

Morgan holds the ball up. "Timothy this is the fifth pitch. You have to swing."

He nods. I close my eyes.

A ding rings out, and my eyes pop open. The ball is about two feet from the plate, but it's legal.

"Run, Timothy!" Morgan yells at the top of her lungs.

He takes off toward me and slides into first. The umpire calls him safe. Morgan slaps her hand on her head and calls time.

She hurries to first base. "Timothy, please don't slide at first again. Run through the bag. 'Kay?"

He nods and she pats his head.

After Morgan returns to the pitching circle, I smile at him. "Thanks for keeping us alive," I whisper.

He grins.

Andrew comes up fourth. His pants are already dirty and both shoes are untied. But neither he nor Morgan seem to mind.

She throws two pitches and he stares at her. She grits her teeth and makes a stern face. He straightens and holds his bat higher.

On the third ball, he swings for the fences. Our dugout and bleachers go crazy. I push Timothy toward second base. "Stop watching the ball, son, and run!"

Carlton is at third base scrolling his phone. He looks up at the excitement and motions for Timothy to keep running. He does keep running—just not fast enough. He falls somewhere between second and third base and Andrew blows past him. How my kid managed to fall instead of the one with untied shoes makes no sense. Maybe it was nerves.

Morgan screams at Andrew to slow down, and everyone else screams at Timothy to get up.

Jeffrey's team fields the ball toward the infield. The second baseman catches it as Timothy hits third base. Andrew jumps on home and everyone cheers.

The ump calls him out. "Passed runner, run doesn't count," he declares from the plate.

Morgan grabs Andrew by the ear and pulls him toward the dugout, giving him an earful while she's at it.

Jeffrey walks smugly to the pitcher's mound as his team jogs off the field in triumph.

It's going to be a loooong game.

CHAPTER 11

Nate

It's déjà vu when Shelby hooks the sticky wires to my arm. I lean back, pleased that it doesn't hurt as much as last time.

Dr. Trenton will be happy to know I haven't so much as touched a piece of furniture except to open a drawer for clothes.

Seriously. Since the house is five times the size of my Atlanta condo, I hired Mom to clean it. She protested at first, then agreed to take payment if I let her cook for me anytime she wanted.

Best deal I've ever made. Maybe one day I'll convince her to try my oven.

"Hey, Shelby, I'm going to lunch at twelve," another PT assistant says.

"Okay, thanks." Shelby smiles at her, then finishes adjusting my machine.

Twelve.

If it's close to twelve here, that means it's close to eleven at home. Or Apple Cart. Technically I live here too.

I pull my phone from my back pocket with the hand that isn't stinging from voltage lines. Yep. It's ten 'til eleven. Timothy's first game is going on right now.

I bite my thumbnail and groan.

"Are you all right? Need me to turn it down?"

"Huh?"

Shelby nods toward the machine.

"Oh no, it's fine. I remembered somewhere I needed to be."

She laughs. "Practice?"

"Yeah, but not mine."

Her face contorts with confusion.

"The machine is fine, thanks."

"It will cut off in ten minutes. Dr. Trenton should be here by then." She takes her hand off the knob and half smiles before making her way to the next guy.

I wiggle my hand, then uncurl my fingers. They're almost asleep. Using my non-dominant hand again, I get on Facebook.

I don't have an account. There are a few fan pages dedicated to me or the Braves as a whole, but Nate Miller as a personal profile doesn't exist. However, Mom is a very active participant.

Anne Miller is my pseudo when I want to stalk people for fun. Or in this case, check to see if anyone posted about the kids' game.

She's still logged in on my phone from the time she borrowed it to check Jim Vann's live weather radar.

Sure enough, she's friends with Morgan. I know Brooke isn't on Facebook, as I've checked many times in the past. I check again for the heck of it. Nope. Might as well click on Morgan.

She has nothing about this particular game, but does

appear very active on Facebook. Mostly complaining about people leaving trash in the Pig parking lot and how tired she is all the time.

"Nate."

Dr. Trenton's voice startles me, and I drop the phone. He picks it up and hands it to me.

"Thanks." I pocket the phone quickly and realize the machine has stopped. Shelby walks over and starts unsticking the cords.

"How are you feeling today?" he asks.

"Much better." I put on an optimistic face.

"Much" might be a stretch, but I'm hoping he will give me a clean bill of health.

"Let's see." He stands behind me and waits until Shelby pulls the last cord and rolls the machine away. "Stand for me."

I stand and try not to flinch when he digs his fingers into my shoulder blade. He mashes around a few minutes, then starts our routine of stretches and pulls. I go through the motions, relieved there is minimal pain.

"Much better than the last visit." He slaps me on the shoulder and grins.

I don't even move under the pressure. My cheeks hurt from smiling so widely. "You think I can start training soon?"

He draws in a breath and picks up my chart. Then he makes some notes and looks at me. "I think you can slowly integrate heavier weights and some pitching to see how your arm reacts." He holds up a hand. "Nothing too heavy. I'll write up a plan and we can Zoom in between visits."

He scribbles some more notes and talks to himself, then writes a little more. "I suggest speaking with your trainer about a revised workout."

I grit my teeth.

"I understand you don't want to show pain, but if you go back to normal too soon, it could make matters worse."

I nod. "Good point. I'll talk with him."

"Be smart and safe, and I'm confident you'll make a full recovery." He extends a hand, and I shake it.

The words "full recovery" are music to my ear. However, I can't get the kids' game out of my mind. As soon as I'm in my truck, I pull out my phone. When I unlock the screen, it's still on Facebook. As suspected, nothing about the game.

I toss my phone on the dash of my truck. My stomach sours at the memory of Brooke riding with me when I first moved to Atlanta. It's a miracle my old truck made it here. Even more of a miracle that it survived my spontaneous trip to visit her on a bad tank of gas.

That was the last time I saw her in person while we were still together.

We'd talked and texted and video chatted plenty the next few weeks. Each time, she acted a little more distant. I assumed it was because she was busy adjusting to college and new classes. Add to that a weird roommate with a very fast lizard, and I'd feel out of whack too.

What I didn't expect was when I wanted to plan a weekend together and she broke up with me instead. All I could get out of her was how our lives were going in different directions and it was for the best. I could hear her crying on the phone.

All I wanted was to hold her and assure her we could make it work. I never got the chance.

Brooke

The pastor asks everyone to stand for the invitational song. I turn my head to hide a yawn and spot Nate across the church. He grins at me. I straighten and turn toward the front. It was an innocent grin. Definitely one fit for church.

But it didn't keep my mind in a churchy spot.

I'm daydreaming about everyone but us disappearing and him dipping me over a pew for the best kiss of my life. Nothing more, just a great kiss.

Still, not the best idea in a Baptist church during Sunday service.

"The Old Rugged Cross" plays in the background. I focus on that, which helps. No romantic vibes there.

Soon the song ends and the preacher closes us in prayer. I bow my head and keep my eyes closed until the final "amen."

I barely have my head raised when Timothy plunges past me, smooshing my legs against the pew. "Watch out, son."

I turn around to Mama shaking her head. She was on the other side of him before he darted away.

"Where's he going?" I ask. Craning my neck while in chunky sandals still doesn't give me a good view of him as he meanders through adults.

"Don't worry, he went to Nate."

Of course he did.

Not that it's a bad thing for him to be with Nate. But it means I will have to be with Nate to retrieve him. God, please don't let him give me that grin again.

That's probably the most sincere silent prayer I've lifted up in this church.

We take our time shuffling into the bottlenecked aisle. Daddy gets lost in the crowd when someone engages him in a tractor conversation. Mama slows down next when someone asks her about pies.

I continue alone, wishing for once my brothers still sat on the family pew. Facing Nate with no allies makes me even more vulnerable to his attack.

Timothy has him cornered by the wall.

"Hey," Nate says when I make it to them.

Timothy turns around to acknowledge my presence for a split second before continuing to blab to Nate. We make eye contact for a moment over his head.

And I'll be dead alive if he doesn't give me that grin again.

I lower my head to hide the blushing and listen to my son recount yesterday's disastrous practice game. He finally stops to catch a breath, giving Nate a chance to respond.

"Hey, my mom has lunch with her book club today, and I'm starving. Would the two of y'all want to go with me to Mary's?"

Not the response I expected.

"Yes." Timothy beams.

"I guess it's fine. I didn't have any grand plans other than maybe grilling burgers." I lift my head slowly to Nate staring at me.

That does not help with the blushing!

"Why don't we go ahead and get a good seat before the Methodists take all the booths?" he suggests.

"Okay, we'll meet you there."

"Mama." Timothy whizzes around to me. "Can I ride with Nate?"

"It would actually make sense for you both to ride with me. Save on parking."

"Great," Timothy answers for us.

"Great," I whisper under my breath.

The only upside to the three of us leaving church together —in the same vehicle—is that most everyone has left already.

Apparently not Mrs. Maudy. She adjusts her glasses and smiles widely at us in the sunlight. I smile back, but keep walking. The guys didn't notice her, so I think we're safe.

"Brooke!"

Don't look, it's a trap.

"Oh, Brooke!"

"Mama, someone's calling you."

I clear my throat and speed up, but Timothy stops. "Mrs. Maudy needs you."

I tilt my head to check, but I'm certain she doesn't need anything aside from a good scratch on her gossip itch.

"Good to see you two together, hon!"

That makes us all turn her way. She waves wildly, then give us two thumbs-up. I groan and Nate chuckles.

"Have a nice afternoon." He waves back.

I make a beeline for his truck, more embarrassed than ever. Nate smiles as if he's enjoying this, although he does unlock his truck so I can find refuge. He and Timothy climb in a few minutes later.

"You must be really hungry, Mama, to run like that."

I laugh off Timothy's comment and stare out the window. It doesn't take long to get to Mary's, but he fills the silence by discussing the game.

"Anyway, I need to work on my speed and not tripping. Could you help me with that?"

"Yeah, buddy." Nate parks the truck and unlocks the doors.

Paul and Ms. Dot are on the other side of my window, waving and smiling. Actually, Paul nods since he's loaded down with to-go plates.

Apple Cart County could use a weird-weather warning to give everyone something else to worry about. They're all way too concerned about who's with who.

I give the two a slight wave, which satisfies them enough to move on. Timothy beats us to the restaurant door and holds it open.

"Thank you, son."

He smiles and waits for us to enter before closing it behind him.

"Timothy, manners will get you far in life. A much more reliable skill than sports," Nate says.

Timothy's face falls as he slides in a booth. Nate slides in the other side. I almost sit by him out of habit.

This was *our* booth a decade ago.

Then I snap back to the present and sit by my son.

"Sports got you far," Timothy says once we're all seated.

"Yeah, but people get old and retire from jobs and sports. You're never too old to be kind." Nate nods across the restaurant toward a group of older people. "Nobody in here thinks of me as Nate the Great. In here, I'm Nate."

"But your jersey's behind the cash register."

Nate laughs. "My high school jersey, not my Braves jersey."

"Still your jersey."

"What I'm trying to say is people who really know you care about who you are, not what you are. Always be kind and real. That's what matters most."

Timothy nods and smiles.

I study Nate as he pulls a menu from behind the napkin holder. If his grin didn't win me over this morning, his humility might seal the deal.

"Hey, sugar, good to see you in here with these sweet peas."

Mary's voice calls my attention, and I look away from Nate before he catches me staring.

"What can I get y'all to drink?"

"Sweet tea?" Timothy whispers to me.

"One glass." I glance at Mary and she laughs.

Nate orders tea, and I order water. She fills us in on what's left on the hot bar. It's not uncommon for certain vegetables to run out quickly during the Sunday meat-and-three special.

Macaroni usually goes first. Even though it's not technically a vegetable, most Southern menus categorize it as such. And all Southern eaters choose it over anything green.

Mary finishes her laundry list of items and smiles at us. "It's so nice to see y'all."

I clench my teeth, waiting on the "together," but it never comes. I exhale in relief and shock. Mary has quite the reputation as the unofficial matchmaker of Apple Cart.

If she isn't hinting about something more between Nate and me, maybe it's all in my head.

CHAPTER 12

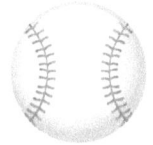

Nate

"How did y'all manage to score an actual baseball field?" I toss and catch a ball a few times.

Morgan huffs. "I had a few choice words with Mr. Jeffrey when he came by the Pig this week." She tosses her hair over her shoulder and continues toward the dugout.

"I think he felt sorry for us." Brooke wrinkles her nose.

"Well, hopefully we can remedy that tonight," I tell her.

"Thanks for helping again," she says.

"Of course."

Bags clank against the metal fence and Morgan grunts. Brooke and I exchange a look.

My heart thumps harder when I look her in the eye. Sharing an inside laugh with her makes me wish we could share more. I miss those moments.

I miss her.

"What are we working on tonight?" she asks.

I palm the ball and come out of my trance. "According to

everything Timothy told me about the practice game, I'd say base running is high on the list."

She frowns. "Sorry about that. There's so much he doesn't know. I could've taught him that, but . . ." Her voice trails off with a sigh.

"Don't be sorry. It's not your place to teach him ball. He's young, smart, and willing to learn. He'll be fine."

Her lips curve into a slight smile. My eyes follow the movement and I allow them to linger on her mouth a little too long.

She turns her head.

Dang it. I got caught gawking.

"I can help them with batting too, and knowing what's a ball and a strike."

She turns slowly and nods.

Morgan comes our way with a bucket. She's waddling stiff-legged with it in front of her. I meet her halfway and take the bucket in one hand. I set it in the pitcher's circle.

"I had that, you know," she calls from behind me.

"Most women would just say thank you."

"I'm not most women."

That she is not. I shake my head and chuckle. Brooke laughs too. We share another glance, and I soak that in before a bunch of dirt-eaters hit the field.

Morgan whistles to call their attention. "Coach Nate has some ideas to help us."

I turn to Brooke and whisper, "When did I become Coach?"

"Morgan has a way of voluntelling others."

"I see."

I cross my arms and make my way to the fence. Jeffrey stands on the other side. He stops near me, chewing a toothpick.

"So I see you're helping with practice." The toothpick rolls across his mouth.

"Yeah."

"You know only parents on the field at games."

"Yeah."

I narrow my eyes. He's trying to run me off and I don't like it. Two can play at this game.

"It's nice of you to find them a practice field."

"I figured they needed rescuing from that bullpen." He laughs obnoxiously at his corny joke.

"I couldn't agree more. That's why I opened up my personal training facility anytime Morgan and Brooke need a place for them."

His jaw drops and the toothpick falls to the ground. I meet his dumbfounded stare and wait for that to sink in.

"I wasn't aware you were letting teams work at your home, with your equipment."

"I wouldn't say teams." I emphasize the S. Really just this team.

I smile, and Jeffrey's nostrils flare. I take a few steps back and wave a hand at him. "But we needed a change in venue. Astroturf and pitching machines can only help us so much."

Jeffrey's entire face turns the color of the Apple Cart Armadillo mascot on a sponsor sign. He may have won the first competition, but as long as I'm around, he won't get the championship.

"Have a good practice." I turn and jog toward the kids.

They listen eagerly as I describe our stations for today. Ethan has practice, so I enlist a few parents to come help and break them into groups.

"Where do you need me?" Morgan asks.

"You and Brooke will stick with me today. I think our coaches need practice too."

She snorts.

"I don't expect y'all to throw strikes, but you have to give them something to work with."

"Yeah, we suck." Brooke twists her mouth, then turns to Morgan.

"I didn't say that, but y'all do need practice."

"You didn't have to, Coach," Morgan chimes in.

"You don't have to call me Coach."

"Okay, Coach." She shakes her head. "Sorry, bad habit."

"You can go first, then."

Her sarcastic smile fades. I give her a ball. "See that torn spot in the fence behind the plate?"

"Yep."

"That's your target."

She narrows her eyes, then goes through the cliché motions most pitchers use. Her foot drags a country mile and takes about as long. I study everything from her stance to her arm, taking mental notes.

The ball makes it to the plate, but wildly.

"All right, let's start with your stance."

"What's wrong with my stance?"

"It's throwing you off balance. I think you're so focused on how you're standing and moving your feet that it's messing with your arm."

She stares at me blankly.

"Are you trying to mimic anyone?"

"I dunno?"

I cross my arms and wait for her to answer honestly. Out of the corner of my eye, I watch Brooke's face glow with amusement and try not to laugh.

"Maybe the pitcher on Ethan's middle school team, and the guy I saw on TV the other night, and sometimes Roy in pickup softball at the church picnics."

I raise one brow.

"That's fair, I see your point." Morgan grits her teeth.

"Can you stand more—" I catch myself before saying "normal" and get in my stance instead. Morgan follows my lead.

"Good. Now when you bring your foot up, maybe don't take so long." I hand her another ball. "Try it."

She squares up, sets, and pitches. She hits just below the spot I told her to.

Brooke gasps.

"I did it!" Morgan jumps and claps once the shock wears off.

"You did. Throw a few more. One isolated pitch doesn't mean you can pitch."

We watch her throw several more pitches, most of them decent.

"Good job."

She lifts her chest and smiles. I scan the field to see what's going on with the circus outside the ring. "Can you help with the kids hitting off tees while I coach Brooke?"

She follows my gaze to the corner of the field. I set up a station for the boys to hit off the tee toward the fence and put Carlton in charge. He seems like a bright enough guy. After all, he is a pharmacist.

But he's also a golfer, and he's got the kids taking golf swings at the baseballs.

Morgan's face sours when she watches him try and get Charlie to start swinging low. "Yeah, someone needs to fix that."

"I think that could be you." I give her back an encouraging pat.

She hands me the glove she's wearing and marches toward Carlton.

Brooke and I watch her a few seconds, then face one another. My pulse picks up when I realize we're only inches apart. I hold up the glove as a makeshift buffer. "Here you go."

"Thanks."

Her fingers touch mine for a millisecond, but it's long

enough to keep me wanting more. She puts the glove on and takes a deep breath. "I've never tried to pitch before."

"There's a first time for everything." I drop a ball in her glove to keep from accidentally touching her again.

"Do I stand like this?"

"A little to the left."

She turns her entire body.

"Not so much."

She turns back the way she was before.

"Just your hips turn." I reach one hand and gently put it on her waist.

So much for not touching her.

My hand falls to the curve of her back and it's all too familiar. Like slipping on my favorite pair of sneakers. It just fits.

I take longer than I should sliding my hand away. Her breathing is heavier, either from the nerves of pitching for the first time or from me touching her for the first time in almost a decade.

I clear my throat to reset. "You watched me tell Morgan, so do what she did."

"I'll try." She goes through the motions and pitches the ball.

It falls short of the plate, but also looks a little low.

"You're a good bit shorter than her. You'll need more power behind that to get it farther and higher."

I hand her another ball. This time it makes it to the plate, but it's still low.

"Too low, huh?" She turns to me with a panicked look.

"Not if we get Carlton to ump."

She laughs.

"It's fine, really. Y'all are both doing great, I swear. It's not easy to pitch, especially to kids."

"Let me try again."

I hand her another ball. It goes the same way.

She throws her head back to the sky. "How in the world do I get it higher?" She drops her head to face me.

"Go through the motions without a ball so I can see what you need to change."

I watch her arm all the way through.

"All right. Bring your elbow up more."

She lifts her elbow in an awkward position.

"Hang on." I stand behind her and cup my hand behind her arm. Then I bring it higher. "How's that feel?" I say, close to her ear.

"Good," she whispers.

"Yeah?" I whisper back.

She slowly turns her head, and for the second time in a week, we're within kissing territory. My throat constricts and I can't get a word out. But I'm not sure what I might say if I could. There are no words for this moment. Actions would speak louder than words.

I dip my head the tiniest bit to put my mouth maybe a centimeter closer to see how she reacts.

"You didn't do all that with me," a familiar voice taunts behind me.

I flinch and drop my hand from Brooke's arm. Morgan stands a few feet back, grinning like a possum.

Busted.

Brooke

Nate is waiting by the park entrance when we pull up. Timothy smiles and waves at him through the back window.

Today is the Apple Cart County Little League Opening

Tournament. I've never been, but heard about it over the years from others.

The teams in our county and surrounding counties' parkball teams play each other in a bracket tournament. Rings and medals are awarded to the last two teams standing in every division.

I'm not so much nervous about how the kids do today as I am for myself. If for some crazy reason we start winning, we keep playing. I don't think Morgan has more than two or three games in her to pitch, and I know she'll look to me as her backup.

Too bad the park board won't allow Nate in the circle to hold me up.

That's probably for the best. If Morgan hadn't walked up at the right time, we may have kissed. Only instead of being alone on his property, we were in the middle of the ball field with families watching.

I don't know which is worse. Obviously, I'm not a fan of PDA. On the flip side, not having a captive audience could lead to a much hotter kiss.

I climb out of the car and blow a stray hair from my eyes.

"Are y'all ready for today?" Nate asks.

"I am!" Timothy hops. He high-fives Nate before grabbing his bag.

My trunk is loaded down with lawn chairs, snacks, and bottles of water.

Morgan has to work the gate, so I offered to bring backup drinks for everyone. She's also been known to forget things.

"Let me help with all that." Nate grabs the cooler and both lawn chairs. I reach for the duffle of snacks, but he beats me to them.

"I guess I'll shut the trunk." I raise an eyebrow.

"Thanks." He smiles.

It's contagious. For a brief moment I smile too, forgetting the reason I was so nervous.

Nate steps in front of me like a pack mule with a chair over each shoulder, a cooler in one hand, and a bag in the other. It's hard not to feel like an entitled diva following him and Timothy, who's carrying a decently heavy bat bag.

We stop at a folding table with a tent covering it. Morgan looks up from her nachos and smiles. "What's up?"

I reach in my pocket for money.

"Save it, girl. Coaches don't pay, but your bellman owes us five bucks."

I frown at her. Despite all my protesting, she still insists on calling me a coach.

Nate scrambles to put down a bag. I hold a hand to stop him. "I got it." I give Morgan a five.

She hands me two bands. "Nate's is the red one. You wear the neon orange to show you can go on the field."

"Thanks."

"The schedule is posted at the concession stand. We don't play for another hour." She tosses a chip in her mouth and chews, then swallows. "If the two of you could get everyone warmed up when they get here, I'd appreciate it."

"Okay."

"Where do you want me to set you up?" Nate asks.

"Oh right. This way." I hurry down the hill, but not at a pace so fast he can't find me. I've already made him stand far too long holding my entire trunk contents.

It's not even ten and several tents already line the fence by our field. I'm sensing a pattern here.

"Should I have brought a tent?" I ask.

"Most people do for all-day tournaments."

My face falls.

"I can always bring one in if y'all need it. Besides, I doubt the Corolla could hold anything else."

"True."

Nate sets down the cooler and drops the chair from that arm. He rotates his shoulder and grits his teeth. I didn't even consider his injury when I loaded him down with my stuff.

What kind of person am I?

"This spot looks great," I lie. It's a horrible view of the field and on a slope. But if it gets Nate to unload, it will work.

He glances around and scrunches his face, clearly realizing the downfall in this spot. Then he smiles at me and sets up the lawn chairs best he can on the slope.

Jeffrey struts our way from the concession stand. His gold watch catches the sunlight, overpowering the rest of his ensemble for once. Between the bright red pants and Armadillos cap, it's hard not to spot him. Oh, and today he's added a fake sleeve.

"Why is Jeffrey wearing a compression sleeve?" I whisper.

"My guess is he thinks it looks cool, but if we ask he'll say it's because he's pitching all day."

I laugh and Nate joins me. We straighten our faces when Jeffrey gets within earshot.

"I guess Morgan filled you in, but the first games are on the board. We're in a pool of eight and it's double elimination."

"Thanks," I say.

He puts his hands on his hips and spits to the side, barely missing my snack bag. I swallow.

"Nice sleeve, Jeffrey." Nate grins at me.

"Thanks. I got it at one of those vendor trucks last travel-ball tournament." He stretches out his arm and admires it. "Should help me with pitching today."

Nate lifts his chin. "Maybe I'll look into getting one."

Jeffrey smiles, then continues toward the other end of the park. I shake my head at Nate.

It's going to be a long day.

CHAPTER 13

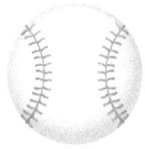

Nate

Jeffrey said I couldn't be on the field, but he didn't say I couldn't help the kids from outside the field. That includes giving my advice to Morgan.

"All these teams are using catchers. I think y'all need one too."

She turns her head toward the kids. Half of them are rolling down the slope where we set up, one of Maribelle's twins is eating powdered donuts, and Tami's daughters are filming themselves on her phone.

The last one disturbs me a little since Tami showed me some of her own videos for TikTok.

"Has Andrew caught before?"

Morgan turns back to me. "Not officially, but he's put on Ethan's gear and played around at home."

"Think he'd try some with me warming him up?"

"Sure."

She lets out her famous whistle and every head turns. Even Reece looks up from his *Harry Potter* book.

"Everyone sit still!"

The kids who were rolling freeze. Morgan may not have the best baseball skills, but she sure knows how to get kids to listen.

"That's impressive," I say.

"Substitute bus drive awhile and you'll learn a few things."

"I bet."

"Andrew, come here."

He stands and dusts the grass off his knees from rolling and hurries toward us. "Yes, ma'am."

Morgan looks to me, and so does Andrew.

"How would you like to catch in the tournament?" I ask.

"Yes, sir."

"Okay, they keep gear in that equipment trailer behind the gate. Take a parent with you to help you find the right size."

He smiles and runs toward the group. He passes us again with Easton behind him. Easton shrugs at Morgan and me.

"Just make sure it will fit him. We'll take care of the rest," I say.

Relief covers his face and he continues following Andrew. Morgan and I discuss where we probably need to play everyone else.

I suggest Timothy for first base since he's left handed and can catch decently. We put Carter at short. Everyone else is pretty much sitting ducks, so we decide to rotate them around.

"I wouldn't put Angel and Precious in the outfield at the same time. They'll start picking flowers."

"Good point," Morgan agrees.

By the time we've settled the starting positions, I hear metal clanking. Andrew comes behind us in full gear.

"I'd probably wear a cup too, just in case," I advise him.

"I have one in my bag," Morgan says.

We follow her to a pile of baseball gear near Brooke's chairs. She opens a girly-looking bag and starts tossing things out one by one. Sunflower seeds. Prime bottles. Feminine products I can't unsee. Tylenol. A romance novel. Finally, a cup. She holds it up triumphantly.

Andrew takes it as she crams the other things back in the bag. "Hey, nobody look! I'm putting on my cup," he announces.

Obviously, everyone looks as soon as he tells them not to. I do think a little better of Tami when she covers her daughters' eyes.

"I'm ready, Mr. Nate."

I nod. "Let's warm you up." I stand and see an empty field. "Morgan, why don't you take the others to their positions and practice tossing the ball to them."

She salutes me and grabs a glove and a ball. I take Andrew to a flat spot near the fence while she does her usual yelling and wrangling of kids.

We warm up a few minutes before I hear a lawn mower and a kid scream. Jeffrey is driving full force toward the outfield while our team is warming up.

One of Tami's girls is in the fetal position by the fence, and Reece poses like Harry Potter squaring up to duel Draco. Andrew tosses me the ball, and I step closer to the fence. When Jeffrey has his back turned to me, I chuck the ball and nail the engine. It sputters and dies. Good thing it backfired loudly, because I read his lips when he spun around to check on it.

Andrew lifts his mask and stares at me. "Boss!"

I put a finger to my lips and wink. He nods and smiles. Morgan snort-laughs, then she and Brooke continue warming up everyone else.

I'm proud to say it takes Jeffrey every second until the umpire is ready for the game to pull that lawn mower off the field. Not one person offers to help him—his coaches, parents, and especially not me.

"You've got this, buddy." I fist-bump Andrew and send him to the field.

Jeffrey wipes sweat from his brow and stumbles my way. You'd think a guy who moves repo trailers for a living wouldn't get so winded pulling a lawn mower off the ball field.

"You." He points the sleeved arm in my face.

"What?" I mentally prepare to deny hitting the lawn mower.

"You can't be this close to the field. You're not a coach."

"I know. I'm a spectator."

"Well, you best spectate elsewhere." His hand falls to his hip. "I can't trust you to not call plays from the sidelines."

I shrug. "Okay."

I brush past him, almost knocking him over with a gentle shoulder bump. I jog toward first base and get Brooke's attention.

"Jeffrey's kicking me out."

"He can't do that. We paid and you're not doing anything wrong."

I shake my head. "It's fine. Tell the kids I'll be watching from outside the park."

She frowns and nods.

"Good luck." I hurry away before Jeffrey can get to me.

We cross paths on my way out. I keep my eyes on the parking lot, not giving him a chance to speak to me.

As long as we play on the same field today, I'll have a perfect view from my truck's toolbox. I climb up and make myself comfortable.

Andrew catches decently, and Timothy makes a few good plays. Carter is looking more comfortable too. I lean back and snack on a bag of sunflower seeds Morgan forgot to put back in her bag. I stuffed them in my pocket to keep the park clean, but they're coming in handy since the concession stand is in forbidden territory.

Morgan delivers one of the ugliest pitches I've seen. It's like she's tossing a horseshoe, but overhanded. Herrington is at bat and his signature golf swing connects perfectly with the ball. I jump in the bed of my truck and cheer along with everyone inside the park. He gets a double.

Andrew is up next and slams the ball, despite another questionable pitch from Morgan. It goes to the outfield and he quickly advances toward Herrington, who runs the bases like a six-year-old girl playing hopscotch.

I bite my thumbnail when Andrew bumps into Herrington between third and home. He yells at him to run, but he's too slow. Andrew picks him up and runs full speed, carrying Herrington in front of him. He sets him down a few feet in front of home plate.

Herrington hops on the base, further proving my hopscotch analogy. Then he skips off, and Andrew crosses the plate.

In all my years playing and watching ball, I have to say that's a first.

Four hours and two trips to the gas station later, I watch the 8U Armadillos exit the field for the last time.

They lost both games but had some good moments. Most kids at least made contact with the ball today, and we had some good catches in the field.

The bad news is Jeffrey's team is still undefeated.

I dip my Quick Stop chicken in honey mustard and focus on Brooke. She's busy gathering all the junk we carried in earlier while Morgan gives the team a speech.

It hurts me that I can't go in and help her carry it out.

Even more than it hurt my shoulder carrying it in. Easton and Carlton come to the rescue, juggling her heavier things with their own.

A few people stay in the park, but most of our team trudges toward the parking lot. Dirty and tired like they're walking the green mile. Brooke has one arm around Timothy and the other looped through her snack bag.

When they get to the fence, I hop down from the truck and meet them. I take the chairs from Carlton and loop both around my right shoulder. I reach for the cooler, but he shakes his head.

"We're headed that way."

I'm relieved I don't have to carry the cooler again, but I'd never admit it to him.

Timothy breaks free from Brooke's arm and comes to me. "Did you see me catch the ball with my foot on the base?"

"I sure did, buddy. Y'all played good today."

"Thanks." He beams. "Did you see both our games?"

"I did."

"What was your favorite part?"

"Probably Andrew carrying Herrington."

The other adults around us laugh.

"I didn't even know that was legal," Carlton says.

"They have to run the bases in order, and they did."

"Something tells me Bubba will be adding that play to the rule book for next season," Aniston says.

I chuckle. "Guess we'll have to wait and see."

Carlton sets the cooler beside Brooke's car. I wait for her to unlock the trunk, then set everything inside. My shoulder catches as I lift the cooler, but I keep a straight face. If she knew carrying her stuff bothered my shoulder, she'd feel horrible. The last thing I ever want to do is make Brooke feel horrible.

"Thanks." She smiles up at me once everything is put away.

"You're welcome."

I turn to Timothy, mainly to break my old habit of kissing Brooke after ball games. It's been nine years since that's happened, but this is the first game I've been to with her since then.

I used to stare blankly into the stadium and imagine she was somewhere in the crowd watching me. Maybe she was, or at least watching on TV.

But she was never close enough for a kiss.

"You did good." I hold out my fist for Timothy to bump. "We'll work on a few things later. Go home and rest."

He hugs me unexpectedly. My heart melts a bit, and I can't blame it on the heat, as it's only March. I've become attached to this kid.

I make eye contact with Brooke over his head. Maybe it's my imagination, but she blinks back a tear. I pat Timothy on the side, and he slowly releases me.

"Y'all be careful going home." I nod toward the field. "I'm gonna stick around and scout some."

Brooke smiles. "Don't let Jeffrey give you a hard time."

I laugh. "Too late for that."

"I guess so." She scrunches her nose back at Jeffrey, then grins at me.

Before I get too carried away, I retreat to my truck. By the time she and Timothy are driving away, I'm dipping another chicken finger in sauce. Timothy waves out the window, and I lift my non-chicken hand.

I thought the two-run carry was the most entertaining part of the day, but Jeffrey warming up to pitch to kids beats that a million to one.

Every pitch starts with a windup. And why is he looking around like he plans on picking someone off? There's no stealing in coach-pitch.

A kid yells something from the dugout, and Jeffrey turns his head. At the same time, the other coach throws the ball back to him. Jeffrey turns just in time for the ball to smack him square in the eye.

He hits the ground like falling timber.

I can hear the gasps from my toolbox perch. Bubba hurries to the pitching circle, followed by the other coaches. The one who threw the ball still stands in shock.

The ump comes on the field and checks on Jeffrey. I can't hear what anyone is saying, but I can tell Jeffrey is mad. They help him to the dugout, and one of the moms pulls out a first-aid kit.

I finish my afternoon snack while I watch Jeffrey get a gauze eye patch. There are a few words exchanged between him and the umpire. Then Jeffrey grabs a glove and ball and returns to the circle.

He pitches half the game before allowing another coach to pitch. It's a shorter guy in an Enchilada T-shirt. He's a better pitcher than Jeffrey. But to be fair, I've yet to see Jeffrey pitch without an eye patch and throbbing pain.

Each inning is back and forth until the opposing team comes out one run ahead. The Red Armadillos, or as Jeffrey affectionately calls them, "the Reds," get last at-bat, but the Grasshoppers hold them for the win.

Everyone in lime green goes crazy, and Jeffrey slings his glove to the ground. His players pout and go through the motions of lining the bases and slapping hands with their opponents.

The umpire comes out with medals for the Reds and rings for the Grasshoppers. It's not hard to pick out Jeffrey's kid from the attitude. He snarls at his medal and doesn't put it on.

I wait for the Grasshoppers to receive their rings, but Jeffrey doesn't. He leads his boys off the field and gathers their things in record time.

More than anything about his coaching abilities, I hate

how he's teaching his team bad sportsmanship. Double congrats to the Grasshoppers on that note.

I toss the empty chicken box in a nearby trash can and hop down. I close my truck door just in time for Bubba to ride by in a Jeep, hitting a nearby mud puddle. Red globs sling across my window and windshield.

A lot of good it did to hit up that fancy car wash last time I drove through Tuscaloosa. I leave the park and settle for the self-serve car wash beside the gas station.

Two familiar kids stand near the edge of the concrete wall wearing jerseys, slides, and boxer briefs. No pants.

I drive a few feet closer and notice Jeffrey's truck parked outside the first bay. He's inside spraying down pants with one hand and holding a cigarette with the other.

He glares at me with his good eye. I smile and keep driving. What's he going to do to me? Spray the mud off my truck?

I pull in the next slot and get out. I'm shoving quarters in the machine when I hear a whistle. Morgan's whistle. I turn around.

"Good news, I've got your balls," she says louder than I'd like.

"What?"

She drops two baseballs from the window. They roll toward me. I shake my head and stop them with my foot.

"Come here." She motions me over.

I sigh and walk away from my truck before putting in the last quarter.

"Brooke and her parents are feeding the team tonight."

"That's nice of them."

"Yep. I wasn't sure if you knew."

"No." I look down.

"I'm inviting you, then."

I lift my head and sigh.

"You know she wants you there."

"If she wanted me there, she'd have told me herself."

"No, not Brooke. She's not assertive like—"

"You?"

Morgan smiles. "I'll take that as a compliment."

"I can't bust up on a team gathering."

"I think the team would prefer it."

I suck in a deep breath and exhale before looking back at her. "I'll think about it."

"You should." She drops the sunglasses from her hair to her eyes and peels out of the parking lot.

Her van moves to reveal Jeffrey's kids playing with the air hose. The older one is trying to shove it down the smaller one's underwear. I shake my head and hurry to wash my truck.

This place makes Waffle House look upscale.

CHAPTER 14

Brooke

"Here's some more burgers." Mama lets the screen door close behind her and brings a pan to the kitchen counter.

"All right." I move them to a platter with the other patties and cover it with tinfoil.

"I hate we missed the tournament. We'd already signed up to bring pies to that farmers' market."

"It's okay. Not much to see."

She touches my arm. "It'll be fine. They're new at this."

I half smile. "Timothy did get some hits."

"See." She squeezes my arm, then moves toward the refrigerator.

"Thanks for helping with all this. I want to keep their spirits up."

"Anytime. You know I love to feed people."

I laugh. That she does, and people love her for it.

The screen door slams, and I turn, expecting Timothy. He's

not the best at letting it close slowly, especially on windy days.

Morgan lifts her chin. "What's up?"

"Hello, Coach Morgan." Mama smiles at her.

"Hey, Mrs. M. Thanks again for having us."

"Of course. Sawyer's always happy to grill."

"What can I do?" Morgan slaps her hands together and scans the kitchen.

I nod toward the table. "You can make sure one bag of each kind of chips is open and get the dip from the refrigerator.

"Got it." She washes her hands and gets to work.

"Thanks for coming early. You didn't have to help."

"Well, as coach, for better or worse, I wanted to help."

I smile. Morgan's had a long day. We only played two games, but it was way more than she's used to throwing. If we'd lasted longer, I might would've had to pitch. That would make things even worse.

"You're a good woman, Morgan." Mama side hugs her.

"Thanks, Mrs. M."

"You will make a good man very happy one day."

Morgan glances at me behind Mama and laughs.

I've thought of setting her up before, but she's never let on like she wants another relationship. Her ex left her alone with four kids, and she's the most independent person I know. I wish I were as strong as her.

If I didn't have my supportive family, I never would've made it as a single mom.

"Where are your kids?" Mama asks.

"They found Timothy outside. Except for Isabella. I took her to the park earlier for practice, then she's spending the night with a friend."

"I don't see how you keep up with multiple kids playing ball at the same time," I say.

"My house is a mess, and we live off overstock cereal from the Pig half the week."

"Enjoy it. One day they'll grow up." Mama's eyes soften as she gives me her sentimental face.

Cars come down the gravel drive. I check my phone, shocked at how fast the afternoon passed. I'm not used to spending half my day at the ballpark.

I grab the tablecloths from the side of the pantry and go outside to cover the folding tables. Daddy is cleaning the grill beside the porch steps, and the kids toss a football between their house and mine.

I'm halfway to the tables when Nate's truck pulls up. My heart catches in my throat. I'd almost invited him when we decided to feed everyone tonight.

Either he chose now to randomly stop by . . . or someone else invited him.

I crane my neck and stare inside the kitchen window. Morgan waves and winks.

Yep, someone else invited him.

"Hey."

I turn to Nate standing a few feet away. The wind whiffs his just-showered scent my way. I suck in the smell as my eyes settle on a clean white shirt tugging against his chest muscles.

"Hi," I manage to whisper.

"Morgan invited me. I hope that's okay."

"Of course." I shake my head to reset my vision. "The kids will be glad to see you."

"Just the kids?" He raises one eyebrow and I swoon.

He should not have this effect on me. Especially in the presence of kids, with my daddy a few feet away wielding sharp grilling utensils.

"We're all glad to see you." I emphasize the use of second person. The last thing I need is for him to realize he still has me if he wants me.

"Hey, Nate." Tami comes out of nowhere.

She's wearing what I'd consider a cross between a cocktail dress and spandex workout wear. Her thigh tattoo is on full display, and she doesn't seem to notice—or care—that her baby is pulling the top of her dress.

I clear my throat to get her attention. She slowly turns from Nate to me, and I nod at her chest. I'd be happy if someone discreetly let me know my bra was showing, but I don't think she gets my signal.

"Uh, Tami."

"Oh." She slaps a palm to her head. "Are y'all like together?"

Nate and I lock eyes. There's a lingering silence between us, and I halfway wish he'd answer one way or another.

"Gotcha." Tami laughs. "Been there. Anyways . . . I'm about to go take a snap break."

"Snap break?" This must be some teenager lingo I haven't heard.

"Yeah, I have a smoke, then a nap."

Nate lifts his chin, then cuts his eyes back to me with a half smirk.

Tami fans a hand. "Don't worry. I pass the baby off to someone before doing that."

I nod. "Good to know."

"Y'all kids have fun." She struts past us and slaps Nate on the butt.

He jumps, and I burst out laughing. He holds his butt and watches her leave with a disgusted face. "I can't say I didn't expect to feel violated today. But I can say I expected it to happen at the park."

I laugh more and he joins me.

More people drive up, and I remember the tablecloths in my hand. I start to unfold one, and Nate takes it. "Let me help you."

He flaps open the cloth, sending his scent soaring and

putting his biceps on full display. I blink and focus on the other cloth still in my hand.

We cover the two serving tables in time for Morgan to come out with food. "Hope I'm not interrupting," she says sweetly.

I give her a dirty look and she bats her eyelashes.

"I can bring out more food." Nate climbs the steps.

I follow him inside, keeping my eyes on the door. I can't look at Nate's butt or Morgan. Both are equally dangerous on different levels.

Mama made small baseball-shaped candies from white chocolates. Nate grabs that tray and grins. "Remember that coffee place we found that had all the chocolate-flavored stuff?"

"Yeah."

"Is it still around?"

I nod. "I still go there sometimes when I'm in Tuscaloosa."

"Huh." He pops a chocolate in his mouth and chews, then swallows. "We should go sometime."

"We should. Timothy's never been."

He looks at me. "I meant just me and you."

My heart beats faster, and I catch my breath.

He grabs another tray and brushes past me in the doorway. I slowly pick up some plates and cups, trying to snap out of whatever trance I entered since he arrived.

Nate laughs with my friends and their kids as he helps set up the food. Then he shakes my dad's hand and helps him push the grill out of the way.

He would fit into my life seamlessly. That is, until he has to report back to Atlanta for ball.

And that brings me back to the reason I chose this solo life for myself and Timothy.

I step onto the porch to Nate's big smile. He does seem happy, and he does live partly in the house down the road.

Could it be possible he wants this life too?

Nate

I stop and catch my breath, then toss the Wiffle-ball bat toward a row of trees.

"That's enough for now."

Some of the boys moan, and others have already lost interest and found the food. Mr. Sawyer sees the game disband and rings a bell on the back porch. A literal dinner bell.

The kids run toward the house, and I lag behind. My shoulder hasn't given me much trouble since earlier today, but I don't want to push it. And I'm getting tired.

Even though I'm in shape, I lack the gung-ho of an eight-year-old. Especially when a plate of burgers and chocolate is within reach.

By the time I make it to the table, Sawyer is finishing the prayer. All the kids yell "amen" and descend on the food like a pack of dogs on a dead squirrel.

I strategically get in line beside Brooke and pile my plate with two burgers and chips. I plan on coming back for dessert, until I watch how many chocolates the kids are grabbing. Brooke puts two on my plate and smiles.

She knows me so well.

When I first moved back, I was skeptical. I thought it was because I'd been gone so long, or because I moved into a much bigger house than where I grew up. I spent more time in Atlanta than here and had all but convinced myself Apple Cart was no longer home.

Then I saw Brooke hanging on the fence across from my house.

Everything changed that day. The house, the town, my mood. This is my home, and it's all because she's here.

I want to tell her that. No, I *need* to tell her that. I just haven't figured out when or how.

The last thing I want is to confess my love and jet off to Atlanta for another season. That's not fair to her or Timothy. I would never ask her to leave her job or take him out of school to follow me. That's unfair.

People start finding seats on the porch and around the yard. Between the kids and adults, the rockers and swings fill up fast. I take my drink and plate to the front porch.

Not until I sit on the swing do I realize Mrs. Margaret might not want people venturing to the front of the house. Southern women can get a little territorial about their homes. They might not want you going in certain areas they haven't cleaned and decorated specially for the occasion.

I'm standing to leave when Brooke comes around the corner with her plate and cup.

"Mind if I join you?"

I shake my head. "No, come on."

She smiles and climbs the steps. I sit slowly, more to the side to give her room. The swing moves slightly when she sits. I smile at her short legs barely touching the ground.

I've always towered over her. After we broke up, I grew another two inches and put on about thirty pounds of muscle, making her look even tinier next to me.

"I'm glad the weather is pleasant for this."

"Yep." I settle back and take a bite of my burger. "Too bad pollen is starting."

"Yeah. Sweet home Alabama. The few weeks we have between cold and blazing hot is covered in yellow dust." She laughs a second, then asks, "Do you still have allergies?"

"Not as bad. The professional fields aren't as rural and allergenic as high school."

She nods and smiles.

"You know what they say?" I cock a smile.

"An apple a day keeps the doctor away," we say in unison.

"Well, I know where to find some apples if I ever need them." I smile wider and nod at the orchard beside us.

"Help yourself anytime." Her eyes widen. "Paul does."

"Still, after all these years?" I chuckle.

"Yeah. If anything, he's gotten worse. Now that he's dating Ms. Dot, he takes her to get pies for dates."

I turn to Brooke and laugh. "I thought they were a little attached lately."

"It started not long after her husband passed."

I shake my head. "Small-town romance. Always a scandal."

She laughs nervously, and I drop my eyes to my plate. Maybe now isn't the best time to suggest we pick up where we left off.

I continue eating and allow her to carry the conversation. Discussing Aniston's ideas for music at the games and the new coffee maker in the hospital isn't ideal, especially when I'd rather talk about us. But for now I'll take sitting on the porch together.

"Mama," Timothy's voice calls from behind us.

We both turn to him grinning excitedly.

"What is it?"

"We're going to have a dance contest, and Miss Aniston says you have to come. She said you're a good dancer."

"Did she now?" Brooke sucks in a breath.

I'm guessing she doesn't dance in front of Timothy. His eyes move toward me as if asking for my help.

"Your mom is a good dancer."

A grin crosses his face, but Brooke shoots eye daggers at me.

"What? You are, or were."

"Were?"

She moves her plate to the side and jumps from the swing. My insides heat up at the old Brooke coming back to life.

"You want to prove it?" I stand to challenge her.

Without another word, she hurries down the front porch and rounds the house. Timothy grins wider as I follow and motion for him to come with us.

Aniston has a speaker hooked to her phone's music. She raises her eyebrows when we come around.

"I'm trying to sell the kids on our songs for the games. They said they need something danceable." She narrows her eyes on Brooke. "That's where you come in, prom queen."

Brooke huffs. "It's been a while."

"You were prom queen?" Timothy asks.

"It's been a while," she says to him this time.

"Who was prom king?"

Without answering that, I grab her hand. As if right on cue, "Shut Up and Dance" blares across the speaker and I sing with it.

Brooke follows me to the center of the backyard. Her eyes twinkle, making my fingers tingle as I hold her. "You hate dancing fast," she says.

"Not with you." I spin her around and dance like a fool.

She laughs when I dip her, and the kids clap and cheer. A few cheesy moves later and everyone is dancing, even Brooke's parents.

Aniston eventually abandons her phone to autoplay when Tami tries to cozy up to Easton. Georgia and her husband are doing some sort of dance with actual steps I've seen on *Dancing with the Stars*, and the kids are jumping and going crazy.

Jack tries to do the worm and Reece runs around with the porch broom. Everyone is cutting a rug until the speaker transitions to a slow song. Most of the kids lose interest, and the adult couples start to slow dance.

I lock eyes with Brooke and try to read her thoughts. This isn't just a slow song for us. It's *the* slow song.

It's the song that played during our prom king and queen dance. Right after I told her I was entering the MLB draft. She teared up, and terror covered her face as our futures became uncertain. Then she ran off crying.

We didn't break up that night, but I can say in hindsight that things were never the same after that. She became guarded and skeptical, no longer totally carefree.

I lost a piece of her that night, and I never got it back.

The song goes into the chorus, and she slides her hands around my neck. I lean closer and start to sway. I dip my head and snuggle my face against the top of her head. Her hair smells like springtime—minus the pollen.

A million memories rush through my brain. Proms, homecoming dances, impromptu dances on the front porch, and a ton of other times when I held her close without dancing.

For one song, everything holding us apart disappears. Nine years, two hundred miles, and all the questions of whether she's with someone or if she wants to be with me.

She doesn't have to tell me, and I don't have to ask. Right now, I know.

Then the song ends and Taylor Swift starts belting out "Bad Blood." I open my eyes and lift my head. This is not the song I want to snuggle to.

Brooke bats her eyes up at me, and everything in me wants to kiss her.

Then I notice Morgan, her parents, Aniston, and a few other random parents staring at us. Everyone is smiling, except for Tami. She's licking her lips. Whether at me or at us together, I'm not sure. Either way, it's gross.

I take a step back, embarrassed at going all high school in Brooke's backyard at a Little League cookout.

Her face reddens as she notices everyone too. Morgan

turns and starts talking to Brooke's parents rather loudly about the game schedule. Others slowly turn too.

I run a hand through my hair and clear my throat. "Want me to help y'all clean up the food?"

"Sure." She shakes her head, as if dislodging another thought.

I nod and walk to the table holding empty chip bags and candy dishes with crumbs. Brooke walks in the opposite direction and starts cleaning another table. Morgan slides beside me and smiles.

"I know what you're up to." I narrow my eyes at her.

"You're welcome." She snatches a stack of plates and walks away.

The night winds down while Morgan and I help Brooke and her parents pack everything inside and Aniston argues song choices with the kids. As the sun dips behind the orchard, people begin to leave.

Timothy, Ethan, and Andrew have roped me into a kickball game. Morgan steps onto the back porch with her youngest daughter and lets out a whistle. Both boys turn like dogs hearing a squeaky toy. Morgan's whistle would probably ruin a dog's ears.

"Let's go, Things One and Two."

They begrudgingly pick up the toys they brought and head toward her.

She palms the back of Andrew's head. "Tell Brooke and Mr. and Mrs. M thanks for having us before you get in the van."

They disappear behind the screen door. I pick up the rest of the balls and bases used for the Wiffle and kickball games.

"I know where those go," Timothy says.

"Where's that?"

He leads me to a trunk in the garage and opens the lid.

"Thanks." I drop everything inside.

Andrew calls "bye" out the back window, and I lift a hand

to wave. Timothy leaves my side to tell him something before they drive away.

I circle the house to make sure we didn't miss anything and run into Brooke.

"Hey."

She straightens and sprays my shirt with a water hose in her hand.

"Oh no."

I laugh. "It's okay."

"Sorry." She wipes her hand down my chest as if it would dry the soaked cotton. "I was watering the daffodils." Her voice trails and her hand rests on my stomach.

I want so badly to kiss her, but it's not the right time. She has to make the first move.

We've gained so much ground this past week, but we're not there yet. I can't steal home. She has to give me the base. That's the way it's got to be. She has way more to lose than me.

"Thanks for tonight," I say. Then I lean down and kiss her gently on the cheek. I step back, letting her hand fall from my stomach, and smile.

She blushes and smiles in return. "See you soon."

I walk backward a few steps. "Coffee sometime soon."

"Coffee," she agrees.

I turn and get in my truck. If I don't go home now, I'll be tempted to stay until her dad flashes the porch lights at me.

Just like the good old days.

CHAPTER 15

Nate

It's nice playing a home game without Jeffrey around.

The Red Armadillos are on the road tonight in Moonshine County, leaving the Gray Armadillos at home to face the Wisteria Mud Cats.

That should make for a fun game.

The Apple Cart Armadillos and Wisteria Mud Cats are the two high school teams in the county and have a heated rivalry dating back to long before I came around. Legend has it that the Mud Cats feed their football players rattlesnake each year before the big game against Apple Cart.

The hatred trickles down to Toy Bowl and Little League too, which is why Bradley is here.

Bradley Manning grew up in Wisteria, but now lives in Apple Cart and has been the county sheriff for a while. Long enough that I think he's coming up for reelection.

"Hey, big dog." Bradley nods to me, then straps on a pair of leg guards.

"What are you doing?"

"Oh, I'm not just here to patrol for potential fights. I'm helping ump to keep all these crazy coaches and parents straight too."

"I didn't know you were an umpire."

He slips on the chest protector without removing his signature cowboy hat—impressive. When it's over his head, he grins. "Got certified last night online."

"Don't you have to go through some kind of process with the county to make it official?"

His grin turns into a mischievous smirk. "I am the county official."

I shrug. Can't argue with that.

"Are you coaching the Gray 'Dillas?"

"No, just helping them practice. Morgan is coaching."

"Morgan Archer?"

"Yeah."

He shakes his head. "Better keep my handcuffs handy. That woman is a handful."

I laugh. "I'll take your word for it."

"Keep her in line for me tonight."

"I'll try."

Bradley starts buckling his gear.

"I'll see you from the sidelines."

He glances up as I walk away and calls out, "Good seein' ya, big dog."

I head to the home dugout, where Easton is giving the kids a pep talk. It's actually pretty inspiring. He finishes on a high note, and I attempt a slow clap, but it doesn't catch on.

They're too young to appreciate a special moment.

Morgan hands him the book and Aniston the lineup.

I crane my head inside the opening. "Good luck, guys. Y'all got this."

They offer fist bumps and high fives. Charlie's hand leaves mine sticky. He immediately picks up a frozen pickle pop.

I slide back from the dugout and wipe my hand down my shorts. Brooke stands near the fence, smiling at me. My knees buckle, and I lean against a bleacher to steady myself. Other than speaking to her briefly Sunday at church, I haven't spent any time with her since she sprayed my shirt.

And we almost kissed again.

I don't want to come off as too eager to be with them. However, she did text and invite me to the game. I can thank Morgan's scheming for that. My phone hasn't seen any sign of Brooke in almost a decade.

Bradley brings the head coaches and the other umpire to the plate and goes over rules. The Mud Cats coach snarls at Morgan like they're opposing gang members.

This should be fun.

On that note, I go to the concession stand and buy a bag of popcorn.

"Wassup, Nate," Tami calls to me from inside the window.

I duck my head to find her scooping nacho cheese with one hand and bouncing a baby on her hip with the other. She's wearing a tight, short jean skirt and baseball heels. That's something you don't see every day.

"Hey, can I get some popcorn?"

"Slim!" she yells over her shoulder.

A tall, slim guy comes to the window. "What you need?"

"Popcorn and a Coke, please."

"What kind of drink?"

I've traveled and spent so much time in bigger cities that I forget "Coke" is the small-town equivalent to "drink."

"An actual Coke is good, or Mountain Dew, if y'all have it."

Slim lifts his chin. "Four dollars."

I pay him and wait as he slowly pours a bag of popcorn and retrieves my drink. He gives me a Gatorade even though I saw at least five types of soft drinks.

I decide it's not worth correcting him and go find a seat near the dugout.

Aniston holds up a bag of mixed candy. Jack and Charlie jump for it, and she stretches farther. "You have to do something good to get candy."

A kid in a Mud Cats jersey runs by and stops at our dugout. "Can I have candy?"

"You're not on our team." Aniston scowls.

"Booger, get over here. You've had plenty of time to pee!" a man yells from the visitors' side.

The boy jerks his head that direction, then runs.

Aniston studies the back of his jersey. "Booger. That gives me one name I needed." She makes a note on the lineup. "No wonder Maribelle quit after one game."

Once Booger is in place, the first batter lines up.

I thought Jeffrey was the most entertaining coach to watch. Well, this Mud Cats guy may have him beat. He doesn't wind up like Jeffrey, but after every pitch, he calls out the count. Loudly.

Some of these kids look like a deer in the headlights. Others get frustrated. It only takes four batters to get three strikeouts.

I'm glad I bought popcorn.

Carter is our first batter. He gets a double off an error. We all clap, and the kids cheer. The next kid strikes out, then Timothy gets a double and hits Carter home.

I don't think I could be any prouder if he were my own son. He smiles at me from second, and I give him a thumbs-up.

Unfortunately, they tag him at home.

We manage to get in two runs in the first inning. The next inning they score one. A bigger kid nails the ball on the first pitch. I guess he didn't want to wait to hear the count.

I wouldn't.

Our kids score one in the second inning. Then the other

team scores one, but Timothy catches a fly ball for the third out. This kid is on fire today.

The boys celebrate when they get in the dugout. Morgan gives them a quick speech about how they're only a point ahead and we need to hold them.

Booger is up to bat. He steps toward the plate and bends at the waist. Everyone groans as he spills his guts on the plate.

Bradley waits until he's done, then brushes the base. I'm a little squeamish already, and when the kid throws up a second time, I turn my head.

The coach talks to Bradley, and Booger goes back to the dugout. Bradley calls the kid on deck to the plate, but he's against the fence holding his stomach.

Bradley calls time. He and the head coach go to the Mud Cats' dugout. From what I can see, most of the kids are bowed over or holding their mouths.

Some kind of virus must be going around.

Bradley nods and talks with the coaches a few minutes before returning to the field. "Mud Cats have forfeited due to sickness. Armadillos win!"

Morgan and Brooke stare at each other in shock. The kids go crazy, until Aniston settles them down. "They're sick. Show sportsmanship," she snips.

Everyone quiets. Maybe Aniston should coach.

She lines them up and gives them instructions I can't hear. Andrew leads the team across the field. They march past the opposing team's dugout saying "good game," then rush back to our dugout.

"Now, you can celebrate." Aniston tosses candy in the air, and they go crazy.

The other team gathers their belongings and helps the sick kids to the parking lot. Slim almost hits me when I'm walking toward Brooke and Morgan. He's carrying a broom and some trash bags. "I heard there was a lot to clean up," he says.

"Unfortunately, lots of throw up," Bradley says.

"I once worked night shift at the Waffle House. There ain't nothing I ain't seen." Slim lifts his chest.

Bradley pats him on the arm. "Get it, big dog."

Morgan glances back at the field, then at Bradley. "I'm glad we won, but bless their hearts. They all got sick so quickly."

Carlton stops packing up his kid's gear and frowns. "We sat close to the other side. Someone said a kid brought gum in the dugout because he wanted candy, then shared it with everyone."

We exchange puzzled looks.

"Was it expired?" Brooke asks.

Carlton's eyes widen. "It was Nicorette."

"Ohhh," we all say.

Bradley slams down the chest protector and straightens his hat. "If you guys will excuse me, I smell someone needing a citation for subjecting minors to narcotics." He rushes out of the park, still wearing the leg guards.

After the shock wears off and everyone continues gathering gear, I speak up. "If y'all want to celebrate, dinner is on me."

The kids scream with excitement.

"What are you cooking?" Morgan asks.

"Nothing, I'm taking y'all out."

Aniston checks her phone screen. "Mary's and Big Butts are closed."

"Waffle House?" Carlton suggests.

"Not after what Slim said." I shudder. "Who likes Mexican?"

Brooke

. . .

I should've thought before I agreed to Mexican.

Somehow I've made it twenty-seven years without eating at Enchilada. Surely it won't make me as sick as the poor kids trying to blow bubbles with Nicorette.

It's not the food that scares me as much as the atmosphere. When you share retail space with a sketchy motel and a liquor store on the county line, it doesn't exactly make people feel safe.

Even worse, the bulbs in "Quality" are out at the motel, so the signs read "Inn The Hole Enchilada."

I wait until Nate gets out to unlock our doors. He meets me at the car. Timothy hops out and stares at the neon lights. "Is this the place on the way to Double Drive?"

"Yeah."

"I saw a Double Drive sign. Who owns that?" Nate asks.

"Earl Ed Mayberry."

His brows lift. "I thought he was in jail."

"He got out on good behavior and started a go-kart and putt-putt place."

"Good for him. I thought he got a bad break going to jail for stealing mail."

"Yeah. The place is pretty fun, actually."

"You should go with us sometime." Timothy peeks around me at Nate.

"I will." He smiles at Timothy.

Then he looks at me and smiles deeper, like he's trying to convey a hidden message, or maybe flirt. Whatever he's trying to do, it's working. I dip my head and follow him inside.

Our group gathers at the door, and a man not much taller than me asks how many are with us. Morgan quickly counts all the adults and kids, then throws out a number that makes his eyes bulge.

"Is it okay to do two big tables and a booth?" he asks in a heavy accent.

"Yep." She turns to us. "Kids at one table, adults at the other."

The host leads us to the dining area and speaks Spanish to a waiter. They pull together a bunch of tables, leaving one walkway in the center of the room. The kids pile around one table and the adults at the other. I pull out a chair to sit on the end, and Morgan jumps in it.

She bats her eyelashes at me. "I guess you and Nate are stuck with the booth. Sorry."

I frown when she drags out "sorry." Sarcastic minx.

"That's fine." Nate takes a couple of menus from the waiter, and we find a nearby booth.

I've barely had time to read the specials when I sense someone standing over me. I open my mouth to say I need a few more minutes, assuming it's the waiter.

No, it's Jeffrey and Bubba. Two more coaches get up from the booth behind us.

Jeffrey crosses his arms, showing off his fake sleeve and gold watch. His eye is still swollen from this past weekend. "What brings y'all here?"

Nate lifts his menu. "Food."

"We won tonight," Jeffrey says with a huff.

"So did we," Nate says.

"*We*? You better not have helped coach."

"I didn't. I said 'we' since I'm a fan. Ask Bradley Manning, I sat on my rear and ate popcorn."

He sniffles. "Glad to know they won. We can't have the gray team ruining the Armadillos' reputation."

He walks by and his entourage follows. I scrunch my face and watch them march away in a line like ducks in a row. Arrogant, ugly, redneck-men ducks.

"Well, that was entertaining," Nate says once they're out of sight.

"And rude."

"That's just sports, dumpling. You've got to overlook it." He flips a menu page and continues browsing.

My mouth drops and two very different emotions get in a bidding war for real estate of my brain.

"What?" he asks when he glances up.

"It's nothing. You called me dumpling, that's all."

"Oh, I'm sorry, I didn't mean—"

"No, it's fine." Without thinking, I reach across the table and grab his hand.

He wraps his strong fingers around my much-smaller hand and my pulse elevates.

The waiter comes back with chips and salsa. "Can I get you drinks?"

I let go of Nate's hand and clear my throat. "Water. Ice water, with extra ice."

"Okay." He turns to Nate.

My heart kicks into mild cardiac arrest as I scan the menu absentmindedly to act as if nothing is out of the ordinary. In reality, everything is out of the ordinary.

My child and I are about to ingest food from Inn The Hole Enchilada, Nate just called me dumpling for the first time in ages, and we were holding hands. Either I'm in some sort of twilight zone, or I'm having an early midlife crisis.

Nate orders sweet tea, and I find the word "taco." I call out the number for what I hope is chicken tacos and hand the guy my menu.

The kids are laughing, and the adults are smiling as they chat.

"I like our team."

Nate turns toward them and smiles. "They're good people."

"It's kind of cool. There's no other situation that would have Tami sharing cheese dip with Georgia."

He laughs. "Or have Georgia eating here."

"Confession." I wince. "I've never eaten here either."

He shrugs. "As long as you don't get the special, you're good." He pops a chip in his mouth. "It's known as a natural laxative."

"So I've heard."

We laugh, and I relax against the backrest. Sharing a basket of chips in a booth alone with Nate feels way too much like a date. And I love it.

A little too much.

This team also brought us together. Not that I wouldn't have crossed paths with Nate eventually. But my kid standing in his yard asking for baseball help made that happen sooner than later.

I thought it was too soon, but I'm warming up to it being a blessing in disguise.

Our waiter delivers the drinks, along with an extra cup of ice for me. I glance at Nate, with his tight T-shirt and chiseled jaw. Maybe I should save myself the trouble and toss the ice on my face.

Nate and I chat casually until eventually we're interrupted by a cloud of smoke, followed by a crackling sound, coming from behind us. A muscled bald man with a handlebar mustache brings a pan of fajitas and my tacos.

"Hot plate!" He all but drops the fajita skillet in front of Nate.

I lean back in case he's dangerous with the tacos, but he isn't. He hurries off and returns with more food for the tables.

"Tacos. Safe choice," Nate comments.

"That was the plan."

He rolls a fajita as I take a bite. "Not bad."

"See, I told you." He bites into his food and smiles.

Loud, annoying laughter catches my attention. Tami is standing in the center of the room, talking to handlebar mustache.

He disappears to the edge of the room, then returns with a microphone.

"What in the?"

Nate laughs. "They do karaoke on weekends. I guess Tami wanted a wild Tuesday night."

"You go to that?" I arch a brow at him.

He laughs harder. "I've gotten fajitas to go on a Friday night."

I sigh, relieved Nate doesn't frequent Enchilada. The tacos and salsa are good, but I imagine a rough crowd here for Friday karaoke.

The microphone squeaks and I almost choke on my water. An older box TV cuts on in the corner with lyrics. The cliché Hispanic beats playing over the speakers are replaced with pop music.

Tami is in her element, jamming out every word to Beyonce's "Single Ladies." Nate and I exchange a look, and he smirks. I bite back a laugh and give it time to pass before attempting to eat more.

We continue eating and chatting about the game. He compliments Timothy and how far he's come in a short time. "I think he's a natural."

He got it from his daddy. I clear my throat and choose not to say that out loud. We're getting along so well, and there might be potential for something here. I don't want to drop a bomb on him until I'm sure he's interested in me, along with the kid plus Apple Cart County package I'm carrying.

"Thank you for helping him."

Nate smiles.

"Seriously. Daddy didn't play ball, and my brothers aren't around much anymore. Not that they were superstars, anyway."

"Come on, give them more credit than that."

I roll my eyes.

"Single Ladies" finally comes to an end and "Strawberry

Wine" starts playing. Maribelle and Georgia jump up and Tami shares the microphone. Nate and I watch with amusement.

"That's a trio you don't see every day."

"Nope," he agrees.

The lyrics make me a little sentimental about dating Nate back in the day. I look down at my plate and try to block out the song.

"You okay?"

I lift my eyes to Nate staring at me. "Yeah." I shake my head. "My tacos are a little spicy," I lie, and blot at a stray tear.

Nate hands me a napkin.

"Thanks."

"I know we both have crazy schedules, but I'd love for just the two of us to have a quiet night in Tuscaloosa soon."

My face involuntarily jerks into a huge smile. "I'd love that."

Maybe one day I'll muster up the courage to say that I still love him.

CHAPTER 16

Brooke

"Hold still." Morgan licks her thumb and wipes at the corner of Andrew's mouth.

He shakes his head out of her grip. She grabs him and wipes the end of her shirt across his face.

"Boy, I am not paying an extra five bucks to have the bacon grease photoshopped out of your photo."

When Morgan finally releases him, Andrew grunts and runs in the opposite direction. "Don't you get grass stains on those pants either!" she yells. She sighs and turns to me. "None of my other kids had a problem getting their ball photos made."

"He's young," I offer.

"Says the woman with a calm kid."

I follow her eyes to Timothy sitting patiently on the bleachers. I smile at him. When it comes to kids who mind and make life easy, I hit the jackpot.

A huge van pulls up to the park, slinging gravel when it

stops. The tall roof and maroon paint make it creepy enough, but the bumper sticker sets it over the top. It's a camera with the words "I Shoot People" in bold block letters.

Jillian jumps out with a coffee the size of a Stanley cup. She slings her long black braid over her shoulder and opens the back of the van, revealing an arsenal of equipment.

"Should we go help her?" I ask Morgan.

"Nah. She's too particular. I don't want to pay for a light reflector thingy because my fingernail accidentally grazed it."

I nod.

"On the flip side, that's part of what makes her photos so good."

I watch in awe as lanky little Jillian loads her arms with anything and everything she might need to snap a few photos on a ball field. All while balancing her coffee cup.

Impressive.

"Maybe she should help us unload our stuff," I say.

Morgan laughs. "Told you."

She passes us and steps effortlessly onto the field. Then she meticulously sets up multiple lights and screens and her camera on a tripod.

Morgan whistles loudly, and the kids circle around. "We're going to take a group photo first. Then individuals. After your individual, you can go to your parents until the game."

She grabs Andrew by the arm and leads him to the field. Everyone else follows. Morgan moves them around a few times, first with the taller kids in the back. When she discovers Jack has huge mud streaks already on his pants, she puts him there too.

Tami's daughters are wearing false eyelashes and their hair curled like this is an elementary scholarship pageant rather than Little League picture day.

"Here, Mama." Timothy hands me his bat bag. I take it to the side and sit on a bleacher.

"No, girl, we gotta be in this too," Morgan says.

I frown.

"You too, Aniston. You're our number three."

Aniston huffs and pushes herself off the fence. "If I had a nickel for every time I've been called someone's number three," she mumbles to me.

I snicker and join them behind the kids. Jillian swaps me up so I can be seen over Reece's tall head.

"You." She points to Reece. "Get rid of your gum."

He stops chewing the wad in his mouth, digs it out, and hands it to her. She scrunches her nose.

"He doesn't get out much," Aniston says.

Jillian goes to her equipment and slings the gum onto a piece of paper. She wipes her hand down her pants and shudders before refocusing on us. "There. Now, everyone smile."

She takes a crazy amount of photos in two minutes' time.

"Great." She checks her camera. "Let's start with individuals."

"Jack." Morgan snaps her fingers. "You and your brother go first before you get any dirtier."

Morgan snatches Andrew by the back of his shirt before he can run off. He pouts. "You're next, buddy. Stay put."

Jillian is every bit as loud as Morgan, if not more. She does a great job getting everyone's attention and making the kids smile. She even helps reattach one of Tami's daughters' eyelashes when it falls off.

Jeffrey's team is lined up waiting their turn when we exit the field. He's wearing his fake sleeve, and all the coaches have on matching jerseys with their names. A little overkill, if you ask me. We settled for wearing our gray "Go Armadillos!" shirts.

The kids all have on eye black and fake sleeves too. Most them are also wearing gold chains with their numbers.

"I'll email you when the proofs are ready," Jillian says to Morgan.

"Thanks."

"The real armadillos are here," Jeffrey gloats.

He cozies up to Jillian, and she shrinks away.

That's our cue to leave. Morgan motions for the kids to find their parents, and I help her make sure everyone has their bat and cap.

"I've got the rest of the birth certificates in my bag. If you can turn them in at the concession stand, that'd be great," Morgan tells me.

"Why do we need those, again?"

She reaches in her bag for some chips and rips them open, grabbing a handful and chomping down before answering me. "This is our first big tournament to host that includes some travel teams. They're real finicky when it comes to ages and making sure everyone is legal."

"I guess that's a good thing."

Morgan swallows more chips. "Yeah, especially with shady folks like Jeffrey around." She pulls a large envelope from her bag and hands it to me. "There's a park board member stationed in the office beside the concession stand today. Take those and Timothy's to her."

"Okay." We part ways and I head to my car.

A copy of Timothy's birth certificate is in my glove box. I printed it last week when Morgan said we may need it. The crisp piece of paper stares back at me when I take it out. In particular, the section that is left blank. Nate is not listed on Timothy's birth certificate.

Shame and embarrassment run through me as I add it to the envelope. We have a few single mothers on our team, but every birth certificate at least names a father.

Except for my son's.

Even worse, I *know* the father and have full confidence he would love and support my son.

I swallow the lump in my throat and shove Timothy's birth certificate in the envelope. I've kept the truth hidden from everyone all these years. Several times I almost told my parents, because I didn't want them thinking I was the one-night-stand type. Especially since the timing of it meant I would've cheated on Nate.

Sometimes I suspect they know the truth. However, they've never pushed me for an answer. I'm forever grateful for that—and them.

I climb out of my car and head for the concession stand. The envelope grows heavier with every few steps. The office door is open, and Luanne sits behind a desk. All I know about her is that she makes the best bundt cakes in three counties and her husband is the local taxidermist. That makes it a little easier to hand over such demeaning information.

She looks up from a stack of schedules and smiles.

"Hi, here are some birth certificates for the eight-and-under league. We're the Gray Armadillos, head coach Morgan Archer."

"Thanks." She reaches for the envelope. "I'll take care of these."

I suck in a breath and slowly let go of it, symbolic of letting out my darkest secret. Although it isn't really. Everyone in this county knows I'm a single mom and always have been. On more than one occasion, I've heard people refer to Timothy's dad as "Bruno" because my family never talks about him.

That never bothered me until Bruno came back to town and flipped every switch of emotion I'd worked so hard to hide.

Nate

I spent the last few days in Atlanta with PT and doctors. It didn't go like I wanted, but for reasons other than my shoulder.

My pitching looked good, and they still wanted to see me on the roster despite some younger guys showing promise in the preseason. But every pitch I threw made me think of the Armadillos. Not when I played for them, but Timothy's current team.

In a short time, I've gotten attached to those kids. Of course, I've gotten reattached to Brooke even more.

I left town this morning on good terms, letting everyone assume I'm headed to spring training soon. The funny thing is the whole time I was there, I thought about Brooke and being in Apple Cart. When I'm in Apple Cart, I rarely think about playing ball in Atlanta.

Maybe I'm done.

The four-hour drive gave me plenty of time to think things through. I came to the conclusion that if I have a shot at Brooke, I'm taking it.

After a quick shower and plenty of caffeine, I head to the ballpark. I have no idea when they're playing, because it's a tournament. As long as Jeffrey lets me in the park, I'll be fine.

When I turn toward the ball fields, cars are parked in the ditch on both sides. I stop at the school and decide to walk rather than chance finding a spot. Morgan's and Brooke's vehicles are near the entrance, which means I haven't missed all their games.

"Nate!"

I jerk my head to Becki Douglas. At least I think it's still Douglas.

"Becki?"

She nods.

"Hey, I haven't seen you since right after high school." I give her a quick side hug.

She smiles. "Good to see you too. You may or may not know, but I'm head writer for the *Apple Cart Weekly* now."

"That's fitting, congratulations."

"Thanks." She clears her throat. "I wanted to see if I might could interview you for a feature story sometime."

"That's very thoughtful." I snap my fingers. "I could get you some game tickets and let you interview more of the guys too. Really make a good overall story you could share online."

"Uh, actually, I wanted to write a story about you moving back and reconnecting with Brooke." She winces.

"Wait, what?" I tilt my head.

"I know it sounds cheesy, but I'm a sucker for a good love story, and—"

I shake my head. "Good to see you, Becki."

I hurry toward the gate, more than a little ticked. Either we're really getting older, or the desire for gossip has trickled down a generation. I expected this crap from the old ladies at church, but not a former classmate.

A teenager at the gate takes my five bucks, and I walk inside. Jeffrey's team is on the field, and Bradley is umpiring again. I've taken maybe three steps inside when Aniston finds me and slaps my arm.

"Everyone is this way."

I follow her without saying anything. Carlton is adjusting a tent, and I help him move it.

"Thanks. The sun is shifting."

"You're welcome."

We settle the tent, and I notice Brooke on the other side. She's spraying sunscreen on kids, and she's wearing shorts. I take a moment to appreciate her legs, which I haven't seen since the day she jumped the fence in a bathrobe. She always got cold easily and has worn pants until today.

Morgan gives me a look that communicates she knows what's up. I press my lips together and give her a firm glare.

I soften my features when I get to Brooke. "Hey."

She smiles. "Hey, I thought you were in Atlanta."

"I left this morning."

"Hey, Nate!" Timothy waves from his spot on a quilt next to Carter. A few more kids sit around them with a stack of Uno cards.

"Hey, buddy. Have y'all played yet?"

"Yes, sir. One game. We lost, but we get to play again."

"That's cool."

I'm preparing to sit beside them when Brooke brings me a chair.

"Thanks."

"You're welcome." She grabs another chair and sits beside me. "We play the next game. We're now in the bottom bracket, but can still 'win' something." She makes air quotes around the word "win."

I chuckle. Like me, Brooke was always competitive. I'm glad to see she didn't let motherhood turn her into one of those participation trophy people.

"We have snacks if you want anything."

"I'm good for now, but thanks." I smile at her, then lean toward the kids.

"Want to play the next round?" Carter asks.

"Sure."

"Easton plays with us a lot, but he's at the hospital today."

I nod. "I haven't played in a while, but I think I can handle it."

Carter half smiles. He shuffles and passes out the cards, adding a stack for me. I take them one by one and watch the boys interact.

This is the best part of baseball, being with your ball family. Whether elementary age, high school, or beyond, the friendships are what make it most special.

In the past few years, I've had a lot of friends come and go from the team, whether through trades, cuts, or retirements.

That gives me more reason to settle down in a place I plan on living forever.

One of the boys plays a card that makes me take ten cards, and I groan. They laugh and keep playing all the crazy cards on me. Before long, I have more than I can manage.

"What are you doing here?"

I look up to Jeffrey. His game just ended, and he came over here? "Shouldn't you be giving a coach's speech to your kids?"

"No time for that on tournament days. Besides, we won ten to two. What's left to say?"

"Not that it matters to you, but I'm playing Uno." I fan my massive stack of cards.

"I told you to stay out of the park."

Brooke stands so quickly that her chair falls. She steps across me and squares up with Jeffrey. Well, best she can for someone a foot shorter than him.

"Nate is doing nothing wrong. He is here to watch and support, not coach." She clenches her teeth like a dachshund trying to intimidate a UPS driver.

As someone who walked a tiny dog for extra cash back in the day, I find the comparison almost identical.

"How can I know he won't be throwing up hand signals or something?" Jeffrey counters.

"Because an Atlanta Braves pitcher would rather watch paint dry than coach a bunch of kids," Bradley booms from the field. He's propped on the fence, scowling at Jeffrey.

I appreciate the defense, although that's actually not true. But Jeffrey believes it, because he growls and walks away.

"That's what I thought," Bradley says. "Now let's get back to some ball." He pulls the umpire mask over his face and marches toward home plate.

Morgan is already on the field. She pitches to Bradley to warm up. Brooke turns to the boys on the quilt. "If anyone has to go to the bathroom, now's the time."

Half of them jump up and run toward the concession stand. Jack takes a few steps away from our spot and drops his pants.

"Whoa!" I jump up and stop him. "What are you doing?"

"I can't wait that long in line."

"Come on." I make him pull up his pants, then help him find the tree line, away from the crowd.

We return a few minutes later. Maribelle shakes her head at him, then twists toward me. "Thanks for that."

"No problem. When you gotta go, you gotta go." I look at Jack. "And you gotta go warm up now."

He nods and takes off.

"You'll make a great dad one day, Nate," Maribelle says.

I sigh. "I hope so."

"I know so, trust me."

The boys take the field in their positions. I settle in a lawn chair near Carlton and Georgia, keeping an eye out for Jeffrey in case he tries something stupid. I don't trust anyone over thirty who isn't a real athlete but wears a jersey.

He stays away from us the remainder of the game. Maybe it's Bradley's warning, or even Brooke getting mad. Whatever did it, I'm thankful.

I'm also thankful the boys are having a good game. Who knows? I may be good luck. And if things keep going the way I want them to, I may soon give Jeffrey some competition for park board president.

CHAPTER 17

Brooke

Bombing the first game is either the best or worst thing that could've happened to us. We are dominating the losers' bracket.

Daddy and Mama came for a few games, then had to go home to work at the orchard. I'm finishing a run to the Dollar Store for more snacks and bug spray. Since I had the best parking spot, Nate let me borrow his truck. It's a huge step up from what he drove in high school.

The one time I rode in it before, I was so worried about people seeing us together that I didn't pay much attention. Now I don't care who sees us—or me—in his truck.

This time I'm paying full attention.

I couldn't be more immersed in Nate's scent if I were a dog rolling in a dead skunk skin. The fact that it comforts me and has such a homey feel scares me a little.

I'm borrowing his truck to buy Doritos and OFF!, not a

marriage license. Although I wouldn't be totally opposed to the latter of those.

A few teams have left, clearing some spaces closer to the fields. I park the truck and suck in the Nate scent one last time. Good thing, since outside smells like sunscreen and dirt.

Armed with my loot, I cross the parking lot and find our little tailgate area. Morgan is under the center of the tent with half her arm immersed in a Yeti cooler. Nate examines her shoulder and rubs it. She rolls her eyes back in her head and relaxes.

"It's a little tight, but you should be fine after icing it a bit." He steps back and sees me. "I'll take those." He grabs the bags and starts dispersing supplies.

Morgan opens her eyes and shakes her head at me. "If you don't take him, I will!"

"Shhh."

She rolls her eyes. I think it's fair to assume everyone can sense something going on between Nate and me. Possibly even Timothy, which complicates things further.

Easton comes up in his scrubs. Aniston stands from her chair and kisses his cheek.

"Hey." He kisses her quickly on the lips. "Hey, Carter," he says louder.

Carter jumps up from lying on his belly in the grass and fist bumps Easton.

"Aniston said y'all keep winning."

"Yeah, ever since that first loss, we've done well," Morgan says. She twists in her chair, then grabs her shoulder. "Oomph, moved too soon."

"Rest for now," Nate scolds.

She leans back and nods, then turns to me. "Brooke, you may have to pitch this next game."

I choke on the water I'm drinking.

"Since this is a tournament, does it absolutely have to be one of you pitching?" Nate asks.

"The way it's worded, you have to be a player's parent," Easton clarifies. "So I couldn't pitch if I wanted to because I'm not yet their guardian."

Nate sighs. "That sucks. You're already helping raise them."

He laughs. "Doesn't matter as long as Bubba's at the park. He holds that rule book like the Bible. That's why I got a copy, to look for loopholes."

My skin burns, and I want to ball up and hide. Nate would be the best pitcher by far, and he *is* a biological parent. I chug water, hoping the cold liquid will help me chill.

It doesn't.

After a few minutes of silence, I speak out of guilt. "I can try and pitch if Morgan isn't better."

"I'll try." Carlton leans forward in his chair.

If you can call it a chair. It's more like a hammock cocoon that rocks and spins.

Morgan and I exchange a look. She jerks her head back at Nate to get his reaction, then reaches for her arm and grimaces.

"That's a good idea." Nate nods at him.

Our eyes meet over Morgan's head. I can read him well enough to see he doesn't trust Carlton can throw a strike. But it's coach-pitch. As long as these kids can hit something, we'll be fine.

The game on the field is winding down, and it's clear who we will face next. This is the last game in our bracket. Either way, we place.

Bradley lifts his mask and wipes sweat from his brow. The players line up and slap hands, spouting out a monotonous "good game."

"Let's get ready, boys." I start gathering bats and helmets to move us into the dugout.

Morgan stands slowly and steps toward Carlton. "Are you serious about trying this?"

"Yeah." He stands and folds his chair. "If I can swing a golf club, I can sling a baseball.

She wavers her head.

"Thanks, Carlton. I know you can throw better than me," I assure him.

"It will be an honor to try." He smiles and grabs a glove.

He's already to the fence when Morgan moans.

"Your arm?" I ask.

She shakes her head, then points to Carlton. He struts to the pitcher's circle, head held high.

"At least he's confident," Aniston says.

"He's something." Morgan sighs. "Someone help me bring this ice to the dugout. I'm gonna coach from the sidelines."

We pile everything into the dugout and set her up near the opening. Carlton warms up with Bradley while Aniston and I check to make sure everyone's shoes are tied.

She hops up from tying Angel's cleat and digs around under the bleacher. "Just making sure there's no Nicorette left over from last week."

"Good call." I give her a thumbs-up.

Bradley calls the kids to the field. Carlton comes and digs in Herrington's golf bag. He pulls out a monogrammed towel and wipes his face. If he's already winded, we're in big trouble. Maybe it's nerves.

Morgan yells out where she wants everyone to play in the field, and Aniston makes note of it in the scorebook.

"Carlton, you can be on first base today, and I'll take third," I tell him.

"Thanks." He adjusts his sunglasses and jogs to the base.

I'm not comfortable coaching third base, but Morgan is close enough to yell at them from the dugout.

Timothy stands at first base, ready to play. I shade my eyes and get a good look at the opposing team. Only half of them have on jerseys and one kid doesn't have a cap. I try to never judge a book by its cover, but we may have a real shot at this.

Their coach starts pitching. The first batter stands frozen for every ball. He's out. The second batter hits a little dribble that Andrew quickly throws to Timothy. He's out.

The third batter could easily pass for a twelve-year-old. His pants are at least two sizes too small, and unless the sun is playing tricks on my sight, I detect a hint of upper lip hair.

No wonder Morgan said we needed birth certificates.

He watches the first pitch, then nails the second one. All our players watch it like a plane flying overhead. Nobody even tries for the ball.

"Get the ball!" Morgan yells.

Half of the kids scramble. Tami's girls are both picking flowers, and pushing-puberty kid is running the bases. He's not fast, but he's rounding second. His coach yells, "Run home!"

The kid stops and stares at the coach, then reverses his steps. He picks up the pace, huffing and puffing. He runs off the field and toward the parking lot.

The coach tosses his cap in the dirt and fumes. "Somebody go get him!" he yells to the dugout.

A man in head-to-toe camo with the same stature as the kid jogs toward the exit. Bradley calls time and walks to the coach. "He need to pee or something?"

The coach pinches the bridge of his nose. "He's never hit the ball and ran bases until now. I think he ran home."

Bradley stares over his head to the parking lot. Then he lowers his chin and opens his mouth in realization that home meant the kid's house.

"Well, they say kids are literal." He pats the coach's arm. "Sorry, big dog, but that's gotta be an out."

He steps back and calls the third out. Our crowd claps, and the kids who are paying attention cheer. Morgan screams at the sisters to stop picking weeds and come to the dugout. The kids hustle back, with Reece picking up the rear.

He's one of the fastest when he wants to be, but right now he's doing that Harry Potter trot.

"Look, we've got them at zero. Let's get some hits and start leading off. We can win this thing. Y'all have been doing good today." Morgan sticks her hand out and little hands stack on top of it. "Gray 'Dillos on three."

She counts down from three, and everyone joins in the chant, including Aniston and me. I hear Nate's voice behind me.

When Morgan is done with her pep talk, I twist my head to him smiling at me from the front bleachers. I smile back.

I wish he could be even more involved—with both the games and our lives. Hopefully one day. Right now, I don't want to put everything on the line and have him leave town.

I face the field and help Aniston keep the kids in batting order. Bad as I hate it, Nate will remain Bruno a little longer.

We won.

I can barely believe it. Of course, it helps when you're in the lowest bracket available and the other team is *Bad News Bears* on steroids. Still, our kids won a tournament!

Nate claps slowly as Bradley lines both teams up on the field. He stops after a minute of clapping alone. Morgan whistles, and most of our parents pull out a phone for photos.

"Y'all can come down for pictures," Bradley announces.

Most parents hurry down the bleachers. Reece's parents, Agatha and Jim, don't move. I stop by them to check if anything is wrong.

"It's okay for us to go on the field now and get better photos."

"Oh, we don't have cameras," Jim says.

"Or cell phones," Agatha adds.

I blink in shock. No wonder they never gave me a contact number. I assumed they hated GroupMe like most parents. What's most impressive is how Reece is always on time for everything.

"I can take some photos of Reece for you."

"That would be lovely." Agatha's lips curve slightly.

When she said the only electronics he's been exposed to are online schooling and old DVDs, I thought she was being sarcastic. Guess not.

I join the rest of the crew on the outskirts of the infield. Bradley has each team lined up across from one another. He stands in the center, still wearing catching gear except for the mask. That is now replaced by his cowboy hat.

"Both teams fought long and hard today. We played a lot of ball, and you guys are the last two teams standing in this division."

Something brushes against my shoulders. I notice Nate from the corner of my eye. He settles right beside me so that our arms are touching.

He could stand anywhere on this field or in the stands, but he snuggles close enough to touch me. That's got to mean he likes me, right?

Ugh. I sound so high school right now.

"I'll start with our runners-up, the Bama Bananas." Bradley calls the coaches forward and hands the one who pitched a bag.

Their coaches are about as mismatched as the kids, with one wearing a work uniform for the local coal mines and another dressed like he came from a tree stand. The one with the bag pulls out a fistful of medals. Each kid steps forward and gets one when his or her name is called. They have a girl on their team as well.

"We should've called people out before the game so I could identify them better," Aniston whispers loudly.

I laugh. She had a time with the book this game. Since a

lot of them didn't wear jerseys and they had to sub once the boy ran home and another refused to leave the dugout, she scrambled to figure out who was who.

She gave them nicknames like Mullet and Inappropriate T-shirt. The kid who ran home changed from Too Old? to Homeboy. She was so proud of that, until he never came back.

Once everyone is wearing a medal, they line up with the coaches for more photos. Everyone claps, including Bradley.

I can feel Nate's bicep flex against my arm as he claps. Part of me thinks he's making it do that on purpose, and the other part hopes he is. I savor the moment until Bradley calls us forward.

Morgan snatches my arm and drags me away from the comfort of Nate. I slog behind her as she grabs Carlton and motions for Aniston to join us too. Carlton grins at the honor. He deserves it. The man may pitch like a golfer, but he somehow got the job done.

"And now for the winners of today's 8U lower bottom bracket, the Gray Armadillos."

Everyone cheers, and even the opposing team gives us a nod of approval. I ignore the words "bottom bracket" and focus on "winners." A positive outlook on life has kept me sane so far, so why abandon it now?

Bradley hands Morgan the bag, and she digs out a ring. It's pink. She frowns, then shrugs. "Andrew."

He hurries up, still wearing catching gear. The rest of the team follows until everyone is wearing a ring. Tami's girls appreciate the pink, but I'm not sure anyone else does.

We clap and snap a ton of photos. I get several of Reece and make a mental note to print some for his parents, since I assume they don't do email either. He poses with the ring up high, then runs to his parents. "Dad, Mom, I got Marvolo Gaunt's ring!"

I haven't a clue what that means, but they all seem excited about it.

The rest of the kids scatter and play around until Aniston makes them help her pick up the dugout.

Morgan gets Bradley's attention before he leaves the field. "What's up with the Barbie pink rings?"

"Oh, this bracket was added last minute after they had more teams sign up."

Morgan narrows her eyes as if needing more explanation.

Bradley sighs and leans closer to us, where the kids can't hear. "They're leftover from a breast cancer awareness softball tournament last fall."

"And we couldn't do any better?" she asks.

"Hey, you're on the park board, not me." He lifts his palms. "I'm just your friendly neighborhood sheriff trying to make an extra buck while keeping the park safe."

Morgan nods. "We appreciate your work."

"Thanks." He gathers his gear and heads toward the fence.

One of Tami's girls comes to her crying. A stone fell out of her ring. She tries to fix it.

Jeffrey walks by, picking up trash. Tami screams his name, and he straightens.

"Why did you give our kids these cheap rings?"

He slings the bag of trash over his shoulder and marches our way like a mad, sports-enthused Santa.

"Those are quality softball rings."

"*Softball*. We're playing baseball."

"Yeah, well your kids are girls!"

She snaps her head like a scene in *Mean Girls*.

"If they'd played softball where they belong, they would get these all the time."

"I told you the sign-ups were full." She grits her teeth.

I stand beside Nate and Morgan in awe, watching the equally matched Tami and Jeffrey go at it with nothing but a chain-link fence between them.

"You should be on time."

"Why don't you get back to work and finish taking out the trash." She pops her hands on her hips and does the head thing again.

"You mean like the time I took you to Double Drive?"

Despite wearing a short, tight skirt, Tami scales the fence in a matter of seconds. I could've used those skills on the cattle gate.

Morgan slides her phone in front of us and laughs.

"Are you videoing this?" Nate asks.

She nods. "I have a whole collection of blackmail footage just in case. Most of it from the Pig."

Nate looks at me with concern. I shrug.

Tami leaps on top of Jeffrey and starts slapping at his chest and face. He drops the garbage bag and holds her at arm's length. Cans and nacho trays roll down the hill in slow motion.

We all watch in shock for a minute. Then Nate shakes his head and rushes toward them. He pulls Tami off Jeffrey and holds an arm out to keep him back.

"Y'all need to stop. We have kids here. And what are all these other teams going to think about our park?"

Jeffrey snorts. "Y'all just don't get it. I made up this bracket to give you losers a chance to win something. If this were travel ball, y'all would've went home hours ago."

My stomach drops as I watch our kids' faces fall. Aniston consoles them, then marches from the dugout.

"Jeffrey, you need to stop. We still won this bracket and earned these crappy American Girl Doll rings." She snarls her nose at a ring on the kid beside her. "And give it a rest with the travel ball. Nobody here cares."

"Fine." Jeffrey huffs, then snatches the bag and stomps away. He stops after a few steps and calls back, "But you'll be the one laughing when my kids get full college rides for playing ball." He turns his back and trudges toward the trash can.

Aniston calls loudly after him, "Whatever you say, but errbody knows those kids aren't going to college!"

Easton puts his arm around her. "Let it go, babe."

She sighs and looks past him to Morgan and me. "This is not what I signed up for."

Morgan snickers, but I sympathize. Who knew kids' baseball would turn into a *Jerry Springer* episode?

CHAPTER 18

Brooke

"Mama, I don't care if we have pink rings." Timothy holds up the gaudy thing and grins. "We earned these."

"Yes, son, you did."

"We did, as a team."

I smile at him from the rearview mirror. It makes my mama heart happy that he's having a good time with his teammates.

His bat and bag stick up beside him, partially blocking my view. Now I get why so many of my friends have SUVs and minivans. I assumed I wouldn't ever need an upgrade with one child. That was before hauling tons of baseball supplies.

Today I even carried a small heater and fan since the weather changes several times during an all-day tournament.

I sigh. It was fun, but I'm glad today is over. We're a few miles from our road, and all I can think about is a hot shower and my favorite pajama pants.

The sign for the orchard comes into view, and I turn down

the gravel road. It crunches under my tires, making me relax. I've long associated that sound with the promise of home.

I park in the garage off the carriage house and cut the engine. "Get your bag, and we'll worry about everything in the trunk later."

"Okay." Timothy hops out and beats me to the front door.

I unlock it and all but fall inside. "Do you mind if I take a shower first?"

"No, ma'am." Timothy drops his bag by the door and goes outside.

How he still has energy is beyond me. I take a quick shower and change into my pajamas, even though it's still daylight. Then I dry my hair and grab a book I read when I actually get a lunch break at the hospital.

I'm halfway to my favorite chair when I hear voices outside. One is Timothy's and the other is an adult. My overprotectiveness kicks into gear, and I burst onto the porch.

"Oh hi, Nate."

He smiles. "Hey."

"Are you two going to work on something?" Seems odd since the kids just played five games, but I've never understood baseball.

"No, I'm here to get you."

I open my mouth, then pause and stare at my fuzzy pink pants. "For what?"

He steps toward me and cocks his jaw into a half smile that makes my stomach swirl.

"I talked to your mom earlier, and she agreed Timothy could come to her house for a while."

"For?"

"Our date?"

"Date?" My eyes widen. So many questions I don't have time to process.

"You agreed to go out with me sometime, remember?"

"I—"

He lifts his hands. "Don't worry, I asked Timothy's permission before I talked to anyone else."

I glance at Timothy. "So you knew about this?"

He nods and laughs.

"Then why did you let me put on pajamas?"

"So you'd be surprised."

"Mission accomplished." I scoff.

"Don't worry, I'll keep him company while you change." Nate sits on the porch steps beside Timothy.

I frown, then look to Nate, then back at Timothy. Both stare blankly as if they're waiting on me.

"Okay?"

I rush inside and throw on jeans and a cute shirt. Nobody said where we're going or what we're doing. I don't have time to fix my hair, so I pull it back and slap on a little makeup. Then I slip on some cute, casual shoes and hurry outside.

"Beautiful." Nate smiles.

"Well, I guess I'm off to Granny and Smith's." Timothy comes toward me and whispers, "It's okay with me if he kisses you."

"Timothy!" My face flushes. He's never said anything like that to me. "I'm not sure I like you thinking about kissing."

"Don't worry, Mama. I'm not kissing people, but you're plenty old enough to."

I point toward my parents' house. "Go."

"Yes, ma'am." He laughs and runs to their backyard.

"I wanted to take you to Tuscaloosa for dinner and coffee, but those games lasted longer than I expected," Nate says.

"How long have you planned this?"

"Since Enchilada."

My lips twitch. They want to smile, but my face is still in shock.

Nate's always had a sweet, romantic streak. He would

surprise me often. The last time we were together, he had surprised me with a visit.

I swallow.

"Since we've had a long day, I thought that tonight a picnic might be nice."

"That does sound nice." I blink, mentally cleansing the past from my view and focusing on the present.

Nate's smile spreads across his face and he holds out a hand. I take it, almost in a trance. It's an odd feeling when something you dreamed about happens.

Over the years, I'd sometimes dream of Nate and me together. What would we be like as adults? What kind of life would we have? It's so similar to my imagination that I bite my tongue to make sure I'm awake.

"Ouch," I whisper.

"You okay?"

"Yeah," I mumble with a throbbing tongue.

He leads me to his truck and opens my door. I hide a laugh at the memory of his old truck. Sometimes the passenger door wouldn't even open from the outside. But he'd always open it for me from the inside, then hop out and help me in.

Some women find it belittling for a guy to help them in a truck. But I have a soft spot for Southern gentleman. Plus, I'm short.

I settle into the same scent from earlier today, along with something cheesy. I sniff the air. "Is that lasagna?"

"Yeah." Nate grins as he turns toward me to back out of the drive. "I had Mom cook."

My mouth waters with anticipation. "I haven't had her lasagna in years. She usually brings a dessert to church dinners."

"She has this thing about food having to be hot, and according to her, Crockpots aren't real cooking."

I laugh. That sounds like Anne.

We slow down near his house, so I assume we're going there. Instead, he stops at the pasture and opens the gate. I wait as he climbs back in, drives inside, and closes it back up.

"I've thought about bonfires ever since the day I saw you again." He smiles at me.

Images of high school come to mind. We used to gather on tailgates with friends and light a fire at the edge of the field.

He drives to that very spot and parks. Definitely nostalgic. I haven't gone this far in the pasture since high school. Mainly because of the bull, but also because I didn't have Nate there.

"Too bad I couldn't get Colt to serenade us. He's in Montana."

"Really?" I hadn't kept up with our classmate and one of Nate's closest baseball buddies, but I'd heard he was still playing music.

"On tour with a country band as their lead guitarist."

"Nice."

We get out, and Nate pulls down the tailgate.

"Yeah, I guess I'm back to being the disappointment of our class."

I laugh. "Hardly."

"As long as you don't think so." He smirks, and I tense.

I haven't been on a date ever in my adult life. Probably because when guys have tried to flirt with me, I would send off a vibe that I wasn't interested. Aniston jokes that I'm covered in anti-interest repellent.

If that's the case, Nate is immune to it.

The real reason is I've never considered having a real relationship with anyone but him. I poured my life into Timothy, my community, and my job. I assumed one day when Timothy was older, I might consider dating.

I never dreamed I'd be lucky enough to actually have a second chance with the guy I've always loved.

"I would never think you were a disappointment," I tell Nate.

"Good." He opens the back door and retrieves the food. "I always worried I wasn't good enough for you, and thought maybe that's why—"

I step toward him and grab his forearm. "Never. I was going through some things and didn't want to drag you down."

Nate sets the food on the toolbox and stares into my eyes. He swallows, and I glance at his throat. His neck is red and so is his face. I feel a pulse in his arm before he slides it toward me and holds my waist with both hands. My heart speeds as he pulls me closer.

"I'd gladly let you drag me anywhere."

He leans down, and my breath catches. Before I can exhale, his lips are on mine. My mouth tingles like it's in shock. I haven't kissed anyone since . . . well, him.

Am I doing this right? Do I still have ballpark nachos breath? Why didn't I brush my teeth before I showered?

Then like all the memories that come back so easily, the memory of kissing Nate meshes with the present. Commercial cheese breath and rusty kissing skills aside, I no longer care.

His hands are in my hair, and I'm snuggled close to him. Like a drunk chugging a fifth of whiskey after almost a decade of sobriety, I'm too far gone.

No matter what happens when this kiss ends, I'll forever be changed.

Nate

Kissing Brooke is like living out my wildest dream. It's all I've thought about since seeing her by the fence.

I run my fingers through her hair and pull her even closer. It still doesn't seem real. Maybe because I committed her kisses to memory so well that I could play them out in my mind.

Pathetic? Probably so. But she was my good luck charm many times, even when she was no longer in my life.

Years flash across my mind, leading to this very moment. All the kisses we shared on her front porch and standing in the bleachers, up to the very last kiss in her dorm room. The one I replayed more times than I could count like a favorite song on a burned CD.

Sometimes the memory was a little scratchy, but there's no skipped details now. It's like her mouth was made for mine.

Like she was made for me.

I could kiss her all night. But I also want to talk to her. So much is the same between us, but so much has changed. I need to make sure this is more than reliving glory days to her.

Begrudgingly, I pull back. Her eyes blink open and I stare into them. Deep chocolate brown, sparkling in the setting sun.

Her lips are full and pink, and it takes all my restraint to not kiss them again. Instead, I lead her to the tailgate and sit down. "Hungry?"

She laughs. Yeah, that was dumb, but better than confessing I've been hung up on her forever. Baby steps, Nate. Don't scare her off.

I climb into the bed and grab the lasagna, setting it behind her, then jump down. "Just a second."

With all the kissing, I forgot everything else. I retrieve a bag of plates and forks, along with a cooler, from inside and shut my back door.

"Here we go." I set everything out and open the lasagna. "You still like the edge pieces?"

"Yeah." She smiles sweetly. "I can't believe you remember that."

"I remember everything." I wink.

She dips her head. Whoops.

"I didn't mean—"

"I know, it's okay." She lifts her eyes shyly, then stares ahead at the field.

I clear my throat. Best change the subject to something less personal. "Did y'all ever come out here after I moved to Atlanta?"

She shrugs. "I think some of them did, but not me."

"We both moved off pretty soon after that last night here."

"Yeah." She turns to me and smiles.

I scoop her some lasagna and slide the plate beside her. Then I fix my plate and sit just far enough to fit the food between us. We both reach for a bite at the same time, almost bumping hands.

"Sorry." I pull my plate back a few inches. "I bet you don't miss eating next to a clumsy lefty."

"Timothy's left-handed."

"True." I smile. "I'm glad. The world needs more left-handed players. I could teach him all kinds of pitching techniques to screw with batters."

She chews slowly and swallows.

"He doesn't have to be a pitcher. He's great at first base."

She shakes her head. "It's not that." Her voice is shaky. "What happens when you go home?"

"I'll probably watch some TV and make myself unpack more." I fork a big bite of lasagna.

"I mean to Atlanta."

"I know." I stab my fork in a bite and turn to Brooke. "I'm thinking of not going back."

"What?" Her eyes widen.

"Yeah." I palm the back of my neck and sigh. "I wanted to talk to you about that. Where I go all depends."

"On your shoulder and arm."

I swallow some food and stretch out my pitching arm. "It did, but the team doctor should clear me any day now."

"So you're going to play?"

"Maybe."

"Why wouldn't you?" She tilts her head in confusion.

I drop my fork and touch her face. "There are more important things than playing ball."

"I agree," she whispers against my palm.

"I don't want to pressure you, Brooke, but I could see a future here, living in Apple Cart with you." I slide my hand away slowly.

"What about Timothy?" The shakiness is back in her voice.

I reach for her hand. "I do have six bedrooms."

Her mouth kicks up in the corner, and she blushes.

"I'm not suggesting we marry right away, but I wouldn't turn you down if you proposed."

She laughs. "Be careful what you wish for, Nate."

"If I could ever be so lucky." I slink my arm behind her and curl my fingers at her waist.

She leans into me and sighs. We sit in silence, staring at the pasture. It's peaceful and nostalgic, and for a split second I forget nine years have passed since we were last here.

"I don't want you to quit playing because of me." She turns to face me.

"It would be my choice."

"Yeah, but you'd be doing it for me."

I shrug. "I mean, you'd be a big factor."

She groans.

"What's wrong with that?"

"I didn't want to interfere with your career before, and I don't want to now."

I stand in front of her, bracing my hands on the tailgate so that she's stuck between me. Her only chance of escape would be to scoot backward, and there's a cooler and lawn chairs blocking her way.

"I've worked my butt off to get to where I am. You of all people should know I wouldn't quit without a good reason."

"I don't want to be the reason." She swallows hard. I watch the muscles in her jaw and zero in on her lips.

"You've always been my reason." I dip my head closer to her and whisper, "For everything."

I kiss her slowly. If she doesn't believe my words, maybe she'll believe my kiss.

CHAPTER 19

Brooke

Last night still doesn't seem real.

I had the best kiss of my life with the only person I've ever loved. Then we spent two hours talking and cuddling under the stars. It was everything I've dreamed of and more.

And now I'm in Sunday morning service, finding it hard to concentrate. One Sunday I'm daydreaming what it would be like to kiss Nate, and this Sunday I'm replaying what it was like in my head.

I could really use a trip to the altar.

Speak of the devil—or angel, in this case—Nate slides into our pew.

"Hey, Nate." Timothy grins and slides down, leaving a Nate-sized space between him and me.

"Hey, bud." They fist bump and Nate sits beside me.

He greets my parents and settles closer to me. My limbs tingle as his big arm brushes against me. I smile to myself and glance his way before staring back at the pulpit.

In the few seconds it takes me to turn my gaze, half-a-dozen people make eyes at us. A few even cover their mouths and lean toward their neighbor. It'll be a miracle if we make it out of here without my name mentioned in a prayer request.

Brother Johnny is barely through the announcement side of the bulletin when Nate stretches his arm across the back of the pew and cups his hand on my shoulder. Warmth shoots down my spine, and I relax against him.

Mumbled whispers come from behind us, which is to be expected. I keep my eyes forward and regain focus on the preacher by the time we start singing.

On the third song, the choir director asks everyone to stand. Nate slides his arm away from me, but stands even closer as we're singing. He holds a hymnal where we can both see it.

I watch Timothy from the corner of my eye. He looks as content as I feel. Maybe this really can work, not just for Nate and me, but for everyone.

I'm almost certain Timothy would welcome the news that Nate is his father. Same for my parents, even though I'm somewhat certain they may know.

Of course, there will be a fair amount of backlash from people in the town. Some blaming me for never telling Nate, and others blaming Nate for getting me pregnant.

Whatever ridicule from the peanut gallery awaits, I can handle. Heck, I lived through moving back here in my second trimester, young and single.

What I can't handle is hurting Nate or Timothy—especially both.

The song ends, and we take our seats. Nate's arm finds its way behind me again, and I comfortably welcome his touch. Brother Johnny resumes his position behind the pulpit and begins his sermon.

Now that Nate is here beside me, my focus has returned. It's like I've gotten my fix and can go on with life as usual.

Brother Johnny talks about Issac and his love for Rebecca. He uses them to make a point about God's plan, but I get caught up in their love story. I can't help but feel like Nate came back at the right time and that we are meant to be together.

When the message comes to a close and the preacher asks us to bow our heads, I lift up a silent prayer. I really hope God's plan for my life involves Nate. If not, He best get started on changing my heart, because it's totally in love with Nate.

The same as it has been for forever.

Nate

I put my arm around Brooke in church. That's pretty much all it takes in Apple Cart to come out as an official couple. Last night went so well, I figured I'd go ahead and rip the Band-Aid off before people started making up assumptions.

Several older people followed us out like a pack of zombies. Also like a pack of zombies, we managed to outpace them. Still, it changed my mind about asking Brooke and Timothy to lunch at Mary's.

At least when you're publicly together in church, nobody talks to you. They only talk about you, then follow it up with a "bless your heart." In the restaurant, there's no way of restraining them.

Before the zombies could wheel their walkers across the gravel, I asked Brooke if they'd like to come to my house for an early dinner.

All afternoon, I've been worrying over making my house

look like someone actually lives here. Turns out that's not easy when you have five-thousand square feet to fill with little more than sports memorabilia and a recliner. Good thing I got Carolina to order some furniture for the place after we closed.

The ancient doorbell rings, and my stomach plummets. They're here. I hurry to the front door and pull it open. Brooke and Timothy smile up at me.

"Watch your step." I take Brooke's hand as they step down into the living room. I joke with my teammates that my Alabama mansion is so fancy, it has front steps inside.

"This place is even more beautiful from the inside." Brooke beams as her eyes scan the detailed molding.

"The kitchen's this way. After we eat, I can give y'all a tour."

They follow me to the kitchen. A crispy scent catches my attention, and I find an oven mitt. It's a hideous fish with an open mouth. Jack gave it to me as a housewarming gift. The dude who owns the hunting camp—not the kid who pees on everything.

Brooke's eyes widen when I pull a pan from the oven. "Uh, is that a glove?"

"Yeah. A first baseman's glove for Timothy."

Timothy gasps, and Brooke scrunches her nose. "Why was it in the oven?"

"To soften it. New gloves are a beast. This will help break it in quicker." I set the pan on the flat stovetop.

She shrugs. "As long as we're not eating that."

"No." I grab a bag of to-go boxes and push them forward on the countertop. "We're eating Big Butts."

"Yes," Timothy cheers.

I pull plates from the cabinet near my head.

"Can I help with anything?" Brooke asks.

"You can fix some drinks. I have tea, Mountain Dew, and stuff in the refrigerator."

She opens it and laughs. "And stuff?" She holds up a bottle of Starbucks vanilla Frappuccino.

"I thought that might do until I can take you out for real coffee."

A smile covers her entire face. My chest catches as she opens the lid and takes a big sip. I love making her happy.

"Mama is addicted to caffeine." Timothy shakes his head.

I chuckle. "You'll understand why when you get older."

Brooke sighs and sets the bottle on the counter. It's already a third gone. She pours Timothy and me tea and moves the drinks to the table. I hand him three plates and forks to carry while I take the food.

I choke back the emotions of how much this feels like a family. Brooke and I may be reunited, but I shouldn't get ahead of myself. Timothy adds another layer to us, and I can't assume his dad will be fine with me having them over like this.

Even if he isn't in his life now, he may resurface when he finds out Brooke is with me. She said Timothy doesn't know him, but she also said she hasn't been with anyone since him. I've seen enough to know how guys get jealous and territorial.

I unbag the boxes and open them in the center of the table. Then I get some tongs and big forks and spoons so we can fill our plates. Timothy asks the blessing, and we start eating.

I'm at the head of the table beside both of them. Although I can't get carried away, it does feel nice to have them here. Most nights I eat in front of the TV or with Mom.

"Timothy, since we're all here, I need to ask you something important."

"Yes, sir." He sits up straighter and wipes macaroni from his mouth.

"Your mom and I had a lot of fun on our date last night. With your permission, I'd like to ask her to be my girlfriend."

His face stretches like he's seen a ghost. Not quite the reaction I'd hoped for. Is that a bad thing?

"Are you kidding?"

"I wasn't, but if it's not okay with you, I might be."

I glance at Brooke. She's all smiles, enjoying her potatoes. Maybe it isn't so bad.

"That's awesome." Timothy's face normalizes. "Can I tell everyone at school tomorrow my mama is dating the starting pitcher for the Braves?"

I cock my head. "I may not say 'starting,' but the rest is accurate." I started three games late last season before my injury.

"Starting or not, it doesn't matter." Brooke pats my hand. "Playing or not, it doesn't matter."

"I'm glad you think so." I wink at her, then take a sip of my tea. "Timothy, what if I didn't play baseball?"

"What do you mean?" He scrunches his eyebrows with confusion.

"If I weren't in the MLB, could I still date your mom?"

"Yeah, but it wouldn't be as cool."

I laugh, and they join me. I watch Brooke for a hint of how she feels about me playing ball. All she has to do is say the word and I'll retire.

A part of me wishes she would.

Brooke

Monday mornings usually have my mind going in a million directions, from getting Timothy ready and off to school to starting a new work week. Or starting a normal work week if I had gotten called in over the weekend. Today is different.

My mind is on one thing—or person—Nate.

Timothy and I ate dinner at his house last night, then talked and laughed for a while. He gave Timothy a new glove, and we toured his house.

It was big and beautiful, but a little sad. So many rooms, some without any furniture. Every room we entered added to my realization that Nate lives there alone.

My parents have a big house, but not quite that big. And they did raise three kids and run a business on the property. We always had people coming and going and eating with us.

Nate said he invited his mom to live there, but she wanted to keep her trailer. That made me sad on several levels.

I know him well enough to know that while he may have everything money can buy, he really enjoyed our company. Of course, we enjoyed his that much or more.

I'm halfway through packing Timothy's lunch for the day when I hear a car door shut. I peek out the kitchen window and see Nate's truck.

My spirits lift when he climbs out and walks toward our door. Before he has time to knock, I swing it open.

Without saying a word, he steps closer and kisses me. I fall into his embrace and kiss him back, then snuggle against his chest as he hugs me close.

I could get used to Mondays like this.

When we pull back, I look up at him. "I thought you were heading back to Atlanta."

"I am. This is my only stop until I need gas." He smirks.

My stomach does a small flip. "Don't get bad gas."

We both laugh at the memory of him almost ruining his old truck by making that mistake.

"Nate?"

I turn to Timothy bounding down the stairs. He hurries to the door and hugs Nate's waist. Nate pats him on the back.

"I wanted to tell you two bye before I go for a bit."

"How long?"

"Several weeks. I need to head down to Florida to start spring training."

Timothy stares at the ceiling as if calculating. Then he shifts his gaze to Nate. "You should only miss a few games, and several practices."

Nate chuckles. "Is that allowed?"

"It's for the Braves." Timothy shrugs.

Nate wraps his arm around me and gives my side a gentle squeeze. I swallow at him touching my waist. For some reason, it resonates different than when he touches my back or shoulders, or even my face and hair. Maybe it's the way he squeezes my side that says we're now totally out of the friend zone.

Whatever the case, I hope he means it the way I take it. He hasn't been gone for more than two days straight since I first saw him again. For all I know, there could be other women anxious to see him.

I mean, obviously there are plenty. I just hope there's nobody there he's anxious to see.

I lean my head against him for a second, then pull away. As much as I'd love to throw all responsibility aside and go with him—or even better, have him stay—that's not possible.

We all have places to be and things to do. Hopefully one day those places and things will align more than they do now.

"Y'all call me whenever, and I'll call and text, too, while I'm gone."

Timothy nods and I smile.

Nate steps onto the porch, and I follow him. He stands on the bottom step and turns to me. We're now close to eye level. My heart jumps near my throat at the memory of how we used to always stand with him one step down. It made eye contact and kissing much easier with our height difference.

He cocks his mouth into a half grin and focuses on my eyes. "I love you, Brooke."

My mouth parts, but I'm speechless. That's the first time he's told me that as an adult.

"You don't have to say anything back, but I had to tell you that before I leave."

I want to say it back so badly, but my throat is hot and clogged like I've suddenly swallowed a lit piece of charcoal. I clear my throat, then manage to squeak out a single-word answer.

"Same."

Not the most thoughtful or romantic response when the love of your life confesses he still loves you after a nine-year absence. But it's enough to make Nate kiss me on the cheek before he gets in his truck.

I sigh as he drives away. And just like that, I'm back to a mundane Monday.

CHAPTER 20

Brooke

The best way to break up anything mundane is for Morgan to text you that she has a surprise for practice.

Per her request, I'm wearing gym clothes and tennis shoes, and I brought a cooler of waters. I'm not sure what she has planned, but at least I'll be comfortable and hydrated.

Timothy squeezes his new glove open and closed. I had to pry it off his hand before he got out at school. I'm not sure if it's more about the glove or that it came from Nate. Either way, he's treated it like we would a prize-winning bushel of apples.

I roll the cooler past several fields used by other teams. Morgan waves me over from the T-ball field. She's got to be kidding. It's little more than a glorified circle of mud with a rickety fence around it.

A swarm of gnats funnel around us as if warning me to turn back before it's too late. I'm more scared of Morgan than gnats, so I trudge on. Timothy follows behind me, coddling his glove.

"Hey, girl. Park that Igloo over here." Morgan fans her hands toward the fence.

I park the cooler and drop the handle. The fence bounces when it makes contact. If anyone has a chance of hitting something over a fence, it's today.

"We're scrimmaging the boys today!" Morgan slaps her hands together and rubs them like she's scheming.

"We're what?"

She scans my Nike shorts and shoes. "You're dressed for it, and everyone else will be too. We've got water. What else could we need?"

"Uh, younger knees and an energy drink?"

She snaps her fingers. "Oh shoot. I could've gotten those out-of-date Monster drinks we chucked when restocking the Pig."

"I think we're good." I wince.

Note to self: Never accept prepackaged snacks from Morgan unless the date is visible.

She grins. I turn and follow her gaze to the rest of the team and parents. Easton in particular catches my attention.

He's dressed in a camo shirt with a flag bandana and eye black. Until now, he's had two looks: doctor scrubs and lawn-care casual. This is the only time I've seen him wear shorts except at the pool, which would explain the huge skin-tone difference in his legs and arms.

"Look at Rambo." Morgan punches his arm. "I like it."

I spin to face her. "Wait, so everyone else knew about the scrimmage?"

"Yeah."

"Why wouldn't you tell your assistant coach?"

Morgan crosses her arms. "Because my assistant coach would not be in favor of it."

I raise a brow. She's got me there.

"I can keep score, or maybe be the cheerleader." I clap my hands and smile.

Morgan frowns and shakes her head. "I have coaches and scorekeepers coming."

"Wait, what?"

Before she can answer, Isabella and a few of her softball friends come from the opposite end of the park.

Morgan wiggles her eyebrows. "Here comes the boom."

She whistles to get our kids' attention. They come running like a pack of dogs. At this point in the season, they have come to expect her signal.

Four teenage girls with long legs crowd around the fence. Every kid's eyes are on Morgan, except for Maribelle's twins. Charlie and Jack stare at the softball girls like Morgan stares at those all-inclusive island-vacation ads polluting her Facebook feed.

"Afternoon, Gray Armadillos." Morgan slaps a bat against her hand. "We are going to play a little practice game tonight. Parents versus kids."

The kids go crazy cheering.

"I don't think they understand," Easton mumbles.

"Are they kids or adults?" Charlie points to the teenagers, bringing his finger dangerously close to Isabella's chest.

She leans back and scrunches her nose. Maribelle slaps his hand down and gives him a stern look.

"They are half-adult, half-kid, and they are our coaches." Morgan smiles. "Armadillos, meet some of the sophomores on the Apple Cart County High School softball team."

The girls wave. Jack is close to drooling as he waves back with a dumbfounded look. I sincerely hope their dad doesn't act this way. As much as he works out of town, Maribelle may be in trouble. Although I'm not certain a lot of women frequent offshore oil rigs.

Morgan hands the bat to her daughter. "Passing the torch to you, Isabella. Take it away, honey."

Isabella introduces her friends Suzie, Ainsley, and Daphne. They split up, and Ainsley and Daphne coach us. Easton pops his neck and jogs in place a little. Either he's preparing for a boxing ring or he had one of those discarded Monster drinks. I narrow my eyes at Aniston.

She takes a step closer and talks from the corner of her mouth. "He found his first gray hair the other day and is trying to reclaim his youth."

I cover my mouth to hide a laugh.

"That's exactly the reaction Adrianne had when he asked her about hair dye."

So much for hiding my laughter. Aniston bites her lip and smiles.

"All right, people. Let's get our teams ready!" Morgan calls.

We join the other adults on the left side of the field and listen for the batting order. It's a little like middle school kickball, waiting for Daphne to call my name. I'm near the bottom of the order, which is to be expected. They put Easton at cleanup batter. Must be the eye black. Or the bandana. Probably the combination of both.

I take my place at the edge of the fence beside Tami, who's wearing high heels designed like baseballs.

"Tami?"

She glances at me, wiping bright red lipstick across her mouth.

"Are you sure you can run in those?"

"Girlfriend, I do everything in these." She winks. "And I do mean everything."

I quickly jerk my head in the opposite direction. Morgan is first batter. She hits decent, and makes it to first. Timothy fields the ball with his new glove, but she beats him to the base.

The next two batters put the ball in play. The pitcher catches Carlton's ball, putting him out. With two on base,

Easton comes up to bat. He slings his batting arm in circles, puffing out his cheeks.

From all the games I've watched because of Nate, guys like that either hit it out of the park or strike out.

He gets up to bat and sways back and forth in his stance. Ainsley frowns and throws a strike. Isabella calls it, and Easton gives her a look. She shrugs.

He hits the next pitch into the outfield. Surprisingly, Angel gets to it quickly. She tosses it to Herrington at second, who gets it to Timothy. Easton is safe, but only because he slides into first base.

Morgan yells "time" and slaps her hand on her forehead.

Daphne rushes toward Easton. "What are you doing, Dr. West?"

"Am I safe?" he asks from the ground.

"You're not supposed to slide at first. You need to run through the bag." She blows a stray hair from her face. "But it counts."

Easton pumps his fist in the air and cheers from the ground. He hops up, then grabs his knee almost as quickly. "Oomph."

Aniston rushes over and wraps an arm around his shoulder.

He grits his teeth and slowly straightens.

"Babe, are you okay?"

"It's my knee again." He narrows his eyes at us. "Can I get a base runner?"

Aniston shakes her head, then glances my way. "Can you bring Carter home from practice?"

"Sure thing." I pat Easton's shoulder. "Get better, Doc."

Aniston gives me a pitiful smile and helps him hobble off the field. Someone starts clapping, and we all join in.

Carlton scribbles something in the scorebook and rips it out. He hands it to Aniston. "Take this by my pharmacy. It's a low-grade painkiller."

"Thanks, Carlton." She takes it with the hand not holding Easton, then waves to us and exits the field.

Morgan reaches for the paper as they pass, but misses. I frown at her, and she shakes her head. "Shame to waste a good prescription on another doctor."

"Still need a base runner?" a man's voice asks from the fence.

Morgan and I face him at the same time. He appears a little older than us, with a slight smile and eye wrinkles, but he's also in much better physical shape than anyone else we have. Aside from the softball girls, of course—and my Nate. Ugh, I miss him already.

"Sure?" Morgan half smiles.

He holds out a hand. "Elijah Bowing."

"Morgan Archer." She shakes his hand.

He smiles. "Firm handshake. I like it."

Morgan notices she's still holding on to his hand and suddenly drops it.

"I'm Brooke. Go ahead and take the base." As he marches toward the field, I call out, "Thanks!"

I take my place in line beside Tami. She lowers her sunglasses and nods toward first base. "Who's the hunk on first?"

"His name is Elijah Bowing. Ever heard of him?"

She drops her jaw. "Uh, yeah, he's like this bodybuilder dude that starts up gyms."

I cock my head. "And he's in Apple Cart?"

"Good thing for us." Tami licks her lips.

I start to reprimand her and try and tame her behavior, but it's no use. My energy would be better spent warning Elijah instead.

And stretching. The last thing I need is to end up like Dr. Slugger.

Tami and I both strike out, which is a surprise to nobody.

I'm a little relieved since I don't want to follow her on the bases—or anywhere.

"It's okay, Mama!" Timothy calls.

I side-hug him as my team goes into the field. They put me in left field and Tami in right. She's every bit as unfocused as her daughters. I wanted to sit out, but they needed me after Aniston and Easton both left. The mysterious gym man is in center field.

Our kids are hitting better. Isabella helps correct their swings, so I give her all the credit. Several get on base, but the adults are better fielders.

We play two more innings and beat them nine to one. I hate that, but they're still smiling.

Morgan whistles everyone in and gives a quick ending speech. "I'm proud of y'all." She nods around. "Adults included."

"I've never played any ball before," Jim comments.

"I can tell," Morgan says. He frowns, and she continues. "But you hung in there, and you got better."

He nods and the sides of his face lift, curving his mustache.

"Neither have I," I say.

Jim's mouth forms a real smile. I squint at Morgan, but she's already continuing with her speech.

"It's tough playing bigger, better people, but we learned some new things."

"Like don't slide at first base," Jack yells.

"You should already know that," Morgan corrects. "But yes, that's one of them." She pats Isabella's back. "And we had some great coaches today. Let's give them a hand."

Everyone claps.

"Isabella, honey, break us down."

She sticks her hand out and the kids circle around. Jack and Charlie shove at each other until both are touching an older girl's hand.

"Gray Armadillos on three!" Isabella counts down and everyone yells in unison.

I remind all the adults of the extra water, mainly because I don't want to roll it all back to my car. Elijah engages Morgan in a conversation, so I sneak past her.

"Mama, can I have your phone and call Nate?"

"Sure." I unzip my shorts pocket and hand him the phone.

He calls while I hand out waters to anyone who will take them. Then I drain the excess water from the cooler and pull it toward the car.

Timothy holds out my phone after I put the cooler in the trunk. "He didn't answer. I left a message."

"Okay, I'm sure he's practicing or eating."

Timothy nods and jumps in the car.

I shake my head to clear any doubts that he's with another woman. He was at our house this morning, kissing me.

Of course he's not with anyone else.

Nate

Yesterday was jam packed with visits to the team physical therapist and doctor, as well as my coaches. They put me on a specific workout plan that will hopefully have my arm in pitching shape by start of the season.

I roll over and blink at the sun coming through my window. It's odd looking out at palm trees instead of fruit and pine trees. And Mom's trailer if you're near the back of the house.

Spring training couldn't be any farther from Apple Cart,

and I'm not referring to distance. It really feels like a world away without Brooke.

I sit up and stretch. Every muscle in my back pops when I arch it. Then my shoulder twists and I lower my arms. That's what I've got to work on.

Good thing I slept so long.

I stand and make my bed, then grab my phone from the nightstand. There's a missed call and voicemail from Brooke.

I listen and smile as Timothy's small voice comes across the line. He says they did good at practice and asks how the Braves are. I laugh.

The man who fathered him is missing out on a great kid. I hope he knows that.

I sit on the edge of the bed and call Brooke. She answers on the second ring.

"Hello?"

"Hey."

"Hi, I'm at work so I only have a minute."

"That's fine. I just saw you called last night."

She makes a cute noise that sounds a lot like a smile. "Timothy called. He said he left you a message."

"Yeah, I heard it." I chuckle. "To be honest, I really wanted to hear your voice."

She sighs. "I wanted to hear yours too."

Something sounds like metal clanking in the background.

"I better go check on that. We have an ornery person waiting in the X-ray room.

"Okay. I'll call you tonight when I get a chance and talk to Timothy too."

"That would be great."

"I love you."

She lets out a breath, then answers with, "I love you too."

I fall back on my bed like a teenage girl rather than a grown man. That's the first time she's told me. Well, the first time since we've gotten back together.

The phone is silent. I hold it back to see the screen and realize she hung up after that. Who cares? That's all I really wanted to hear.

I spent half the drive to the airport and most of my flight analyzing why she didn't say it back yesterday on her front steps. She said "same," so I guess that counts. But "same" is not the same.

"Same" is the response you give when you're indifferent about something.

Someone says they want sweet tea. "Same."

Someone says they prefer country music. "Same."

Someone says they love you. Then you need to say it back.

I drop my phone and fold my hands behind my head. Brooke is the only person who makes me like this. Sure, I want to please my coaches and my mom, but it's more seeking their approval than affection.

I used to never question Brooke's love for me. That is until she pushed me away.

Things are great right now, but the slightest fear bubbles in the back of my brain that her feelings don't run as deep as mine. Either that or she wasn't ready to say she loved me in front of Timothy.

I choose to believe the Timothy excuse and hoist myself from the bed. Time to work on my professional life again.

"Nate the Great-Grandpa." Aaron lifts his arm and smirks.

I nod and turn in the opposite direction. He's a hotshot young pitcher who's too cocky for his own good. Many days I've come close to knocking that smirk off his face —permanently.

Two things have kept me from it thus far. The memory of Mom's voice quoting "do unto others" and my public image.

The media would love nothing more than to post stories of a starting pitcher beating down the young guy brought in to possibly replace him.

My time and effort are better spent working on my arm to keep my position and knocking Aaron's ego instead of his face.

"What's up, brother?" Ace waltzes up from the corner and slaps me on the back.

"Hey, man."

He grabs a pair of dumbbells while I stick my arms inside a resistance band. "What's your poison right now?" he asks.

"Fifteen."

He grabs a pair of fifteen-pound dumbbells and puts them in front of me, then gets a heavier set for himself. He starts overhead squats, while I work on my shoulder techniques.

I've always babied my arm, and now I'm even more cautious. I can't help but notice Aaron maxing out across the room. He'll regret it when his shoulder turns to rust.

"How was your little vacay in the country?" Ace asks in between his sets.

"Good."

"It's gotta be better than that. You've had a stupid grin on your face since you've gotten in town."

I laugh. Ace was one of my first roommates. We lived in a trashy apartment. Unlike me and Dom, our other roommate, he came from money. He could've lived in a nicer place, but took a deal with his dad for spending money instead.

"Okay, great." I grit my teeth through the last reps in my exercise. "You ever miss Nashville?"

He shrugs. "No more than going home to visit. I've been away so long, it's no longer like home."

I set down the weights and reposition the band for a new exercise. Weight rooms were always a stress relief to me. The noise of metal meeting hard rubber and guys grunting out one more rep energizes me in a Neanderthal way. Oddly enough, I prefer the weight room to my actual condo back in Atlanta.

Once or twice I almost put an offer on a house outside of town. A few buddies with families live in the suburbs nearby. I even went as far as going to one home with a Realtor.

But it didn't feel like home.

Another house on twenty acres came up for sale, and I kept making plans to go look. When it sold to someone else a week later, I was relieved.

That let me know the only reason I'm in Atlanta is the Braves. And the only other place I want to be is with Brooke. On some subconscious level, I believe that's what drew me back to Apple Cart.

I got all nostalgic about the house I bought, idolizing it as a child and playing ball in the field across from it. Heck, I wasn't sure Brooke still lived in town. But her family's orchard was down the same road, and that was all it took to sell me.

That town, that orchard, and that field always belonged to us in my heart. Nowhere else could ever compare. Not even a stadium full of cheering fans.

CHAPTER 21

Brooke

Aside from bulk apple deliveries to their Piggly Wiggly, I haven't been to Moonshine County since we played them in high school. Unless you count our celebratory meal at Enchilada, which is barely across the county line.

Now I'm at their baseball park for the first time.

It's about what I'd expect. The only things offered at the concession stand are boiled peanuts and fried Twinkies. Although a lot of adults keep pulling beer from coolers since this is a wet county. Oh, and there's a few women shaking cocktails under a tent.

I pull my sunglasses down and squint. Sure enough, that's Tami with them. I don't know what surprises me more. The fact that she went up to random strangers for a homemade drink or that they gave her one.

She lifts a red Solo cup when she sees me and smiles. I fake a smile and look away. This should be an interesting night.

Morgan slides beside me and sighs. "I just found out we're not playing Nicorette again." She tosses a few peanuts in her mouth and chews before continuing. "This team is supposed to be better."

I nod. At this point I'm more worried about the crowd than the team. Moonshine County has a certain reputation, but I've never experienced it so up close and personal. The combination of warmer weather and Little League has this place looking like a People of Walmart fashion show.

Charlie is gawking at a girl whose shorts could qualify for blue-jean panties. Maribelle covers his eyes and calls to Morgan and me, "Do we know what field we're on?"

Morgan checks her phone. "Field three." She looks around and nods toward the field.

A younger group of players runs by on their way to the concession stand. I shake my head to make sure I'm not hallucinating. Nope. Their caps say MF. That's highly inappropriate.

Only when they pass us do I notice "Sponsored by Moonshine Furniture" on the back of their jerseys. Still, inappropriate.

Our group heads that way, except for Tami, who is content with her new friends. Maybe she will stay in Moonshine.

"Some of those kids are huge!" Timothy gawks.

"Shh." The last thing we need is for him to scare everyone before we even throw a ball.

Georgia tiptoes over mud toward us. Her face is scrunched like she smelled a fart. In a place like this, she could've smelled anything.

"Everyone's here." She huffs. "I was hoping this was the wrong park."

I raise a brow. "We're not in Kansas anymore, Dorothy."

"Apparently not." She lifts her foot and grimaces at mud caked on the side of her white sneakers. "I brought the kids some candy for later." She slides a box out of her Bogg bag.

"Thanks."

I turn my attention to the field. Timothy makes a good point. Some of those kids are close to my height. I haul my lawn chair to the dugout. One of the coaches yells something foreign and half the kids nod.

"Is that Spanish?" I ask.

Morgan leans closer and listens. "I'm no Don Quixote, but that scruffy kid did answer him with "sí, señor."

She takes a step back and whistles. The kids stand at attention. "Grab a glove and go to the outfield. We need to warm up."

The kids jog onto the field, except for Reece. He trips on his Harry Potter robe. I help him stand. "Sweetie, why are you wearing this again?"

"I keep it in my bat bag for good luck. When we got out, I saw a bunch of people in costumes, so I thought I should put it on."

I bite back a laugh. "I think this county has a different kind of style is all. Why don't we put it back in the bag, and you can dress up after the game?"

He unclasps the front and takes it off. I pat him on the back as he hurries onto the field, capeless.

Aniston steps in the dugout and turns an ear toward the field. Her eyes widen and she stares at me. "I knew it!"

"What?"

"That's Guatemalan Spanish." She grins.

"And how would you know that?"

Aniston stands tall and proud. "I backpacked through Guatemala one summer in search of the perfect plantains."

"That's strange."

She frowns. "Maybe, but he just warned the tall kid to watch out for Ethan's arm."

My eyes dart in the direction of the kids. Ethan is warming up with Herrington. He does have our best arm and plays catcher. I sigh. "Want to coach first base tonight?"

"I'd be delighted." She smirks and marches onto the field.

Morgan whistles and everyone runs to the dugout. She follows, eating a few peanuts on the way. "What's Aniston doing in your spot?" she asks.

"She speaks Guatemalan Spanish and knows what the coach is saying."

"Boss!" Morgan holds up her hand for me to high-five.

I do, then wipe my hand down my shirt. The peanut oil is dense. I snarl at a greasy stain on my clothes and reach for the book. "I'll do her job."

I start calling out the lineup, while Morgan straightens her ponytail behind her cap. The kids gather against the fence and semi-listen to her pep talk.

"And Miss Aniston is at first base today. Listen to what she says. She speaks the coach's language."

"She speaks Chinese?" Precious blinks in amazement.

"Spanish—Guatemalan, to be exact," Morgan corrects.

"I didn't know guacamole was a language." Jack cocks his head.

"Just line up. Timothy, you're first."

Timothy takes the field and Reece hops on deck. I just pray we make it to Andrew in the inning. Something tells me these kids can field.

A few plays later, I'm proven right. We make it to Andrew, but barely manage to score one run. The next round they rack up five. These kids are such heavy hitters, we can't get the ball in time.

At the top of the second, Morgan huddles everyone around. Aniston comes in the dugout with her intel. "He tells them to always go for home, and if nobody's on third, the base closest to it. If we can load the bases, we have the best shot at scoring a run." She wavers her head. "Or if anyone can hit more than a single, that would be great."

I frown at her. She shrugs.

"Okay, so that's offense. I have a game plan for defense,"

Morgan says. "Do y'all remember Isabella and her friends who practiced with us?"

"Do we?" Jack says. He smiles at his brother, and Charlie wiggles his eyebrows.

Morgan clears her throat. "When they were your age, they won by rolling the ball." She glances at the players to make sure everyone is watching, then takes a ball. "You gently toss it underhanded."

"Like a Quaffle!" Reece wiggles with excitement.

"Get your mind off waffles, son. We can eat later."

He gives Morgan a mean look. I try not to laugh, as I'm sure he was referring to the ball in *Harry Potter*.

"But underhanded, like you're bowling. Let the ball roll hard on the ground to the next player. Keep your gloves to the dirt, and scoop it up."

"Is that legal?" I ask.

"Yep."

Out of nowhere, Bubba steps into our dugout.

"What are you doing here?" Morgan crosses her arms. "Spying on the competition?"

"No, my nephew plays for the 6U and they just finished a game."

He sits on the edge of the bench beside Angel. The wood creaks and it bows under his weight. "Look, I don't have anything against y'all. To be honest, Jeffrey is a little intense."

"A little?" Aniston and I comment at the same time.

"I move trailers for him, but he's even worse at the park than there. He thinks we should win every game no matter what."

"Obviously," Morgan mumbles.

Bubba stands, and the bench readjusts, bouncing Angel in the air an inch.

"Anyways, good luck to y'all. We're going to Waffle House with my sister's family."

"Thanks," I mutter.

Some of the kids wave. Aniston gives me a curious look, as if she's not sure whether to believe him. The kids watch him leave.

Morgan whistles. "Focus. Just because he said 'waffle' doesn't mean we're thinking about it."

I laugh.

"You focus, too."

"Yes, ma'am." I straighten and bite my bottom lip to keep from laughing again.

After all the waffle talk, the first batter jogs onto the field. Aniston stands at first and gives me some kind of weird signal. I'm clueless, but she ends it with a thumbs-up.

We hit better, which I attribute to Aniston's smack talk. Whatever intimidation factor she and Morgan have over the kids, I don't. They come to me for candy and ice packs.

The score is now four to five, but we have to play defense. Morgan glances at me from third base and puffs up her cheeks. Most people wouldn't pick up on it, but she's nervous.

Their first batter is one of the bigger kids. He gets two strikes, then slams the ball to the outfield. Angel stops picking a flower and grabs the ball. I hold my breath as she turns her hand and bowls it hard as she can toward third base. Carter scoops it up at short and tags the runner as he rounds second base, full speed. Morgan pumps her fist in the air and cheers.

The coaches are dumbfounded, and one of them yells some foreign obscenities. At least I think so from Aniston's reaction. We continue with this plan, only allowing them two runs.

It's now four to seven, and we've got another at-bat. Morgan and Aniston smile widely as everyone jogs into the dugout.

"Good job. We scored more runs than them this inning!" Morgan claps enthusiastically.

She starts high-fiving everyone. When she gets close to

me, I purposely stare at the book and pretend to write something. I've had enough peanut oil for one night.

We're back to the top of the order. Timothy puts on his helmet and grabs his bat. I hold on to the end, pulling him back. When he turns, I let go and pat him on the helmet. "You've got this, son."

He grins and struts onto the field. Morgan takes a deep breath and pitches. He hits the first ball and makes it to second. We all cheer.

The momentum continues, and we manage to score four runs before they get three outs. Morgan comes to the fence as the kids are getting their gloves. "All right, Gray Armadillos. This is it."

They hurry onto the field. She stands by the fence, and Aniston joins me. The score is now eight to seven, with us in the lead.

The other team isn't batting as well this time, and Aniston laughs.

"What?"

"Remind me to tell you what all he's saying later."

"Would you need to repent afterward?" I ask.

She wavers her head.

"I'll take your word for it, then."

She laughs harder.

Our rolling technique continues to prove successful until they get back to the big guy. He chokes down on the bat and snorts. His nostrils flare like a bull. Good thing our jerseys are gray and not red.

He hits the first pitch deep into the outfield. Angel covers her face with her glove. Time stands still as every eye follows the ball. It lands perfectly in her glove.

Our team goes nuts. And so does their team's coach, but in a different way. His speech pattern goes into overdrive, reminding me of the time I tried to listen to an audiobook on double speed. Except my book was in English, with a more soothing tone.

Aniston grabs me and hugs my neck. I'm still in shock. We beat the big, scruffy Moonshine Mariners.

"Champs on three." Morgan sticks out her hand, and ten dirty little hands slap on top.

She lets Angel count them down. We all yell, "Champs!" Someone growls in the background, but I'm afraid to see who.

"Let's get out of here before someone slashes our tires," Easton suggests.

I nod.

"Carlton is coming from work and said he'd buy us all a celebratory dinner at Catfish Camp!" Georgia beams.

Crap, Georgia. I'm so ready to get on the brighter side of the county line. But the kids are excited. Maybe that's her plan, since they didn't care for her fancy dark chocolate truffles.

"Let's get a move on," Morgan says.

The adults have everything packed up, so we travel in a pack to the entrance of the park.

"Where's Mama?" Precious asks.

"I'll get her." Easton frowns at me and Aniston. "She may need a doctor."

He meets us in the parking lot with Tami hanging on him. She's holding her baseball heels in her hands and laughing through hiccups.

"I better drive her," he says.

"You're not riding alone with that!" Aniston protests.

"Then she needs to ride with you. I'll take her kids and ours."

"Okay." Aniston takes Tami to their van, while Easton gathers her girls.

I climb in the car with Timothy.

Georgia's Mercedes slows, and the window lowers. "Follow me." She grins, then zips the window.

I do as I'm told. Timothy grabs my phone. "Mama, Nate called us."

"You can call him back." I smile to myself. We haven't talked since last night.

"There are no bars."

"I hope not. Catfish Camp is supposed to be a family place, but you never know around here."

"No, Mama, no signal bars."

I lift my chin in acknowledgement, then refocus on the back of Georgia's SUV. "We'll call soon enough."

I grip the wheel. Every day we talk for at least a quick minute, and he texts me throughout the day. I know Timothy wants to tell him about the game, but I simply want to say "I love you" and hear it back.

Every second I regret not saying it in person before he left. But I was caught off guard and didn't want it to sound like a desperate attempt at keeping him. When he told me the next night on the phone, I had to tell him back.

Georgia puts her blinker on beside a light-up sign that reads "Fresh-Caught Cats."

"They serve cats?" Timothy snarls.

"No." I laugh. "It's short for catfish." *Dear God, I hope that's true.*

We park in a gravel lot that's poorly lit. Lights from inside somewhat show the way to a metal building with a catfish above the door. Rustic letters spell out "Catfish Camp" under it.

Georgia parks beside us and comes to my door. "Carlton is inside getting us a table."

"Okay." I stare at her a minute.

"Oh yeah." She moves aside so I can get out.

Timothy and Herrington follow behind us, talking about video games. I triple-check the lock on our car just to be safe.

Sounds of voices and silverware greet us as soon as we open the old screen door. The inside is actually cozy and welcoming. *Thank you, God!*

I have to admit I expected something along the lines of Enchilada, with hush puppies instead of chips.

"Welcome to Catfish Camp. How many?" a middle-aged woman greets us.

"We're with the team." Georgia grins.

"Okay." She gives us a puzzled look, then smiles. "Right this way."

We follow her past the tables and booths, through a swinging door. If we end up in a kitchen, I'm leaving.

No kitchen. It's a back room full of men. Huge, tall men. Georgia's jaw drops, and the woman nods toward the tables. About twenty pairs of eyes study us.

"This is the only team here," the hostess says.

"Yeah . . ." Georgia presses her lips together.

"I think we're the first ones here of our team," I say.

"Let me get y'all a table." The woman laughs and leads us to the front.

Carlton stands and waves. He's sitting at two tables pushed together in the corner. Georgia waves at him and trots in front of us. "That's our team," she says to the hostess.

"Gotcha." She grabs several rolls of silverware from a bucket and follows us.

Georgia and Carlton do this weird greeting where they touch cheeks and kiss the air. It has Victorian British vibes. The woman places a rolled napkin in front of every chair. More of our people arrive and find us.

Once the silverware is in place, the lady says, "I'm Marsha, and I'll be serving y'all tonight." She pulls a pad from her back pocket. "I can start getting drink orders, then y'all can help yourselves to the buffet."

She goes around the table taking orders. I'm too slow to sit down and get stuck between Tami and Morgan's drama queen daughter, Sofia. That should be fun. Tami orders black coffee, then immediately falls asleep on the table.

"Where were you when we came in?" Georgia asks Carlton.

"In the corner watching that." He points to the opposite wall. It's one of those fake mounted fish that sings and moves its mouth and tail. Carlton laughs when it begins a new song. "Have you ever seen one of those?"

"Yeah," I say dryly.

Then I semi-smile to not sound so cold. I'm glad we won and that I have something to eat other than boiled peanuts, but I'd much prefer eating at home with Nate and Timothy rather than having drunken Tami crowd my space.

Easton clears his throat and offers to pray. We all bow our heads and listen best we can among others talking and the fake fish belting out "Don't Worry, Be Happy."

When everyone stands to fix their plates, I take my phone and check the signal. It's not halfway bad, so I stand. Marsha stops with a tray full of drinks. When she comes close to me, she glances at the phone. "Women's bathroom, second stall, is about the only place you'll get good service."

"Thanks." I smile.

"That way." She tilts her head to the right.

I squeeze through the crowd corralled around the buffet that includes many of the tall guys from the other end of the restaurant. Now that they're standing, I can see "Apple Cart County Community College" and a basketball on their clothing. No wonder she laughed at us saying we were with the team.

There's a clog near the end of the buffet, and I almost get stuck between two guys twice my height digging in the cracker barrel. I squeeze through and see a sign for the restrooms.

A picture of a fish with long eyelashes and lipstick catches me off guard, but also gives a clear sign I've found the right restroom. The door opens to Adrianne, Morgan's sister-in-law.

"Hey, girl." Her makeup eerily resembles the fish on the door, except it makes her look pretty instead of scary. "I don't think I've seen you here before."

"First time." I nod.

"We bring Grandpa Joe most Fridays. It's his favorite spot."

"That's sweet. We're with Timothy's baseball team. Just played a game at Moonshine Park."

"You look good to come from there." She wrinkles her nose.

I laugh. "Good seeing you."

"You too." She smiles and shimmies past me.

I enter the restroom, and another woman comes in behind me. When the first stall comes open, I tell her to go ahead. She beams like I'm a good Samaritan. In reality, I'm waiting on the magical service stall.

When the girl in it walks out, I rush inside. I lose a bar when I sit, so I stand and call Nate.

He answers right away, but it's loud. I stretch upward and gain another bar. Since I don't want him on speaker, I stand on the toilet seat.

"Hey." The toilet beside me flushes.

"Where are you?"

"Catfish Camp."

"Sounded like a toilet."

"Their bathroom, to be more specific."

The woman who honored me earlier with a sweet grin gives me a scowl when she sees me standing over the stall from the mirror above the sink. I drop my gaze to the toilet and hope I never see her again.

"Where are you? Sounds loud," I say.

"Some burger joint with pool and music. Remember Ace? He finds them in every town."

"Vaguely." I met Ace maybe twice when Nate moved to Atlanta. They started in the minors together.

I smile. "Before I forget, Timothy wants you to know they won by a run and that he did good."

"Great."

"And I wanted to say I—"

I hear another woman say his name. I catch my breath and listen intently as she asks him for an autograph. Slight relief washes over me, as it could've been much worse.

"Here you go," I hear him say.

"Sorry, Brooke. What were you saying?"

"I just wanted to say I love you." I say it loudly to make sure he can hear it above all his background noise.

"I love you too." His voice is smooth and caring.

It carries over me like a warm blanket after a rainstorm. I shift my weight to get a better stance on the toilet.

"I'm glad they won. How was your day?"

"Good. I'm just tired."

"Me too. I pitched some today, so after we finish eating, I'm going to ice my shoulder."

"Please don't overdo it and hurt yourself."

"That's the beauty of being hurt, the damage is already done."

I sigh and shake my head. Classic Nate.

I hear someone announcing food and people claiming their plates. "I'll let you eat. I probably need to get back to our table too."

"Okay. Tell Timothy we can talk tomorrow during the day since he's not at school."

"I will."

"I love you," we say in unison.

Then we share a laugh.

"Bye." I cut the call, but am still laughing when the bathroom door opens. A teenage girl stares at me like I have three heads. I jump down and squint through the crack in the door. Once she's in the other stall, I make my escape back to crazy town with all the kids, Tami, and that annoying fish on the wall.

CHAPTER 22

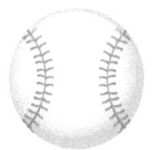

Nate

I barely say "bye" before the phone cuts out. Brooke is in a bathroom, and I'm surrounded by loud talking and some cheesy cover band playing AC/DC. The noise and the crowdedness makes me miss her even more.

Some woman came by and asked for all our autographs on a napkin, then stuffed it in her bra. That's the kind of crap that makes me stay away from places like this. I much prefer a little kid wanting me to sign his cap.

After eating low-key meals in Apple Cart, I'd almost forgotten how hard it is to eat a quiet meal. Unless I get takeout, which I normally do.

But Ace wanted me to come out with him. I refused his offers of clubbing and beach bars, so we settled on a pool hall. We used to splurge on burgers and play pool for cheap entertainment as rookies, and he knows I have a weakness for nostalgia. As well as bacon cheeseburgers.

I take another bite of my food and try to drown out the

noise. Funny how that skill works for me on the mound, but not always anywhere.

It's nights like this I miss Dom. He was my other first roommate and an awesome catcher. A few years in, the Dodgers snatched him. Last year he retired and moved back to the Dominican Republic to coach young players. That was always his goal, and I admired him for it. I'm not certain if Ace has a goal, other than to live life like one big party.

Needless to say, Dominic and I had more in common. Except for him being the oldest of eight boys and me an only child. Plus, he had a great father figure. And thinking of that makes me miss Timothy too.

I almost choke on my tea when Ace slaps my back. "Come play some pool." His perfect teeth shine in the dark lighting.

"Let me finish my food first."

"Eat, sleep, work out." His voice is monotone.

"I don't sound like that."

He laughs and slaps me harder. "Come on man, live a little. We're not even thirty yet."

I push back my chair and start to stand.

"All right, you're in."

"Nope. Going to the restroom." I stand and drain my tea, then pass him.

He boos behind me, but stops when I take a few steps. I hear him talking with a woman and shake my head.

This is one guy I don't see settling down. Dom, definitely. Me, Lord, please, with Brooke. Ace, never.

I pull open the heavy metal door to the restroom and open the door to a stall. After I'm done, I rush to wash my hands. My goal is finishing my meal and heading home before something crazy happens with Ace. Because it always does when he's involved.

As I'm grabbing a paper towel, I see a woman standing behind me from the mirror. I flinch and turn around when I recognize her from earlier.

"Ma'am, this is the men's restroom."

"I know." She does something sensual with her lips. "And I'm no ma'am."

I exhale in frustration. This doesn't happen to me often, but when it does, the women are relentless—and crazy.

"If you'll excuse me." I wipe my hands and shift to sidestep her.

She presses herself closer until we're about an inch away. Then she pulls the napkin from her cleavage. "You forgot to write your number."

"No, it's on there. Number sixteen." I tighten my lips, showing no sign of amusement.

"I meant your phone number."

Obviously, but I don't give that away.

She reaches for my belt and I shrink back against the counter. I could move this woman with one finger, but that would do one of two things. Either give her the impression I'm interested or have her report me for physical abuse. Regardless, I won't win.

I have no choice but to resort to distraction. "Let me fix that for you." I take the napkin from her hand.

I turn and drop it in the sink, then twist the faucet. Water flushes the napkin, and she shrieks.

Luckily, she's so focused on the napkin disintegrating that I slide by her and out the door. Ace is at our table with a woman on both sides of him when I return.

In my estimation, I have about two minutes before the bathroom barracuda either slings a drink at me or keys my truck. I pull a hundred from my wallet and slap it on the table. Then I pick up my plate and head for the door. A hundred dollars should more than cover the cost of that plate.

I hurry outside and climb in my truck. Only when I'm safely at a red light about a mile away do I relax and stuff a few fries in my face.

I have somewhat of a reputation for stealing plates both on and off the field. But it's always for a good reason.

The light turns and I drive toward my condo. Nine years ago, I left Pool Pub in Atlanta with a half-eaten burger on a plate. Back then, it was a huge sacrifice to leave a twenty, and my truck barely made it to Tuscaloosa.

This time feels eerily familiar, except I comfortably left a hundred, I'm in a nice ride, and I'm going to my luxury condo by the beach. That should make it better, but it doesn't.

Nine years ago, I was on my way to see Brooke.

It would be the last time I saw her in person before our breakup, but I had no clue. Still, I don't regret going.

I'd follow Brooke to the ends of the Earth as long as she wants me. Good thing she's in Apple Cart, which isn't too far from me.

It's also much quieter, and I can live a normal life. To everyone there, I'm Nate Miller, or Anne's son. And the only autograph I've signed for anyone over fifteen was on a Chipper Jones jersey.

I arrive at the Florida condo, aggravated I'm not in Apple Cart. I should be thankful I'm able to join spring training, but I miss Brooke.

My burger and fries are reduced to crumbs. After I park in the deck, I open my door and shake them from the plate. I may as well take this plate inside. I did pay for it.

Round, white, and heavy, it's the same kind of plate I ran out with years before. Funny how things change and stay the same all at once.

The blankness of it makes me miss Brooke even more. Many nights I'd stare at the words she scribbled on the original plate with a permanent marker. She'd kissed beside the message, leaving a red lip stain.

Over the years, the lipstick faded, and I found myself doing all I could to preserve the plate best I could.

Whenever I moved my stuff, I'd pack it separately and carry it myself. If it ever broke, I imagine I'd try to glue it back together.

On some level, that's what I'm trying to do with our relationship. Except this time I want the glue to be extra strong. Not like when we were young and let busyness and distance keep us apart.

It's close to ten when I unlock my front door. Brooke may be in bed, so I settle for sending her a message instead of calling. She sounded tired earlier, which I assume is common for someone who works at a hospital all week, then takes a bunch of kids to the Moonshine County ballpark.

I set the plate on my kitchen counter and shoot her a text.

> Wanted to say I love you one more time.

I hit Send and go to my room for a shower. When I return, the text remains unread. Knowing my luck, Timothy will read it in the morning.

That's fine. I have no reason to hide my love for his mother. And if he thinks that text includes him, all the better. The little guy has grown on me.

I open the sliding door to my balcony and step outside. The air is sticky, but the cool tile under my bare feet makes up for it. I pull a patio chair to the railing and prop up my feet.

They're terribly ugly. Big and blistered, with a crooked toe from an old sprain. Brooke's feet were always so dainty and small, and she kept her toenails pink or red. Everything about her is equally adorable and gorgeous. I wish she were here.

I lean back into the cushioned chair and crane my neck and look at the stars. A habit I've formed since being back in Apple Cart. In Atlanta, I have to settle for a barely visible moon among city lights.

Lots of people go into the Georgia mountains to camp and hike on the weekends. I never understood why until I'd lived in Atlanta a while. They want an escape from the noise and the constant movement of things.

Buying the Apple Cart mansion was my way of escaping. Or so I thought. But after reuniting with Brooke, I believe we could be happy anywhere.

I sigh and mentally play out scenarios if my arm doesn't live up to expectations.

If that happens and I choose not to retire, there's a good chance the Braves might trade me. There's also a chance they could send me back to the minors. That would mean less of a chance at bouncing back to my current status.

What would Brooke think of that?

Would she be willing to uproot her life—and Timothy's—for something less stable? Even if she were, would I let her?

Like Timothy, I never had a father in my life. Also like Timothy, I grew up in a great community with an awesome mom and plenty of people who had my best interest in mind.

Worst case scenario, Brooke leaves me again. If that happens, I still want to do all I can to encourage Timothy's love of ball. That kid has some raw talent.

A slight breeze cuts the muggy air and makes me yawn. Ace is probably catching his second wind, but I'm ready to wind down. Maybe I am an old man at twenty-seven.

I retreat through the glass door and lock it behind me. When I check my phone, I see a text from Brooke.

> I love you too. Good night.

She follows that with a kissing, winking smiley face. I grin at the message while I brush my teeth. Again, she has me acting like a teenage girl.

Maybe this is karma for me laughing about how ridiculous some of the girls at our high school used to act.

Whether karma or my own weirdness, it doesn't much matter. I fall asleep quickly with a stupid grin plastered across my face. Even better, I dream of Brooke.

CHAPTER 23

Nate

Every time my phone makes a sound, I jerk my head to check if it's Brooke. Ninety percent of the time, it's reminder dings or some telemarketer.

We talk every day, but with our odd schedules, never at a set time. Monday night she worked late, Tuesday night Timothy had practice, and Wednesday night they went to church.

I've been working out and meeting with people at random times. I pitch a little here and there, and I eat lunch with some of the team every day.

Maybe if I ate lunch with Ace every day, he'd quit trying to get me to go out at night. I didn't care for it back in the day, and I really don't care for it now. He's one of those loyal and fun friends, but our commonalities pretty much end with baseball and burgers.

I'm back in Atlanta to check in with the doctor one more time before I pitch a spring training game. After my appointment, I headed for the interstate. I've been packed all morning so I wouldn't waste any time going back to the Atlanta condo. The only stop I made was at Buc-ee's for gas and a bathroom break. Naturally, I left with a massive fountain drink and Beaver Nuggets. That's a necessity.

Now the Beaver Nuggets are long gone and I'm speeding through downtown Apple Cart.

A siren bleeps behind me. I glance in the mirror and see blue lights. Freakin' Bradley Manning.

I roll my eyes and pull over. He's cocky to a fault, which means I can't act mad. That will send him on a power trip and he will assert authority. I roll down my window and wait for him to reach my truck.

It's hard to read his face with those *Top Gun* glasses. He frowns. "Nate, why were you driving so fast? If a deer ran out of the woods, you could've wrecked badly. God forbid a log truck enter the road."

I swallow the urge to insist turkey would be more common this time of year, and that loggers post signs where they're working.

"I'm sorry, Bradley. I've been in Florida and flew into Atlanta earlier, so I'm ready to get home."

An unexpected grin crawls across his face. He laughs a little, then smiles wider. I blink, worried what this might mean.

"So you're calling Apple Cart home again?"

"I always have."

He scribbles something on a paper and pushes it through the window. "Welcome home, big dog. I let you off with a warning." He straightens his sunglasses and points at my face. "From now on, let's channel all that speed into pitching."

"Yes, sir." I wait until he turns away before rolling up my window and crawling back onto the road.

I near my house soon enough, but I pass it and go toward Brooke's. Timothy spots my truck and waves wildly.

He meets me when I park at the edge of his grandparents' house. I wave back, then glance at Brooke's house.

"Hey, Nate!" He hugs my waist.

"Hey, buddy, good to see you." I hug him and pat his back.

It's nice to get such a welcome greeting. We pull away, and he tells me what I'm about to ask. "Mama is at work. Granny picked me up from school."

"Okay. How is ball going?"

He shrugs. "We're getting better. I could use a little work on my short hop though, especially when Coach Morgan has us roll the ball."

"What do you mean roll the ball?" I raise my brow skeptically.

"That's how we beat the team that fielded better."

I shake my head. "Winning is good, Timothy, but learning to play the game correctly is more important."

He nods slowly, as if mulling it over before agreeing.

"Why don't you get your glove and we'll work on the short hop." I point to him. "Not for rolling the ball, but for true grounders."

He smiles and nods bigger this time, then disappears into their house. I lean one arm against the door of my truck and sigh. Between the flight and appointment, then driving like a maniac to get here, I've barely had a minute to catch my breath.

Timothy returns with a ball and the mitt I gave him. I grab a glove from my toolbox.

"Take a few steps back." I motion where I want him in the yard.

I throw some balls and comment on his form, letting him know what he's doing right and what can improve.

"Have you practiced this any since I left?"

"Some high school softball girls helped us on the T-ball field. One of them played first and showed me some stuff. I throw a ball against the barn and catch it sometimes too."

I grin at the memory of throwing the ball for myself as a kid. At least Timothy has the broad side of a barn to work with. I would toss the ball on the roof of our mobile home and let it roll off. More than once, I had to admit to Mom that's why her wind chimes got so tangled.

"You're doing good."

"Thanks." He stands a littler straighter after my compliment.

Brooke's car pulls beside us and slows. She sticks her head out the window. "This is a nice surprise." She continues into the garage.

I toss Timothy the ball and signal him to hold it, then follow her car. By the time she opens her door, I'm standing beside it.

She gets out and smiles widely. I grab her face and kiss her gently for a second, then hug her close. Her hospital scrubs give off a stench of cleaning supplies and rubber. But her hair still has the usual floral, springy scent I find intoxicating. I lean back and smile down at her.

"I didn't expect you to come out here."

I shrug. "I convinced the team to let me have a couple days off after my appointment."

"Have you seen your mom yet?"

"Nope. You were my first stop." I tap her tiny nose with my fingertip, then step back for her to shut the car door.

"I have some chicken and rice in the Crockpot if you want to stay and eat."

"I do." My nerves flare when I hear those words come from my mouth. It probably would've made more sense to say "sure" or "thanks." Even a head nod would've worked. But I've spent four hours alone in my truck today, daydreaming about what life married to Brooke might look like.

Luckily, she didn't sense the weirdness in my word choice. She yells for Timothy to come inside, and he meets us in the living room.

Brooke's carriage house has a homey feel not yet present in my mansion. She has pictures and Bible verses hanging on the wall. Cookie-smelling candles stay lit on the mantel and kitchen counter whenever she's home. And she has actual curtains and throw pillows.

I used to think of those as women things, but they're starting to grow on me. I'd never admit that to anyone and risk lowering my masculinity. But living in an actual house, especially one the size I own, is different from a sleek city condo. A little coziness could make it more comfortable.

Brooke sets her purse on the couch and heads toward the tiny kitchen.

"Do you need any help?" I ask.

"No, all I have to do is slice the chicken and put everything on our plates."

"I can fix drinks." I follow her.

I'm not wired to sit and have people wait on me, even if I am a guest. That's one thing Ace never understood. He'd tell me to relax whenever we were at an event. I'd go refill my own drinks and throw away my empty plates instead of leaving them on the table.

He'd argue we were major leaguers and didn't have to do that anymore. In my mind, what you do for a job and how much money you make has nothing to do with how you act.

I pour everyone a glass of sweet tea while Brooke fixes bowls of rice and chicken.

"Timothy was catching good today."

"I know he was happy to see you too. When did you get in?"

"Maybe thirty minutes before you. Not long."

My mouth goes dry as I watch Brooke carry our plates to the table. From the mundane conversation about our day to eating dinner together, I get a glimpse of what being married to her might be like.

And it's wonderful.

The only problem is I have a whole team celebrating the recovery of my arm. I'm an actual contender for pitching Opening Day. That might complicate things if I were to elope.

"What time do y'all practice tomorrow?" I ask, after deflating my own daydream with reality.

"Seven." Brooke sets forks by everyone's bowls, and I pass out teas. "Timothy, you want to pray?"

Timothy bows his head and thanks God for the food, baseball, and me coming to eat with them. My heart inflates like I'm the Grinch catching on to Christmas. He's one special boy, and I'm honored he thinks so highly of me.

"Y'all start at seven?" I ask as we eat.

"Yeah, Morgan wanted to hold out for a bigger field. It was either that or the T-ball field again. We couldn't do it right after school since most of us work." She drinks some tea, then adds, "More like all of us work except Tami."

I shove a forkful of chicken and rice in my mouth and try not to imagine how Tami fills her day.

"Why don't y'all come to my place around five-thirty when everyone gets home. That way you can be done before seven, and you and I can have that date in Tuscaloosa."

Her closed lips curve into a faint smile as she chews.

"Mama, that sounds like a good deal for all of us," Timothy says.

We both laugh.

"It really does," Brooke agrees. "Sold!"

Brooke

Cars line the edge of Nate's yard as everyone arrives for practice. I watch Tami hoist her youngest on her hip and tiptoe down the hill in her heels. This time they're covered in black leather instead of baseball leather. She wobbles a little with the baby, and I stand in case I need to run and try to catch her.

After a few close calls, they make it to flat ground and the baby coos happily. I sigh with relief. That will be one resilient child. Good thing she didn't bring her to the game in Moonshine County.

Half the kids are in their own little world, and the other half crowd Nate, asking about the Braves. Morgan walks up to the group and lets out a whistle so loud that Nate plugs a finger in his ear.

The remaining kids come running, and chatting parents pay attention. Morgan turns to Nate with a face that silently says, *You. Are. Welcome.*

I swear, she would've made a great teacher. Or prison guard.

Nate slaps his hands together and scans the group, who now have their full attention on him.

"It's good to be back with y'all. Coach Morgan and I had a talk, and I've come up with some things to help with what each player needs to work on."

Morgan nods as she paces behind Nate with her hands laced behind her back. She's totally giving me prison guard vibes.

"As usual when we practice here, I have some stations. When you're at my station, we'll work on what I think will help you most." Nate points across the field. "Fly balls will be over there with the dads."

Easton, Carlton, and Jim wave. I narrow my eyes to make sure I'm not seeing things. Nope. Jim is wearing a hard hat, and he doesn't work at the mines. He's a military recruiter. I hope the hat is in relation to recruiting for the army and not because he's that cautious of fly balls.

Although, that would explain why his son ducks at anything flying overhead and why he wears a Harry Potter cape. Maybe I should suggest Reece join the homeschool co-op in Wisteria when our season ends. Some more outside influences besides his parents might do the boy good.

"Miss Brooke and Miss Aniston will help inside with the tee." Nate hooks a thumb toward the building behind us. "Coach Morgan and Ethan will help toss grounders." He emphasizes the word "toss" and gives Morgan a look.

She looks like a kid with her hand caught in the cookie jar. He'd mentioned last night he needed to talk to her about rolling the ball on purpose. I join Aniston across the yard and try not to laugh. Very few people attempt to correct Morgan, and even fewer people earn her allegiance to their ideas.

"Okay. You two go inside to Brooke and Aniston." Nate taps Timothy and Carter on the arm. "I want Jack, Charlie, and Herrington with Morgan first." They go to her. "Reece, you'll start inside with me." Nate tosses a ball back and forth in his hand. "The rest of you start with the Village People."

The kids give him a blank stare. But the rest of us burst out laughing.

"Go to the dads." Nate points to the field.

As the kids run that way, Easton lifts his hands as if asking why everyone is staring and laughing at them. He's wearing a straw cowboy hat and boots while standing next to Jim. If only he knew, he'd rethink his grass-cutting wardrobe.

Nate turns to us. "I'll have Morgan whistle when we want to swap stations."

I'm not sure she heard him, since she's still doubled over snorting at the Village People comment.

Aniston and I regain control more quickly and go inside to our station. We have our own kids first, for better or worse. I can't decide as they correct us on how to put the ball on the tee. Both do pretty well, and Timothy announces what Nate told him to watch for with bad swing habits.

They're pretty much practicing together. I honestly think we're just warm bodies to keep the balls coming at a steady rate, which is fine by me.

Nate climbs in the other side of the batting cage with Reece. I listen as he holds a bat and explains how it works like Harry Potter's wand. Weird, but when he tells Reece to cast a spell, the kid hits better than ever.

I'm in awe the rest of practice when Nate finds a way to personally motivate each kid on what he or she needs to work on. He even told Tami's girls that if they do good on the field, he will get their mom to video them and make a TikTok. They liked that idea a little too much.

Thankfully, Timothy is more motivated by candy than the allure of becoming a social media star.

Practice runs smoothly with everyone rotating through each station and having their one-on-one time with Nate. Around six-twenty, we wrap things up with a quick prayer.

I hug and kiss Timothy, and he climbs in Aniston's van. She was happy to let him spend the night so that Nate and I could stay out as long as we wanted. Then I hurry home to change into something a little nicer, and Nate does the same.

My hands are so shaky, I can barely touch up my mascara. Nate and I are going to eat in Tuscaloosa, just the two of us. So much of that makes me feel eighteen again.

And I love it. But not nearly as much as I love him.

CHAPTER 24

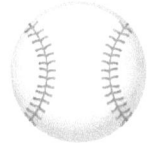

Nate

Typical for anyone living within an hour of a larger city, we spent half our drive to Tuscaloosa discussing where to eat. I suggested all the nicest restaurants I found on Google when I couldn't sleep the other night.

Brooke never liked making final decisions, but she perked up when I mentioned Italian. I love that I can still read her expressions after all this time.

We ate at a nice little Italian place downtown, then walked to the coffee shop that opened not long after we graduated high school.

"It's crowded tonight. Maybe we should go someplace else," Brooke suggests.

I shake my head. "This is one of the few coffee places I like, and I have memories here with you."

She smiles sweetly. I wrap my arm around her back and squeeze in line. I really am a sucker for nostalgia.

I scan the room, both surprised and content at how little

it's changed. There are a few extra photos on the wall, since Alabama has won several national championships since I've been here. They added a wall of coffee mugs and updated the card readers at the register. But that's really all that's changed.

I'd like to think the same for Brooke and me. We're older and well into our careers, unlike before. She's a mom, and I'm mulling over the decision to retire from ball every few months. More like every few hours since I reunited with her.

Still, we're the same people and have the same feelings for one another.

When we get to the register, the barista grins and wags a finger at me. I stare at his hand, wondering what I've done wrong.

"You're Nate Miller, aren't you?"

"I am." I clear my throat. "You look familiar too."

I'm not just making conversation. He does look familiar.

"I've worked here for almost nine years. Finally saved enough to buy the place."

I turn to Brooke, and we smile.

"You want fries with that?" we say in unison.

I face him again, and he laughs, clearly not remembering.

"We don't have fries, but we have some pastries."

I chuckle. "Chocolate coffee is fine."

Brooke orders a vanilla cold brew, as I assumed she would. She always favored vanilla over chocolate and got hooked on cold coffee our last summer together when it was so hot.

I take out my card, but he waves it away. "On the house, man. It's rare we get to serve an MLB player."

I try again, but he stops my hand and slides a card from his pocket to cover the cost.

"Thanks, that's generous." I nod, and we move aside for others to order.

It's so crowded that we can't find a table. But that forces

us outside, and we take a stroll by the river. The sun is setting behind the trees, and the weather is just right.

I take Brooke's free hand in mine and exhale. It doesn't get much more relaxing than this. Why Ace prefers playing pool and dancing with random women over walking with someone like Brooke is insane.

"How crazy is it that 'fries with that' guy owns The Coffee Loft now?" Brooke's eyes widen as she turns to me.

"I'm actually not that surprised."

"Really?" She does that cute thing where she wrinkles her nose.

"Would you have ever thought I'd have started as a pitcher for the Braves?"

"Yes." She smirks.

I kiss her on the cheek. "I appreciate the vote of confidence, but aside from you and my mom, I'm not sure anyone else had that much faith in me."

We walk in silence a moment. The sun lowers enough for streetlamps to glow faintly. We're getting close to my truck, so I slow the pace. Brooke sips her drink, then speaks.

"I never questioned your talent or drive. That's why I removed myself from the situation so you wouldn't have anything holding you back. If you weren't going to make it, it wouldn't have been because of me."

I chug my coffee, glad it's no longer steaming hot. We talked briefly about the breakup on our first date. She mentioned how she didn't want to hold me back. I managed to keep the conversation light and assure her that wouldn't have happened, mainly through kisses. If she gets on a tangent again, I'll have to kiss her right here on the walking trail.

I'm not a fan of rehashing the past. What good will that do?

"Brooke." I squeeze her hand in mine. "Please stop saying you would hold me back. I don't like it when you put that on me, making assumptions I would've quit ball if we stayed together. I never wanted to choose between you and ball."

She stops walking, pulling me to a halt. We turn toward one another.

"I know," she whispers.

"Then why?" I whisper back.

Tears pool in her eyes and she sniffles. What in the world could make her cry? Was it something I said? A bad memory of our breakup? I don't get it.

She blinks, allowing a few tears to fall. Then she swipes at the corners of her eyes with her thumb and glances around the walking trail and park. "Can we talk somewhere more private?"

"Yeah." My voice is hoarse, and I'm shocked it even worked.

I drop her hand and wrap my arm around her tightly. We walk snuggled together toward my truck. It's only a few yards away, but my stomach is a mess by the time we get there.

I chuck my coffee in a trash can beside the parking lot, even though about a third of it is left. My body can't handle any more sugar with Brooke in this condition. I'm a nervous wreck and I don't know why.

Not knowing is probably why. What is wrong?

She hops in my truck as soon as I unlock the doors. I climb in my side and close the door. I twist to face her, but she stares blankly out the windshield.

"I broke up with you because I got pregnant."

Forget my stomach. Now my entire body is hemorrhaging. I analyze every conversation and interaction we had at the end of our relationship. Just as I did for months after she ended things.

Only this time, I take a deeper dive into her mannerisms and excuses for not seeing me. It's all starting to make sense. But why?

Brooke is a porcelain doll, stiff and expressionless in my passenger seat. I narrow my eyes, as if I could read her better that way. For once, I have no idea what she's thinking and why.

Several excruciating minutes pass before I process everything and gain my composure.

"I'm shocked you cheated on me, but I admire you for telling me after all these years. I still love you."

A sad laugh-cry comes from her. She shakes her head and turns to me. Her eyes are dull and lifeless, making her still more doll-like than human.

"I never cheated on you."

I tilt my head, more confused than ever. "But you said you got pregnant when we—" My heart rate accelerates to an unhealthy level.

We were together one time. Like *together* together. We both knew we should wait, and we both wanted to. But at some point we both wanted to not wait more.

Did I regret it? Yes.

Not at the time. I'd never felt more alive, and I'd always planned on marrying her one day. However, our relationship changed after that. She became distant, and then she didn't want to be with me. I blame myself as the guy for allowing it to happen. If I hadn't, we may have never broken up in the first place.

I'm pretty sure we're now on the same page, but I need her to say it. Her chest rises and falls, and her neck gets red and splotchy as she watches me figure it out. Still, I need to hear it from her.

"I'm Timothy's dad?"

She nods slowly.

Wow. An eighteen-wheeler could plow over me and my head wouldn't spin so fast.

That explains so much. The kid loves me. I love him. He's left-handed and good at baseball. He loves baseball. It pretty much explains everything except for Brooke keeping him a secret from me—and me from him.

A string of curses dances in my head. Unlike a lot of athletes at my level, I don't have a dirty mouth. I keep them inside, even though a bomb like this could make a preacher cuss.

Instead, I crank the truck and back out of the parking lot. When I glance past Brooke to see if it's clear to enter the road, she blinks at me with her mouth half open.

Is she shell-shocked? Good for her. How does she think I feel?

We're on down the road, stopped at a main intersection light, when she breaks the silence.

"Nate, please talk to me."

"I don't think you want me to," I answer.

The light turns green. I white knuckle the steering wheel and gas up my truck. Some kid in a sports car beside us lays on his gas.

Just great. Punk thinks I'm wanting to race. I slow down and let the kid pass. Then I take a smaller side road when I get a chance.

"Say something." Her voice is shaky.

I wait a minute and mull over different responses. This news cuts deep, hurting me even more than our breakup. I'm furious, but I still love Brooke—and Timothy. I don't want to talk, but she's not going to let up until I do.

Of all the times to be stuck in a truck together.

"I can't believe you kept this from me so long." I glance at Brooke.

The doe-like sweetness is back in her eyes. Although there's an underlining sadness and no twinkle to them. I clear my throat and look back at the road.

"I missed the first eight years of my son's life. I missed nine years with you. We could've been a family all this time."

Brooke

I am the scum of the earth. I kept my son and his father from one another for almost nine years.

Okay, that makes me worse than scum. I am whatever kind of scum grows on scum, with a big pile of dog poop on top. Even Tami is a better parent than me right now.

The veins on Nate's neck bulge, as do his biceps. Normally, the biceps would turn me on, but they are bulging due to his kung-fu grip on the steering wheel.

There's nothing I can say to make this any better, and it's all my fault. Nate is furious at me.

I'd feared he might be mad about me not telling him, but the more I watched them together, the more I was sure it would all smooth out and everyone would be happy with the news.

Wrong. So wrong.

He's mad that I kept Timothy from him for so long, and he has every right to be.

I've spent my twenties raising him with the help of my parents. I was there for his first steps, words, day of school, pulled tooth, and everything else that comes with raising a child. All the while, Nate was playing ball and had no idea the child even existed.

How selfish could I be?

Apparently, very.

I sink against his leather seat and drain the rest of my coffee drink, which is now watery vanilla slush. It gives me an instant brain freeze. I welcome the headache for once, because I deserve to feel pain.

For eight and a half years, I acted as if raising Timothy alone was noble of me. I changed career aspirations and moved back home. I gave up any extra hobbies or romantic life to focus on him.

In my mind, this was my penance for getting pregnant. I'd allowed myself to go too far with Nate, and this was my fate.

In hindsight, it wasn't the burden I'd made it out to be. My parents were nothing but accepting and loving. As was our community. Even some of the older ladies who'd whispered when I'd come home pregnant crocheted baby quilts and loved on him in the church nursery. The church gave me a baby shower like they would any expecting member, and my cousin helped me paint a nursery.

Maybe I'd secretly wanted them to judge me. At the time, I felt ashamed and wanted to be blamed. I could've lived with those consequences.

What I couldn't have lived with was bringing down Nate's career with it.

Only now do I realize he deserved to know the truth. I can't make decisions for him, and I took away his right to do so by keeping Timothy a secret.

Heck, as much as everyone loved on me, they would've loved on me even more had they known the baby was also Nate's. His mom would've helped out too.

Oh crap. Poor Miss Anne! That's another yard of yarn I've yet to unravel. How will she react when she realizes she's had a grandson all this time?

I bury my head in my hands and swallow hard.

I don't lift my head until we're close to Apple Cart County. Nate hasn't said a word in probably half an hour. My pulse races, and I fidget with the ends of my hair.

We turn onto the road leading to both our houses. Nate finally relaxes his grip on the wheel. I'm sure his shoulder is sore from all the tension. He passes his house and drives straight to mine. He parks in front and kills the engine. The darkness and silence are more than I can take.

"Nate, I never meant to hurt you." My voice is so shaky, I barely recognize it.

"I know," he whispers.

I sigh and throw my head back against the seat. "This sounds so stupid now, but at the time I really thought I was doing what was best for you. I didn't want you to quit ball, and you would've, wouldn't you?"

I twist my head to face him. The veins in his neck slowly sink back to normal. He shrugs, then lets his shoulders droop like a whooped puppy. "You're probably right. I wouldn't have wanted you to quit school and follow me. But I would've asked you to marry me either way."

I close my eyes. Luckily, I'm fresh out of tears. If not, they'd be flowing like a creek after a rainstorm right now.

The biggest irony is I quit school anyway. I went to JuCo in Apple Cart, but not for teaching. If we had stayed together, I could've gone to school online or even delayed the wedding. It would've been hard to stay apart, but he would've been in our lives. Timothy would've had his daddy.

"I'm a horrible person. I love you more than anyone, and in trying not to hurt you, I hurt you more."

I suck in a breath. Saying that out loud is oddly therapeutic. At the same time, it stings.

For the first time since I dropped this bomb on him, Nate reaches for my hand. His is sweaty and stiff, yet offers comfort. The fact that he even wants to touch me gives me hope.

We sit quietly, staring out the windshield for a moment. His hand relaxes, and he rubs the back of my mine with his thumb. I breathe in and out slowly, my heart rate returning to a safe speed for the first time in an hour.

"Brooke, I love you more than anything. And I love Timothy too, even more now that I know he's mine."

He sighs and continues rubbing my hand. Our eyes meet, and the sadness in his breaks my heart. I want to ask where we go from here, but bite my tongue. I've made enough decisions about us for a lifetime. It's time he gets to drive.

"I wish you had told me. It hurts—really, really hurts. I'm not going to lie and say I'm not mad you kept this a secret, but I realize how scared you must have been."

He reaches his other arm across the truck and cups my cheek. "I hate that you went through all that alone. We could've done it together. We are more important than ball or anything else. Timothy is more important than anything else."

He stares at me as if waiting for a response. I nod against his hand. He's right. However, I'm struggling to string together words, since I'm still trying to process all that's happened between us in the last hour. He slides his hand from my cheek and drops it on top of our intertwined hands, adding more warmth and comfort.

"Who else knows?" he asks.

"Nobody. Not even my parents."

"How is that possible?"

I turn my gaze toward the big house. The only light visible is from the spare room upstairs that Daddy uses to watch TV.

"I suspect they know. I'd prefer that to them thinking it was a random guy at school."

"Why didn't you tell them?"

I sigh and turn back to Nate. "They would've told you and Anne. Then it would've defeated my plan to keep you on the path to playing MLB."

He looks back toward the road, then at me. "Oh man. I was so focused on being a dad that I didn't even think of what Mom's going to say."

"She'll probably hate me too." I laugh nervously.

"Brooke, nobody hates you. We all love you, and Timothy." He squeezes my hand. "I wouldn't have handled it the way you did, but I wasn't pregnant and scared either."

"What do we do now?" My chest tightens.

This question has so many layers I pray he can untangle. I'm tired of thinking and want him to come up with a solution. I'm also a little afraid he might run back to Atlanta and leave everything as it was before coming back here.

"That's a good question. I need to think and pray a while. This is going to be big news when it breaks, and change Timothy's life. We need a good plan for telling him and our parents."

I press my lips together, mulling over what he said. He didn't mention anything about the two of us. I want desperately to ask, but I've done enough damage tonight.

He leans over and kisses me gently on the lips. Our mouths linger for a few seconds, then he breaks away. The moonlight outlines his silhouette, and we're too close together for me to read his face.

"I have to go back to Florida. We can talk while I'm gone. Please don't tell anyone without me. This will be life-altering news for everyone, especially our son."

My stomach flips when he says "our son." It gives me hope of us becoming a real family.

He pulls away and cranks the truck. "I'll wait until you get inside safely."

That's my cue to leave. I open the door, a little shell-shocked at the abrupt departure. As I'm climbing down the tall truck, he leans toward me and says one more thing.

"Good night, Brooke, I love you."

"I love you too, more than anything." I force a smile and shut the door.

I walk the few feet to my porch and go inside. Right after I close the door behind me, I hear his truck drive away. I don't allow myself to watch him leave.

Instead, I go straight to my room and fall back in the bed. I stare at the popcorn ceiling and try to do what he said he would do this week—think and pray.

My prayers sound stressful to match my thoughts. I shed a few tears and squeeze the life out of a throw pillow before finally falling asleep.

CHAPTER 25

Brooke

Either a giant woodpecker now lives nearby or someone is persistently knocking on my door. I blink my eyes open and push onto my elbows.

I'm on my stomach, lying crossways in the bed with no cover, unless you count all the throw pillows piled on my body. I yawn and pull a strand of hair stuck to my cheek by either sweat or dried tears.

I stagger to stand and stretch. I'm still in my nice jeans and silk shirt from last night. The silk is now a crumpled mess to match my hair.

My natural inclination would be to pee, brush my teeth, and look in a mirror before facing the world. If only the pesky noise would give me a minute.

Someone yells, convincing me it's not a woodpecker. I stumble downstairs and hear my phone buzzing from the living room. I'd tossed my purse on the floor on my way upstairs, which would explain why I didn't hear my alarm.

"Coming," I yell at the door from the bottom of the stairs. Straightening my shirt, I hurry over and swing it open to Aniston. Timothy and Carter play outside a few feet back.

"Morning." She raises a brow and smirks mischievously. "Looks like someone had a good night."

I exhale laboriously and collapse my shoulders.

"Oh." Her expression goes from insinuating to questioning.

"What time is it?"

She holds up her phone. I read nine-thirty. I never sleep past eight-thirty unless I'm sick, even on vacation.

"Are you okay?" She nods back at the boys. "Do I need to take him to your mom?"

I waver my head. "Are you in a hurry?"

"Nope." She shakes her head.

She's wearing gym shorts, an oversized T-shirt, and flip-flops. However, that's typical for Aniston and doesn't mean she isn't busy. Half of her parenting vlogs feature her with a messy bun and well-worn makeup.

"Come in." I drag her inside by the sleeve of her shirt and shut the door.

Her van isn't cranked, and the boys will be fine outside playing. That's my justification for using her to unload some baggage before I break down under all the weight.

"Want some coffee?"

"Uh, sure?" She follows me to the tiny kitchen just off the living room.

I turn on the coffee machine and frantically pull K-cups from the cabinet, spouting off all the flavors available.

"Are you okay?"

I don't answer.

"You're acting a little scattered. Which is cool, if you're me . . . but it's a little out of character for *you*."

I drop a handful of K-cups on the kitchen table and collapse in a chair. "I have a major problem."

"What's wrong?" Her eyebrows thread together and she frowns.

I bite my bottom lip, remembering how Nate told me not to tell anyone until we came up with a plan.

"I can't tell anyone."

"Then how will you get help?"

I drop my head on the table and moan. Aniston ruffles my head, then sits in the chair beside me. I lift my head enough to see her and fold my arms under my chin.

"What if I guess what's going on? Then you won't have to tell me." Her mischievous smirk is back.

I like that idea, so I nod.

"Okay." She slaps her hands together, causing me to flinch. "Nate has a side piece in Atlanta."

I scrunch my forehead, then laugh when I realize what she means by that. "No!"

"Good, didn't think so." She stares at the ceiling for a beat. "Timothy's dad found out you're dating Nate."

I sit up. What a conundrum.

"Yes," I answer hesitantly.

"And how did that go?"

I take a deep breath. This is weird, and trying to skirt around the issue is even weirder.

"Timothy's dad loves Nate."

"Cool. Most people tend to be fond of handsome pro athletes. So he's jealous, then, right?"

"I wouldn't say jealous."

"Then what? Afraid Timothy will like Nate better than him?"

"Not that either."

Aniston pulls her long blond hair behind her head and lets it fall as she makes a frustrated noise. "You're killing me, Smalls! What's the problem?"

I close my eyes and silently pray she's good at keeping secrets. I've got to talk to someone close to me, but who doesn't have any relationship with Timothy or Nate. And I know for a fact Morgan can't keep a secret.

"Nate is Timothy's dad."

"I knew it!" She covers her mouth and shrieks.

"You didn't know it."

She moves her hands to the table. "May as well. I assumed it was him."

A hissing sound comes from the kitchen counter and Aniston jerks her head that direction.

"That's the coffee maker. Want anything?"

She flicks a caramel cappuccino K-cup my way. "But don't change the subject. Spill the tea while you make the coffee."

"Promise you won't tell a soul? I haven't told Timothy, or anyone else. We're waiting on the right time and way to do it."

She makes a cross motion over her head, torso, and shoulders.

I stand with her chosen flavor and start the machine as I give the facts only, not the detailed version of our last day together, taking a pregnancy test about a month later, and how I hid the father's identity.

"You should've told him. It would've turned out just fine."

"That's what he said last night." I groan and slide the coffee mug toward her.

"Thanks."

I nod and choose a vanilla pod for me.

"Everyone will be happy."

"I know, but you're missing the point."

"What?" She sips her cappuccino, then widens her eyes. "Let's see. The father of your child is the love of your life, who also happens to be rich, handsome, and athletic. Oh, and he and the boy love each other already. What could go wrong?"

I wait on my coffee to drain into the mug, then join her at

the table. "You didn't see his face. I hurt him more than I ever could've thought. It was horrific. And can you imagine delivering life-altering news to people you love?"

She clears her throat. "You mean like when I told Willow and Carter they would have to live with me because their parents died instantly in a plane crash?"

"Sorry." I stare at the table.

She touches my arm. "Hey, I wasn't meaning that as a jab against you. I'm just saying sometimes we have to say the hard things." She sighs. "Morgan was actually the one who had to tell them their parents died."

"Yeah." I stare at the tablecloth, remembering when that happened.

"It will be hard, but you'll get through it." Aniston gives my arm a squeeze before letting go. "There's no way I could've kept this a secret eight years."

I sit up and glare at her.

She lifts her hands. "I can now. I mean if I were you and it were me, and I had a kid."

"I understand." I allow my face to soften. "It was hard keeping it from my parents, but I suspect they know. They've always been supportive and never condemned or shamed me either. That made it easier." I slump down in the chair and glance out the window. "Nate coming back and living a mile away made it hard."

"I bet." Aniston sips her drink, then licks her top lip.

"There were days I wanted to tell him, even before we got involved again. It never seemed like the right time." I swallow some coffee to soothe my scratchy throat, then continue. "Last night we were walking in a familiar place, drinking familiar coffee, and talking about the past. It was too much pressure to keep it all in."

"You did the right thing."

"I hope so."

"You did." Aniston sets her mug on the table and leans

closer. "There's a reason they say the truth hurts, and sometimes it also hurts the person giving the truth."

I look her in the eye and frown.

We both glance out the window when we hear the boys laughing. They must be on the porch and possibly about to come inside.

Aniston faces me. "What do you want to do with Timothy? No offense, but you look like crap on a stick and could use some rest."

I laugh. "None taken. He can go to my parents'. They plan on going to the game."

She drains the last of her drink, then stands. "Tell you what. I can let him fish with Easton and Carter if that's fine with you, then bring him to the game. If you're still not up to it, he can go home with your parents."

On impulse, I spring from my chair and wrap her in a hug.

Aniston isn't the huggy-feely type, but she wraps her long, skinny arms around me. "You're welcome," she mumbles against my hair.

I let go. "Sorry about the hug."

"In high school I would've kicked you." She smirks. "Now I kinda like it."

I smile and follow her onto the porch, where the boys are chasing a frog. It jumps under the steps, and they lose it.

Timothy looks at me with concern. I must *really* look a mess. I wrap an arm around him. "I'm not feeling well, but Aniston said you can go fishing at her house with Carter and Dr. West."

His eyes light up and he nods enthusiastically.

"Why don't we pack you some more clothes and your baseball stuff. I'll catch up with y'all later."

I lead him inside while Aniston and Carter wait on the porch. Once we have him packed, he scans me up and down, as if silently assessing my condition. "Mama, are you okay?"

I nod, a nonverbal lie. "I need to rest. I had a rough night last night and didn't sleep well at all." That isn't a lie.

He hugs me, and I wrap him tightly, kissing the top of his head. I can't believe I deprived Nate of such a special boy. Considering this, I'm both shocked and thankful he reacted as calmly as he did.

Nate

Last night I couldn't sleep.

I tried all the tricks like melatonin gummies and staying off any screens, as well as what all the older people in Apple Cart swear by: warm milk, a shot of apple cider vinegar, and the hum of a box fan.

Nothing helped.

If anything, apple cider indirectly made me think of Brooke. That led down a deep trail of what could've beens, with me imagining our lives had she told me right away about Timothy.

In my mind, we would've married by the holidays and took a Christmas honeymoon. She would've moved to Atlanta, and I would've come up with some safe and clean living situation or died trying.

Whenever she wanted, she could've continued school in Atlanta or online. Worst case scenario, I would've convinced Mom to come live nearby and help with the baby. We would've made it work.

What's haunting me now is that we never got the chance to try.

I ate breakfast and lunch with Mom today. Partly

because I needed a distraction. However, it also helped comfort me to be with the only family I've always had within reach.

She just left for her usual grocery store trip, leaving me in an empty house with thoughts that are anything but empty.

I chug a bottle of water and crumple it in my hand, then toss it in the trash can. I lean against the kitchen sink and scan the oversized eating area. This house was large and impersonal before, but that's amplified by a thousand since I know I could have a family here.

The night we all ate together made it more like home than ever. I want that again. I want them here with me, forever, not just to share an occasional meal.

I'm not going to call or text Brooke today. I made myself promise I'd allow time to process things.

I reach for another bottle of water and notice the one sheet stuck to my refrigerator. It's the schedule for Timothy's games. I want to go watch my son.

Before I talk myself out of it, I grab the water and head for the garage. Halfway there, I realize I'm sock footed and turn around for some shoes.

The game is at our park in thirty minutes. That will give me plenty of time to get there and say hi to the kids. But I won't be there early enough to make things awkward between Brooke and me.

In a small town, if we don't talk, other people will—about us not talking.

Thanks to virtually no traffic, I arrive a little early. I sit in the truck a few minutes and watch for Brooke. Morgan walks my way at one point and I duck.

What am I doing? My long body is hunched on my floorboard. *Idiot.* Like they can't see my tall, bulky black truck in the parking lot.

I push myself back in the seat, groaning as my shoulder pops. Brooke will spot me eventually unless I watch the entire game from my truck. Again, that would make me look like a stalker.

Unless Jeffrey has me thrown out again.

I get out and pass a 6U game on the way to our field. Timothy spots me before I find any of our team.

"Hey, Nate!" He hugs me.

I hug him back as always, but this time it hits differently. Before, he was a cute kid I loved and admired. Now, he's my son. Technically he was always my son, but now our mutual admiration makes sense. And it chokes me up a bit.

Maybe coming here was a mistake?

Morgan whistles, and Timothy lets go of me to run to the dugout. I laugh, happy for her distraction from my too-deep moment.

"Hey, slugger."

I turn around to Aniston. She has a mischievous look.

"Hey." I nod at her, then cross my arms and turn toward the field.

She steps closer to me and whispers, "I know."

I ignore her. But inside I'm sweating. Does she know what I think she knows?

"I won't tell," she adds in another whisper.

I cut my eyes her way and find her staring at me. She takes a step away but keeps talking. I stay stone cold, arms crossed.

"Nobody else knows, not even Morgan."

My rigid posture relaxes slightly when she says Morgan doesn't know.

"Brooke was a mess when I brought Timothy home this morning."

That gets my attention. I face her and blink. "Where is she now?"

"Still at home. She was so upset, I pressed her to talk. I pretty much guessed it out of her, because she said she couldn't tell anyone. For what it's worth, she feels horrible about keeping this a secret so long. Nobody knows but me, and nobody will." She salutes me. "Scout's honor."

"You were a Girl Scout?"

"Heck, no!" She holds up her hand. "Pinky swear?"

I sigh and hook my pinky with hers.

"Ouch," she says.

"Sorry. Your fingers are wiry."

She shakes out her hand.

"You know, I lived through both parents dying and didn't take it well at all. When I heard the news about my sister and brother-in-law's plane crash, I wanted to die too." She shuffles uncomfortably. "I had nobody left but Willow and Carter. Then they tell me I need to come raise them. Me, a hippy backpacker, raise two kids." She laughs.

I chuckle a little too.

"Scared as I was, taking in those two and moving back here was the best thing that ever happened to me." She sighs and shakes her head. "Would I bring Jennifer and Luke back? In an instant. But we don't get to go back, we only get to go forward. Life isn't always as it should be, but we can make it into what it needs to be."

I stare at her. That's the most profound thing I've ever heard Aniston say. Of course, I've never spent much time around her. When we were in high school, she stayed away from the crowd and gave condescending jabs at all the athletes and people who actually cared about school.

"That's very wise and thoughtful."

She smiles at me. "It took a while, but I finally realized everyone has problems, even the ones who seemed perfect in high school."

"I hate you didn't hang out with everyone more. You'd see none of us had that easy of a life. I barely remember my dad."

Aniston frowns. "I bet that makes this Timothy bombshell even worse."

I nod, then pop my knuckles. The crowd cheers as two of

our players score. Aniston claps, and I join her. I came to watch the game, but haven't paid much attention until now.

"I want what's best for him, no matter what."

"It will work out. He needs both of you, and you two need each other. She still looks at you like she did in high school, you know."

I smile. "I do."

There's those two words again, strung together like a lasting promise. Maybe I can say them to Brooke one day and have them declare my lifelong allegiance to her—and Timothy.

We stand on the slight hill watching the game. It's nearing the end, and I need to decide if I want to stick around or go home.

At the top of the last inning, I turn to Aniston. "I want to protect Timothy at all costs, so you can't say anything to anyone."

"I won't." She half smiles.

"I'm leaving tonight. I don't want to burden Brooke by showing up at church in the morning."

Aniston's face falls. "I think you two really need to talk."

"We will." I glance toward the field one more time. "When I figure out what I'm going to say."

Before she can respond, I head for my truck. In a perfect world, I would stay. I would hug Timothy and kiss Brooke after the game. Then we'd all eat dinner together and relax on the porch.

But as Aniston pointed out, life isn't always as it should be. I do know what it needs to be, but I need to figure out how to get there.

CHAPTER 26

Brooke

This time when I hear a knock, I go straight to the door.

It's Aniston with Timothy and Carter. They all come inside. Timothy rushes toward me, talking about the game. He ends with asking how I'm feeling.

"A little better. I've mainly laid around and read in my room."

"Nate was at the game." He smiles.

I glance at Aniston. She gives me a look that says we need to talk, then she eyes the boys.

"Your parents were at the game, but Timothy wanted to ride with us since we stopped by Double Drive for milkshakes after the game."

"How much do I owe you?" I start toward the kitchen, where I last left my purse.

She lifts a hand. "It's fine. Your dad gave him money for hitting the ball, which more than paid for it."

I roll my eyes.

"I wanted to check on you anyway."

I watch the boys chatting on the couch, then inhale and hold my breath a second before letting it out. "Timothy, why don't you show Carter your new game?"

"Oh yeah!" He runs upstairs with Carter behind him.

I collapse on the couch, and Aniston sits on the opposite end.

"You look depressed. I'm not sure staying home was the best idea for you."

"Today I identify as a librocubicularist."

"Huh?"

"Someone who reads books in bed. It's very therapeutic. You should try it sometime."

Aniston shakes her head. "I'm good. I have caffeine and cookie crack."

I pull my knees to my chest.

"I saw him at the game, and we had a little chat." Aniston sighs.

"What did you say?" I glare at her.

I've never been known for intimidation. She laughs, proving I still can't pull it off.

"I could tell he was nervous being there, but he really wanted to watch Timothy."

"Okay, but what did you say?"

"Long story short, he knows I know."

I smack her across the face with a throw pillow. She shoves it back at me.

"You said you wouldn't tell!"

"I won't, but the man looked like someone had run over his dog."

I groan and shove my fingers in my hair, now thankful I made myself shower.

"I know, and you know I know, and he knows I know. That's all. No more knowing. I won't even tell Easton."

Aniston lifts both hands as if surrendering. I really want to trust her, but my stomach is knotted to no end. I haven't eaten anything except one bowl of cereal around noon, so that might be it.

"If you tell anyone else—"

"I won't." She salutes me. "Scout's honor."

"When were you a scout?"

She rolls her eyes and mumbles what sounds like, "You two deserve each other."

"What?"

"I said you two were made for each other. You need to talk."

"Cliché as it sounds, it's complicated. I can't go over there with Timothy home. He'll want to go, and then it will be awkward."

"You don't have to worry about that. He's going back tonight. He said he didn't want to make church weird for you."

I drop my feet to the floor and toss my head back against the couch.

"It will all work out."

"Don't put false hope in my head, Aniston."

"I'm not, but it will. Take me, for example." She sits taller and runs her hand down her side like Vanna White presenting a letter. "Would you have ever pictured me living in Apple Cart, engaged to a doctor, raising two kids?"

"No, not at all."

"Yet here I am."

"And when we were in high school, where would you have pictured me in ten years?"

She shrugs. "Living on this farm, married to Nate."

"Exactly." I shove a finger toward her face. "So what makes you think it will happen that way for me?"

"Because as weird as this sounds, I believe in fairy tales and happy endings. Even though Jennifer's life was cut short, she got a fairy tale with Luke. I don't deserve Easton, but I have a fairy tale with him. If anyone deserves a fairy tale, it's you, Brooke Marshall. You've always been a kind and hardworking person, and you deserve to be with Nate."

Tears fill my eyes. I sniffle. "I thought you hated me in high school."

"I kinda did." She scrunches her nose. "But I hated everyone who was happy and had both their parents. That was my own hang-up. You were always nice to everyone, and you and Nate had something special."

"So many times, I wanted to tell him." I sigh and wipe my tears. "Then he got moved to the majors, and finally he got to start games. Every time I came close, his career advanced. I couldn't risk ruining everything he'd worked for."

She scoots closer and rubs my arm. "I'm sure it would've been fine."

I shrug.

"There's never a good time to give life-altering news. It's best to just get it out in the open quickly, like ripping off a Band-Aid." She mimics ripping one from her leg. It's so dramatic, I flinch.

"Well, I did tell him . . . finally. And now the ball's in his court—or on his field might be the better metaphor."

Aniston moves a pillow off her and twists toward me. "The man loves you, and he'll be back. He had to go to back to Florida anyway, so it's not like he's leaving you."

"But what if he decides to never come back here? What if all this is too much, and it's easier for him to go back to life without us?"

She laughs. "I don't think that's possible."

"But Timothy doesn't yet know, so it would be the easiest option." I tilt my head and frown.

"Honey, if we took the easiest option, not a one of us would be dealing with Little League right now."

I sigh. "True."

Aniston stands, then pats me on the head. "Are you going to be okay if I leave?"

I nod. "I have Timothy."

My throat closes on the last syllable of his name. I do have Timothy, as well as my family. I know I have Morgan and Aniston, and any number of people in town, at work, and from church too.

That had always been enough for me. Until now.

I pray Nate doesn't decide to stay in Atlanta. I want him in our lives now more than ever.

Nate

The season is starting this week, and Coach is talking about starting me on Opening Day at home.

That's a huge honor for any pitcher. After all I've been through, it's even more of an honor. I've literally worked toward this my entire life.

I rotate my arm a few times and step out of the bullpen.

We have several good pitchers who can easily get us a win. All younger than me too.

According to statistics, we start to decline at twenty-six. Considering I'm coming off a bad injury and on the back end of twenty-seven, it's a miracle I'm still here. Add to that the superstitions that loom over the baseball world, and I'm even more shocked I'm a contender.

I grab my water bottle and chug lukewarm water as I walk toward the field.

Staring at the mound brings up memories of the first game I pitched in the majors. It was three seasons ago, when we still had Dom as our catcher. That was the most emotional day I'd had in a while. Happy, excited, nervous, and grateful—all in one ball of emotions.

It was an odd mix of feelings that gave me an out-of-this-world tingle. Like I was an invincible superhero who could conquer anything.

I've been chasing that high ever since, afraid I'd never feel it again. I hadn't, until I saw Brooke again.

My chest tightens at the thought of her.

We haven't talked since that night. And I can't decide if going to Timothy's game was good or bad.

I got some valuable advice from Aniston. I also got to see Timothy and the boys play ball before I left.

On the flipside, Brooke was so hurt, she didn't even go to the game.

It was like when we were ten and Paul got a shipment of new baseball cards at the General Store. He kept them locked up behind a glass, and you couldn't touch them unless you bought them. I'd put my face to the glass and stare at the details. Being so close, yet so out of reach, made me want them even more.

Same with Brooke, except on a much higher level.

I lean against the wall in front of a huge State Farm logo and pull my phone from my pocket.

It's Saturday afternoon and I just threw some awesome strikes. For the first time in months, my arm doesn't hurt. There's a good chance I'll actually throw the first pitch in the Braves' season opener. Six-year-old me would pee his pants at this news. I should be elated. Instead, all I can think about is Brooke.

She's third on my call list. Right under my trainer, who follows Mom. I click her photo and hold the phone to my ear.

My stomach buckles as it continues to ring and ring and ring. Right before I hang up, she answers.

"Hello?" Her voice is a little rushed.

"Hey, Brooke."

Silence. A small twitch churns in my chest like a tiny hammer hitting my heart. Clearly, I will need to carry the conversation.

"I hope you're having a good day. I wanted to call and say I love you more than anything. I love Timothy too."

A sniffle comes across the line. I hope it's sinuses, but I'm more certain it's tears. When she speaks, it confirms my suspicions.

"We love you too." Her voice is shaky.

Now my heart completely breaks knowing she's hours away and I can't hold her while she's hurting. Even worse, I'm the source of her hurt.

"I'll be back in Apple Cart as soon as I can. The season's starting. But I want us to talk as much as possible. I want to talk to Timothy too, maybe FaceTime or something."

She exhales into the phone. A few long seconds pass, then she speaks. "I want that too. But you can't tell him over the phone. We've got to make it as normal as possible." She lets out a tense laugh. "Not that any of this is normal."

"Yeah, but whose life is normal?" I wipe my brow and adjust my cap.

"Funny, Aniston said pretty much the same thing to me recently."

"Yeah, she's a lot wiser than she's let on all these years."

This time her laugh is genuine, and it makes me smile.

"Whatever you decide is best will be what's best for Timothy. I'll give you full control of this since you're the one who really knows him."

She groans, and my stomach drops.

"I didn't mean anything by that other than you do know him best."

"I know." She swallows. "I already feel guilty for keeping him from you this long."

"It's fine. It did sting, but I get it." After a long pause, I try and lighten the mood. "Besides, there's plenty of MLB players with secret babies." I chuckle.

"In a weird way, that helps a little."

"Good, because I love you both, and I want us to be a family."

"I want that too," she whispers.

"I want us to talk while I'm gone. I want to talk to Timothy and assure him I'm coming back. But you talk to me about anything at all—including the big news, if you want. I'm here Brooke, forever."

My heart beats faster, as if the word "forever" climbed from my chest up my throat and out of my mouth like a throttle.

"Now that the hard stuff is out of the way, I also wanted to say y'all can use my shop and property for practices and stuff."

"Thanks."

"There's a key to the shop and my house hidden in the ceramic frog's mouth by the pool."

She laughs. "I wondered why you kept that ugly thing out there."

"It seemed like a convenient location for hiding small objects."

And that's the only reason I kept it, especially out in the open. Paul gave it to me as a housewarming gift not long after I moved in. I'm almost certain he came by to snoop so he could gossip about what I'd done with the place. Most people hadn't been inside the mansion in years. But he left me a heavy ceramic frog that he said would ward off bugs.

That's not true. I've shaken spiders and caterpillars off the thing several times. However, with all the crap Paul sells, I consider myself lucky.

"We won't use your place unless necessary."

"No, I insist. You go there anytime, for any reason. I hate not being there to help them."

"Thank you, Nate."

I straighten my cap and turn from the setting sun. "Of course."

"I wasn't talking about your property." She swallows again. "Thanks for not hating me."

"Brooke, I could never hate you. Even when I wanted to hate you, I couldn't. Trust me, hating you would've made the first few years after our breakup so much easier."

"Hating you would've made my life easier too." She almost laughs, but it turns to a sigh.

"The only easy thing I've done in my life is love you, and that's the only easy thing I want to do."

"I love you too." Her voice is less stressed.

I relax my shoulders at her calmer tone.

"Nate, can we go ahead and get your comments?" a voice calls from outside the field.

I turn to a reporter standing at the bottom of the stadium seats. "Yeah." I hold up my finger for her to wait.

"That's a sports reporter wanting an interview. I gotta go, but I'll talk to you soon."

"Okay, love you."

"Love you too." I cut the call and head for the gate.

Time to get back to work.

CHAPTER 27

Brooke

I never thought I'd stick my hand down a frog's throat. At least it's a fake frog. I ease my fingers into the ceramic mouth and fumble around until I feel something wiggle.

"Ahh!" I jerk my hand out and wipe it down my shirt.

"What's wrong?" Timothy bends down and stares at the frog.

A small worm slithers out of the frog's mouth. He laughs and picks up the creature.

"Let it go someplace else."

He moves toward the grass with the worm in tow, while I untuck my T-shirt. I stretch the end enough to form a makeshift glove over my hand before going back in there.

Growing up at an apple orchard, I've seen my fair share of worms. I also have a dad and two brothers who like to fish and taught me how to bait my own hooks. But I'd prefer to see the worm before I feel it.

I cup my covered hand around a keychain and pull it out.

My shirt is stained with pollen and dust, and the two keys look the same.

With only two, it shouldn't be hard to find the right one. I walk to the garage and try both. Of course it's the second one.

Smothering heat welcomes me when I step inside. The fluorescent lights make a slight buzzing sound as I flip the switch. First thing I do is cut on the air conditioner and realize I probably should've gotten here sooner than twenty minutes before everyone else.

All the equipment is in the usual locations and ready for use.

I fan my face and try to push the larger door up to let out some of the pent-up air. It's even heavier than it looks. I grit my teeth and squat lower to give it an extra push.

After another shove, it lifts.

"Hello, darling." Morgan grins at me from the other side.

"You showed up just in time."

She laughs and crosses the threshold. "I could tell from the slight shaking it had to be your scrawny butt in here trying to lift it."

"How do you know it wasn't Timothy?"

She cocks her head toward the pool. I crane my neck and find him chasing something.

"He was trying to get a lizard with a worm in its mouth."

"Well, that takes care of that." I step back and scan the space. "Any plans for tonight's practice?"

"Use all this nice stuff." Morgan laughs. "But Ethan's coming to help too, since he doesn't have practice."

I glance around the room as I fan my face. "We did hit the jackpot with this facility."

"More like you hit the jackpot with the owner." Morgan elbows me and winks.

My face flushes. We have one major kink to work out, but it is nice to know that Nate is back—especially back with me.

"What about him starting in the season opener?"

"Hmm?"

"I'm sure he told you already." She fans her hand dismissively.

No, he hasn't told me.

"I saw the YouTube clip this morning." She pulls out her phone and brings up a video.

It's hard to tell much with her horribly cracked screen, but I can distinctly hear Nate talking to a reporter about the game.

"Morgan, this says he's a probable starting pitcher."

I take her phone and click to start the next suggested video. A younger guy talks to the same woman about pitching on Opening Day.

Morgan grabs her phone and shoves it under her bra strap. A little disturbing since I didn't notice where she had it before. I possibly held Morgan's boob sweat.

I wipe my hand down the shirt soiled with fake-frog-mouth dirt and worm slime just to be safe.

It's hard not to think about Nate starting on Opening Day. That's been his dream for as long as I've known him. Along with most every baseball pitcher, I imagine.

Although I want him here with us, I can't let him do anything to jeopardize that. He's not getting any younger, and he already survived one injury.

"So I'm thinking you in the batting cage with the tee, Ethan helping with form, Easton and Carlton helping with fly balls . . ." Morgan pauses.

I turn to her staring at me.

"You with me, Brooke?"

"Yeah, just thinking."

She opens her mouth, but voices interrupt us before she can speak. I drop my shoulders and sigh in relief. Everyone else showing up for practice possibly saved me from Morgan's meddling.

I can't take another heart-to-heart about my feelings.

Aniston already guessed what was going on between us. Although this is more about Nate pitching, the whole Timothy deal is still the underlying factor of everything.

If Morgan finds out, we may as well print it in the *Apple Cart Weekly*. It may take a week to come out, but that's plenty of time for it to spread through the Pig and Adrianne's hair salon.

Why do we still have a paper? We'd be better off letting Morgan be the town crier.

Georgia walks up, all smiles, rolling the golf bag behind her. "Ladies, how's it going?"

"Where's Carlton?" Morgan asks.

Her face falls, but she ignores the question.

"We're good, Georgia. How are you?" I smile.

Then I slip Morgan a side-eye. It doesn't work. She crosses her arms as if waiting for an answer.

"He had a medical emergency."

"He's a pharmacist," Morgan huffs.

"Yeah, well some of the dishes for a bride's china registry still haven't arrived and her shower is this weekend."

Morgan narrows her eyes. I swallow a laugh. Every large pharmacy in the South also has an even larger gift shop. Georgia often brags about the items they offer at her husband's store, so I assume she's the one making this a big deal.

"As urgent as that sounds, I planned on him helping with fly balls tonight."

"I can help with that." Georgia beams.

Morgan looks her up and down, then turns to me. I fold my arms over the stains on my old shirt. Georgia is dressed like a professional tennis player, but with high-heel sandals instead of tennis shoes.

She smiles at us and pulls a golf club from the bag. "I still have this driver in here. I can hit the balls up for them."

Morgan lifts her hands in defeat. "Fine by me. I need to

work with them on grounders, and you'd break an ankle trying that."

Georgia grins and turns, pulling her bag with her. I watch her ponytail swish as she trots toward everyone else.

Morgan shakes her head, then turns to the crowd clogging up the garage door opening. She lets out a loud whistle, and kids and adults all stand to attention.

My phone rings on my way to the group. I veer off and go toward the pool when I see Nate's name. I answer it and sit in a patio chair.

"Hey," he says.

"Hey, how's your day been?"

"Good, but tiring. I've got another workout, but wanted to call real quick and make sure you got in."

"Yeah, we're about to practice now."

"Good. Just keep those keys with you if you want. Nobody else should need to get in before I'm back."

"I can do that." I stare at my shirt in relief at not having to reach in the frog again.

"Good. I've got to do some more strength training tonight. If everything keeps going so well, they may start me Friday."

"That's awesome!" I try and sound surprised enough to make him think this is new news, but not so surprised to make him think I don't think he can start.

"I'll call y'all later. Love you."

"I love you too."

He hangs up and I stare at the phone for a beat before standing. Morgan is splitting people into groups across the yard. This probably looks like a three-ring circus compared to whatever Nate is used to at the Braves.

He must really love me to want to come back.

I rush around like a chicken with my head cut off, making sure Timothy has all his baseball gear.

Tonight is the first game in the season-ender. We play against the other park team our age for the title of Apple Cart County 8U Baseball Park Champs. Not the most coveted title, unless you're an eight-year-old boy going up against Jeffrey's stacked travel-ball players.

We've practiced Monday, Tuesday, and Thursday nights for this. Our kids have improved plenty, and it's been several weeks since we've faced Jeffrey's team.

As stressed as this makes me, Aniston is worse. She made Morgan sign an agreement saying she won't have the kids roll the ball. She claims Angela Basset, a local lawyer in town, signed it too. I think she's bluffing, but she did give Morgan a warning glare.

My phone rings, and Timothy answers it. I glance at the clock on the kitchen oven. It must be Nate.

"It's Nate." He grins.

I nod and smile. He'd called me earlier and said he wanted to FaceTime Timothy before his game.

Timothy plops down on the couch and talks to him. I hear bits and pieces of the conversation as I rush back and forth, packing waters and wiping up crumbs from Timothy eating a snack.

The way these tournaments work is the first team to take two out of three games wins. We play one game tonight and in the morning for sure, then possibly a tiebreaker after that.

"Mama, Nate wants to talk to you."

My stomach buckles for a split second. Surely he isn't wanting to talk about *that* over FaceTime. Just in case, I snatch the phone to where Timothy can no longer see him.

"Hey."

"Hey, I mentioned a penny I got when I was Timothy's age. I want him to have it for good luck."

"Now?" I glance at the microwave.

We really need to leave in a few minutes.

"It's in my bedroom on the dresser. Not hard to find. Use the other key on that ring to get in."

"Okay." I look at Timothy. "Grab your bag so we'll have time to get the penny."

"Good luck tonight."

"Thanks." I glance at the stairs, where Timothy is running toward his room. "I gotta go. Love you."

"Love you too." He smiles.

I smile back and end the call.

My mom mode kicks into high gear as I pack a Bogg bag with all the things. Then I dig in my purse for Nate's keys I stowed away. When Timothy comes downstairs with his ball bag, I'm armed and ready to go.

Without saying anything, we rush to the car and drive to Nate's. I park and leave the car running for Timothy to have air. "This will only take a few minutes."

He nods, and I hurry up the path. I unlock and push open the heavy wooden door. It's much thicker than most doors and has a lot of carved detailing that I'm sure adds to the weight.

My biceps pulse as I shove it closed behind me. Nate's master suite takes up one whole half of the upstairs. I hope the penny is where he said and easy to spot. Too bad it's one of those souvenir pennies from a machine. Otherwise, I'd be tempted to pull one from my purse.

I take the stairs two at a time, which isn't easy with short legs. I'm out of breath by the time I reach Nate's room.

It's dark and big, but more lived in than the only other time I've seen it. When he gave us a tour of the house, there were basic furnishings and curtains. He's now added a large area rug, some lamps, and a few wall hangings.

A slight flutter skips in my heart at the thought of him making this place home. The thought of him making Apple Cart home.

I cross the room to the dresser. Sure enough, the penny is front and center, as if he left it there for me to find. As I'm reaching for it, I see something in the mirror above.

Is that?

I drop my hand and go to his bed. There is a nightstand with a lamp on each side. One table also has a small picture of us at senior prom, as well as a plate.

The plate.

It's a dingy white restaurant plate with a faint kiss mark at the bottom. Above the lip print is "Brooke's Home Plate" in my handwriting.

I stand frozen, staring at the plate. It's on a small easel. How long has he had it on display? Did he do this hoping I'd find it today?

Either way, the fact that he kept it in pristine condition after all this time with all his moving around leaves me in awe.

"Mama!"

I jerk my head toward the open door. Timothy's voice calls from downstairs, "Did you find it? We need to leave."

"Yep, coming!" I yell back.

I shake my head to try and shake the shock and dash toward the dresser. A minute later, I'm jogging downstairs with the penny.

But all I can think about is the plate I gave him the last time we were together.

CHAPTER 28

Nate

"Miller, get off the phone. We need you to warm up."

I shove my phone in my bag and out of the way. Easton promised to put the kids' game on Game Changer for me.

This is Timothy's final tournament for the park-ball championship. If I can't be there, I at least want to keep up with it best I can.

"What's going on?" my pitching coach asks.

"Nothing."

I shrug off the questions and head toward the pen. My arm has been on fire this week—in a good way. I've been throwing sick pitches and it's barely bothered my shoulder.

"Nate the Great!"

I turn toward the seats and find a little boy rushing toward the barrier. An older woman comes behind him, trying to keep up. He's barely above the wall, but reaches a souvenir ball over. "Can you sign this?"

"Of course." I take the ball and smile. "Uh, do you have a pen?"

"Here." The woman hands a marker to me.

I scribble my signature. "What's your name, son?"

"John."

I write "To John" more legibly above my name. Then I blow on the ball to dry out the marker before handing it back.

"Thanks." He lifts his head and smiles, showing a few missing teeth.

"Thank you so much." The woman presses her lips together sweetly.

"You're welcome, ma'am. I hope y'all enjoy the game."

She nods and takes the kid's arm as they walk away. Most likely to keep him from venturing off too far ahead.

I remove my cap and run my hand over my hair. Now that I know Timothy is mine, I can't stop thinking about him, or missing him. I miss Brooke even more too, knowing we created this precious person together.

Aaron walks by, popping his knuckles. He bumps me slightly with his shoulder. I know it's intentional. I choose not to say anything and let him keep walking. I'm starting, so nothing he can say matters much now.

He's just as good as me, if not better. A small part of me wonders if the coaches aren't rewarding me for coming back from an injury. Even worse, if they're throwing me a bone since this might be my last time to shine above him.

I puff up my cheeks and blow into my hands. I'm starting in the opening game. I had to claw my way off the injured list.

But all I can think about is a Little League game. I stare at the time on the scoreboard. Timothy's game is just starting. A lot of good that does me when my phone is out of reach.

I continue to the bullpen and begin warming up. I hear the announcer give out the starting lineups. My pulse ticks higher when my name is called and the crowd cheers, but I try to keep my focus. Fireworks shoot around us with every name announced.

I take a pause while the National Anthem is sung with a giant flag flying in the background. I hold my cap across my chest but only half hear the song. Everything is a blur against the adrenaline of soon taking the mound and everything waiting for me back in Apple Cart.

When I'm finished with my pitches, I make the walk to the dugout with our catcher. The crowd cheers. I wave and nod, scanning the stands.

Our manager meets me at the dugout steps with a goofy grin slapped across his face. He pats my shoulder as we continue walking in our respective directions.

I rub my chin as my cheeks climb to a smile. This is the moment I've waited for all my life.

I'm barely inside when a hard squeeze falls on my shoulder. I turn to Ace shaking it.

"Opening Day starting pitcher! That's what I'm talking about."

I smile.

He plops down beside me and rips open a bag of sunflower seeds. "Why are you not more excited?"

"I'm not a super excited guy."

He laughs. "Yeah, but you look like someone ran over your dog and kicked the carcass."

"My mind's elsewhere. That's all."

He scoffs. "Well, you best get it in the game. We need you."

I nod. "Noted."

I smile, but this time it's forced. My gaze falls to the small pile of sunflower seeds Ace spits to the side. It reminds me of when the kids played the team that chewed Nicorette and got sick. I laugh, causing Ace to stare at me.

"Good. You found a good mood. Stay that way."

I ignore him and focus on the ballpark in front of me. We're called to take the field a few seconds later.

Ace hurls a wad of sunflower seeds in the corner and grabs his glove. I grab mine and jog toward the mound. I only faintly hear the crowd, as I've learned to tune them out.

When I hit a mound, it's like living in a bubble. Pitching is my escape. The only time I let any outside influence rattle me was early on when Brooke broke up with me.

Until now.

My hand sweats inside my glove and my stomach knots. As much as I want to be here, I really want to be somewhere else.

Specifically in Apple Cart with Brooke and Timothy.

I throw the first pitch. A strike. The second, a little outside. I pitch more strikes. He fouls one, but I get him with my heater.

Good start.

We continue the inning, allowing only one run. Two of the three outs were by me at the plate. I should be elated.

But I'm not. This suddenly feels like I'm living out someone else's dream. Maybe my old dream.

Whatever the case, it's not delivering the high I've been chasing. An inner struggle of guilt for not feeling grateful and guilt for not being where I belong rolls through me.

The batters get ready, including my DH. I fumble for a ball. It's time to do what I planned on doing one day. I just planned on it being a few years down the road.

I roll the ball across my palm and stand. I look at Aaron across the bench. He's ready. More ready than me.

I grab a pen from the corner of the dugout and scribble something, then hustle toward the manager. I walk up to him and hand him the ball.

"What's this?" He frowns as he stares at it.

"Turn it around."

He spins the ball to see what I wrote. "I'm through. For

Love of the Game." He snorts. "What the Billy Chapel is this?"

"My retirement letter."

"Whoa, whoa, whoa, Miller." He stands, knocking the chair over. "You struck out two players in the opening inning of Opening Day. And now you want to retire? Are you on drugs?"

"No, but I have a family I need to get home to."

"I'll move your mama's trailer here myself if that's what this is about."

"Not my mama, the love of my life."

He rolls his eyes. "Good Lord, I thought baseball was the love of your life."

"It was just a placeholder." I nod toward Aaron. "He's ready, and he wants it."

"And you don't?"

I shrug. "I already started the game. Checked that off my bucket list."

"Even after all you've been through with the injury and stuff."

"If I truly thought y'all needed me to win the game and this season, I'd stay. But there's a lot of talent on this team, and my heart is elsewhere."

He shakes his head and laughs. "There's no coming back from this."

"I know. But I've put in my years." I look at Aaron on the bench. "Time to retire and give someone else a shot."

The skipper leans closer to me. "If you think I should put in Aaron, I will, but I want one more inning out of you."

He tosses the ball back, and I catch it. I grin and turn it over in my hand.

"Maybe I'll draft something more legit about my retirement and submit it to the team?"

He nods. "That would be wise."

I walk back to the dugout, half-deflated, half-happy. This next inning will be my last to pitch.

Might as well go out on top.

Brooke

"Mama, Nate isn't pitching this inning."

I lean to the edge of the booth to get a better look. Mary brought in a large TV for this very occasion. And from the crowd of people eating around it, I'd say it's here to stay.

"It's fine, Timothy. MLB players aren't known for pitching full games."

He spouts out a few semi-familiar names from history of guys who pitched complete games.

"That's a very low percentage of all the games among all the teams of all time."

He frowns, then nods. I lift my lips to try and convince him it's fine. I stroke his hair and try to ignore my nerves firing with worry.

Is Nate injured again?

If it happened on the mound, they might announce it on TV. But if he's suffering silently in the dugout—as Nate would—there's no way of me knowing.

The last thing I want is for him to be in pain. Lord knows I've caused him enough emotional pain lately. He doesn't need his shoulder to bum out too.

"He did a great job when he did pitch. They're probably letting him rest," my mama reassures Timothy.

He half smiles at her and my dad in the other side of the booth. I doubt they're letting him rest as a reward for getting so many outs in two innings. That's a typical response from my mother, but one I don't argue with for the sake of moving on. Anything to pretend Nate isn't hurt.

Mary brings food to our table. Daddy unrolls his fork, then stops when Mama gives him a look.

"I'll pray," he says. He clears his throat and blesses the food, adding in a thanks for Timothy's team playing hard. This is a typical Daddy response, since they got beat. I silently pray for Nate.

As soon as Daddy says "amen," he digs into his chicken. Timothy eats a few fries, but in a zombie-like state, with his eyes glued to the TV across the room.

I almost tell him to eat and not worry about the game, then decide better. In between conversations about what time the game will start tomorrow and what needs to be done with apple fritters, I catch myself sneaking peeks of the TV.

"Mama, does Nate have his phone in the dugout?"

I laugh. "No, sweetie."

Daddy and Mama laugh too.

"What?" he asks.

"It's a rule," Daddy clarifies.

"As soon as the game is over, can I call him about our game? I need some strategies for tomorrow."

"As soon as this game ends, you'll be in the bed." I nod at the TV.

He groans.

"We have to be at the field at nine tomorrow to warm up. You need your sleep."

"Okay." He rests his head in his hand and lazily bites into a chicken tender.

"I'll bring over some apple muffins for breakfast, if that helps. I have to get up early and make a ton anyway," Mama says.

"So you won't be at my game?" Timothy asks.

She wipes her mouth and glances at me.

"Why don't y'all win the first game, so then Granny and Smith can have a later game to watch."

Mama moves her napkin to reveal a smirk.

"I like that idea," Daddy agrees.

"Me too." Timothy perks up for the first time since he announced Nate was on the bench.

How awesome it would be for us to beat Jeffrey's team. However, based on tonight's performance, it would take a miracle.

CHAPTER 29

Brooke

The dew brushes my ankles as I drag a cooler through the overgrown grass around the parking lot. This would be a great time for Jeffrey to run the lawn mower unannounced. Except he'd only want to cut the field and inconvenience everyone practicing.

Timothy bounces ahead of me, anxious to get the day started. How long of a day will be determined after this first game.

If we lose, it's over. If we win, we play the Red Armadillos one more time for the championship.

Of all the games we've played this season, including tournaments, today is the most pivotal. It's not the cheesy rings or even ending the year on a win that's my motivation. It's beating Jeffrey's team.

He needs knocked down a few notches.

Morgan steps toward us with a value-size bag of off-brand

cheese balls. She holds it up for me, but I wave it away. "I haven't even finished my coffee." I take a sip from the cup in my hand.

She shrugs and lifts a fistful of puffs to her mouth. Andrew and Timothy file off toward the batting cages.

"We've got a lot of work to do. Where is everybody?" She scans the parking lot behind us. "I told them to be here at nine." She eats more puffs, then turns to me as she chews. "I want to practice so we can beat those snobs."

I let out a huge sigh.

As if right on cue, Jeffrey and his entourage of overgrown idiots march our way. Morgan wipes cheese dust down her leg and rolls up the bag. By the time they reach us, her arms are crossed so tightly, she's crushing the puffs.

Jeffrey rips his Pit Vipers off and narrows his eyes. Between his smoldering stare and the dramatic reveal, it's like watching a Michael Jackson music video.

"Are y'all ready to get this over with?" His voice is soiled with sarcasm and a dash of confidence.

"Excuse me?" Morgan snaps back.

Easton and Aniston come up with their wagon.

"What's going on?" Easton grins.

Either he's oblivious to the tension or he's playing dumb for amusement's sake. Knowing Dr. West, it could be either. Whatever the case, it causes Jeffrey to stand down and continue toward the concession stand, minions following.

"Let's get to work!" Morgan throws her hands up, dropping the cheese puffs.

Easton and Aniston nod. We hurry to the batting cages and find Andrew pitching to Timothy. Easton takes over pitching, and the rest of the team trickles in a few minutes later.

I chug my coffee, and the last drop hits my stomach like a bolt of lightning. Maybe I should've taken Morgan up on those cheese balls. Empty stomach or not, I know it's my nerves.

I watch the rest of the kids hit, then take our cooler to the dugout. Jeffrey has his arsenal on the home side, which leaves us with the less desirable visitors' dugout.

Bradley comes out of nowhere, hands on hips, cowboy hat tilted down, like he's a Western gunslinger, ready to draw at a moment's notice.

"Has anyone flipped a coin?" He looks at me, then across the field at Jeffrey.

"Not to my knowledge." I answer.

Jeffrey stays silent.

"All right, since Jeffrey made his team home, looks like your team can be home next game." Bradley tips his hat to me.

Jeffrey cackles and returns to his dugout. He doesn't even have to say "like there's going to be a next game." His laugh says it for him.

I try and ignore him and hope for a miracle. Our kids hit well in the cage. They're now warming up in the outfield with Morgan, Easton, and Carlton.

Bradley puts on his protective gear to umpire, then reattaches his sheriff's radio. The crowd starts filling the bleachers, making it become real. This could very well be our last game of the season.

I pull out my phone and hover over Nate's contact. I'd texted him congratulations late last night after their win. He texted me back "Love you."

I wanted to call and talk to him about it, but decided to wait. He didn't pitch but two innings, and the game ended pretty late. I'm sure he's tired, and I don't want to bring up anything that might upset him about not finishing the game.

Baseball is stressful! Especially when you have two different guys playing on two very different levels at the same time.

Bradley calls Morgan and Jeffrey to the pitcher's circle and lays out the rules of the game. I snatch her cheese puffs and eat a handful. They taste like cardboard dipped in parmesan. I frown and grab a Gatorade to wash them down.

We have first at-bat since Jeffrey weaseled his way to being home team. I stand by first base, a ball of nerves with every play. The game goes by in a blur.

Jeffrey's voice scrapes my ear like fingernails on a chalkboard. He has to say something with every pitch.

"Elbows up . . . You've got two on you . . . Good eye . . . Fifth pitch . . . Load up."

I crane my neck and blink at the sun. This is getting annoying. But the good news is some of his heavy hitters aren't performing as well as usual.

We're tied up with one inning to go. Morgan stretches her arm. I don't see her lasting another game. She gives me a tired grin from the pitcher's circle.

Our starting batter is up and gets a double. Everyone cheers, and I hold my waist so I don't throw up. Timothy is up next. He pops up, and they catch his ball.

"It's okay, son, good hit." I say it just loud enough for him to hear me.

He gives me a sad nod and hustles to the dugout. We only score two runs before Jeffrey's team is up to bat. We've got to hold them.

Jeffrey is now wearing his fake sleeve as if he needs it for the closer. I bite my thumbnail from inside the dugout. Maybe he's feeling the pressure as much as me, because he looks a little distracted.

In between pitches, I follow his gaze toward our bleachers. Tami sits at the top in a miniskirt, eating a pickle-sickle in a very suggestive manner. Jeffrey's next pitch bounces in the dirt.

The kid holds the bat, and Bradley calls him out.

"That was the fifth pitch! Why didn't you swing?" Jeffrey

yells.

Bradley comes toward him with a stern stare. Jeffrey wiggles his jaw as if trying to contain more outbursts, but stops when Bradley faces him.

They have a few words on the field, then Bradley goes back behind the plate. Jeffrey's son, Conner, steps to the plate. I count at least three necklaces between gold chains and bedazzled gems on the kid. He's also outfitted with a fake sleeve and Pit Vipers, which I find strange for batting.

The Red Armadillos have two outs, one run, and one guy on first. Conner fouls two balls right away. Jeffrey goes into critiquing mode, showing him how to swing from the mound.

I watch Bradley, who has taken an annoyed stance. His radio buzzes. Something about a suspicious person at the Pig. He calls time and lifts his mask.

"Sheriff Bradley Manning, repeat the Pig report, please."

"Suspicious individual parked an RV behind the Piggly Wiggly in Moonshine County."

He rolls his eyes. "Ten-four, out of my jurisdiction." Bradley lowers his mask and yells, "Play ball!"

I'd like to think that mistaken call was God smiling on us, because it took up enough time to rattle Conner. He swings at a terrible ball the next time.

"You got two on you. Buckle down, load up, big grip, and let 'er rip." Jeffrey might as well read aloud a book of annoying dad advice for baseball.

Morgan snorts beside me.

Conner nails the last ball. I squat down and close my eyes to shield myself from the opposing team's cheers. Instead, I only hear Jeffrey's voice. "Run, crazy boy, run!"

I blink one eye open to Conner staring at the bat in his hand. Or half a bat. The top end is at Bradley's feet. He literally "let 'er rip" and broke a bat.

He's in such shock that our team has enough time to field the ball to Andrew, who tags Conner before he even takes a step. Andrew then stands on home to intimidate the other kid running, even though Conner was a clear third out.

Bradley raises his hands and calls, "Ball game."

Everyone on our side cheers, and the dugout goes crazy. I'm pretty sure someone spilled Gatorade in my hair, but I don't care. Our kids run off the field, and Timothy dives in my arms.

Bradley grins at Morgan and me. "Don't get too excited, we start the championship game in ten minutes. You can stay where you are, but Gray Armadillos are home team next."

Morgan smiles back tiredly and lifts her left arm. Unfortunately, her right arm is already immersed in a cooler. Not good at all.

Nate

I turn into the park on two wheels. I started driving nonstop as soon as I could leave Atlanta.

We negotiated my official retirement. On top of all the rushing around, between last night's win and thinking about the next chapter of my life, I couldn't sleep. I'll crash eventually, but right now I'm running on the adrenaline of getting to Brooke and Timothy.

My truck jerks when I slam it in park. I cut the engine and jog to the entrance. I have my five dollars ready to enter as quickly as possible and can barely stand still long enough for the teenage girl to attach my armband.

The 8U field is visible from where I stand, and I find Brooke at first base. Oddly enough, Carlton is pitching. That can't be good.

I hurry down the hill and find Morgan sitting in the dugout with her elbow on ice.

"What happened?"

She perks up. "Hey, stranger. Just joint crap that acts up. I hope to get back in there soon."

I nod. Precious comes up to bat. Carlton throws her two balls that are semi-decent. She doesn't swing. He tells her to swing at the rest.

She hits a dribbler that's a foul. Tami yells from behind us for her to "kill it." I shake my head at her voice ringing in my ear.

Annoying as that is, it must work, because she slams the ball . . . right into Carlton. I seethe in sympathy as he grabs his crotch and buckles at the waist. Bradley calls time and helps him off the field.

Good thing he owns a pharmacy. He will need more than ice for that. Bradley settles him on the bleachers, and Georgia rushes to his side with a bottle of water.

Bradley sticks his head in the dugout. "Morgan, you've got a few minutes to figure out a new pitcher. Any parent will do, but we can't delay the game too much longer. People are getting antsy, and I don't want to have to arrest anyone today."

She nods and sighs. Bradley returns to the field, and Morgan stands. Her elbow is swelling, and she grits her teeth.

"Morgan, you can't pitch." I put a hand on her shoulder to halt her.

She laughs. "So we're left with Easton? I can't let Aniston or Brooke do it."

Enough of this. Brooke may kill me later, but I have a chance to save the game and get out everything I've been wanting to say all at once. Rip the Band-Aid.

I march to the pitcher's mound and stare at Bradley. "I'll pitch!"

Several people start to cheer. He waves a hand to shush them. Bubba stops midway from walking on the field.

"You can't pitch. We need a parent," Bradley answers.

Bubba nods at him and holds up the rule book. He returns to the dugout, satisfied.

"Then I qualify, because I'm Timothy's dad."

It's so quiet, I can hear a ball hit from the cages across the park. People stare and whisper. Brooke's face goes pale. She comes from first base in slow motion, gawking at me like I have three heads.

"Brooke, I'm sorry. I know we said we'd announce this together at the proper time, but I can't let this team down. I can't let you down anymore, or Timothy."

I turn to Timothy, who's up to bat, blinking with confusion.

"Son, I'm sorry. I didn't know until recently."

I turn back to Brooke. She's now at my side. "When did you get here?" she asks.

I half grin. That isn't the first thing I expected her to say.

"Just now. I wanted to come earlier, but I had to turn in my retirement letter first."

"What?" Bradley yells. "Dude, you were on fire last night!"

"None of your business." I narrow my eyes at him.

He lifts his palms and takes a step back.

I retrieve a ball from the pocket of my hoodie.

"This is the ball I wrote on last night before I took myself out of the game." I get down on one knee. Brooke covers her mouth and tears up. "I don't have a ring yet, but I thought this could be a placeholder."

"Wait!" Timothy yells from the plate.

My heart stops. Should I have okay'd this with him first? My chest pulses as I watch him hurry to the dugout. He returns with the ugly pink ring they won in a tournament. He hands it to me. "Use this."

I take it from him and study his face. With me on one knee, we're eye to eye. He looks happy. At least I hope.

"Are you okay with this? With me marrying your mom and being your dad?"

He lunges toward me and gives me the tightest hug ever. I hug him back, and everyone cheers.

"I wanted it to be you," he whispers.

"Me too." I kiss his cheek, then stand.

"Since I now have a ring, you can have this." I toss him the ball.

"I'm through. For Love of the Game," Timothy reads.

"That's from his favorite movie," Brooke says.

"It's what I say is my favorite movie in interviews." I wink at Timothy. "It's really *Sandlot*."

He laughs. "Mine too."

I raise a brow at Brooke and hold up the ring. "What do you say?"

"I thought you'd never ask."

I put the thing on her finger, then stand and dip her for a kiss. She laughs and wraps her arms around me. Everyone claps as we kiss. I hear a blubbering noise nearby and look up to Bubba ugly crying. I quickly look away when he pulls up his shirt to wipe his face.

"Oh, come on! What is this, *Never Been Kissed*? Let's play ball," Jeffrey snarks.

Morgan whistles and we all come to attention.

"Thank you." Bradley salutes her. "Congratulations to the Millers. Now let's play some ball!" He lowers his mask and squats behind the plate.

Timothy tosses Morgan the ball. She catches it and makes a slightly pained face. He waits until she puts it in his bag, then takes his place as next batter.

I pitch my first non-professional game since high school, and I love every minute of it.

We defeat Jeffrey's team ten to one. His son scored their only run, which hopefully shielded him from Jeffrey's wrath.

Bradley lines everyone up and presents fake gold rings and medals. Brooke stands beside me, proudly wearing the even uglier pink ring. First thing on my to-do list now that Little League is over: buy my fiancée a ring like she deserves.

EPILOGUE

Nate

A lot has happened in a short amount of time.

I gained a son and a fiancée, and announced my retirement from baseball. Timothy gets out of school soon, and I'm pumped to take him to some Braves games and show him around the stadium.

But first, I have a surprise to deliver.

For the first time on a trip back from Atlanta, where I've been wrapping things up, I stopped somewhere besides Bucee's. Although many claim that place has everything, they don't have diamond rings.

I went to a jeweler downtown and picked out the most beautiful, shiny diamond I could find. The saleswoman wrapped it in a tiny box with a perfectly tied red ribbon on top.

It's currently taking up residence on my dash. Every time I glance that way, I can't wait to give it to Brooke.

I never intended to propose without a ring, but I couldn't

wait. Once I announced Timothy as my son, then my retirement, I continued with the confession vomit and proposed. Thankfully, it all worked out, since I didn't want to waste another ten years—or ten minutes—without Brooke in my life forever.

The sign for the orchard comes into view, and I sit straighter in my seat. Gravel crunches under my truck as I pass my house and drive to Brooke's.

A large balloon arch stretches over the entrance to their farm. The top of my truck scrapes the center. I wince as red circles bounce behind me in the road. I'll have to answer to Morgan later.

I park behind the Millers' bigger house, where cars line the drive going to Brooke's carriage house. Morgan and Aniston stand beside a sign with "Congratulations, Gray Armadillos" in a happy font.

The ring box shines in the sunlight on my dash. I start to put it in my pocket, then decide it's too bulky. I rip off the ribbon and dig out the ring. It fits nicely in the corner of my jeans pocket, making it easier to keep my surprise.

"That's too close to the house," Aniston says when I get out.

"It's the only branch tall enough." Morgan points to the tree beside them.

I step toward them. "What's going on?"

Both women turn to me and sigh. Aniston holds high what looks an awful lot like a papier-mâché armadillo. I frown.

"It's a piñata," Morgan offers.

"Give it here." I take the pathetic-looking creature and cross the yard.

Morgan and Aniston follow me in silence. Brooke's brothers' old basketball goal stands at the edge of the yard away from the cars. There's no net and the pole is rusted, so nobody pays it much attention. I hold the end of the rope and toss the armadillo over the hoop, then secure the rope with a knot.

Morgan claps. I turn and smile. "You're welcome. Where's Brooke?"

Aniston laughs. "Getting the cake ready."

"What's so funny?"

Morgan and Aniston exchange a look. I head toward the kitchen, running into Timothy on the way.

"Daddy!" He leaps, and I catch him.

I never get tired of hearing him call me that.

"Hey, buddy." I wrap him in a huge hug, then let him loose.

"You made it before the party."

"Yeah, I did."

"Reece said he's bringing stuff over to teach us all Quidditch."

"Did he now?" I blink and make a mental note to offer up a kickball game instead. "Come with me a minute."

We continue to the kitchen. Andrew dashes down the porch, slamming the screen door. I catch it on a bounce and go inside.

"Brooke?"

She turns and smiles widely. We meet halfway in the kitchen. I wrap her in a giant hug and give her a quick kiss since her mom and several kids are rambling in the house.

"How's your day been?"

"Good." She nods behind her. "Just trying to make the best of our cake."

"Yeah, Morgan and Aniston mentioned something about the cake."

She breaks from me and takes my hand. We go to the counter. I stare at a huge iced armadillo.

"Wow."

"Yeah." She sighs. "All the local bakers were booked up or out of town, so we had to use the nearest Walmart bakery. I asked for a cake with "Gray Armadillos" in gray icing. I meant a sheet cake . . . not an actual armadillo."

"Very *Steel Magnolias*."

She laughs.

"Well, I can't do much about that, but I do have something that should brighten your day."

"Coffee?" She smirks.

Instead of answering, I dig my hand in my pocket and get on one knee. Brooke's hands go to her mouth as I pull out the ring. It shines in the sunlight beaming through the window. Timothy laughs happily behind us.

"This is the ring I wanted to propose with, the ring you deserve."

I take her left hand and slide the ring up her finger. She smiles down at it, then up at me. "Nate, it's gorgeous, and it fits perfectly."

"I took a chance that your hand was the same size as when we got class rings."

She laughs through a few tears. I stand and take her hands in mine. She leans against me, and we hug.

"What's—" Her mom's words turn to a gasp when Brooke holds out her hand. "Nate, that's so pretty."

"Thanks. I hate I didn't have this when I proposed." I give Brooke a squeeze. "I didn't want to wait."

"This calls for a celebration." Mrs. Margaret rummages in her kitchen junk drawer and finds a marker.

She hurries out of the house. I kiss Brooke, then we both hug Timothy. People start gathering in the backyard.

"I guess it's party time," I suggest.

"Yeah, a lot to celebrate." Brooke smiles and leads me outside.

Her mom stands by the banner, beaming. Underneath the "Congratulations, Gray Armadillos," she wrote, "And Nate and Brooke!"

We all laugh.

"What's going on?" Georgia asks.

Brooke shows her the ring. More people come to see it and shake my hand.

Morgan comes out with the ugly cake and sets it on a picnic table. She whistles, and the kids come running. "If it's okay with y'all, I think Coach Nate needs the first piece." She wiggles her eyebrows at me.

We've already had a few discussions about me coaching next year, as well as running against Jeffrey for park president.

She stabs the armadillo's tail with a cake server and cuts out a square piece. It's red velvet inside. Angel screams, and the rest of us laugh. Very *Steel Magnolias* indeed.

I take a bite and nod. "Tastes better than it looks."

"Maybe that can be your groom's cake," Brooke teases.

"As long as you're the bride, it doesn't matter." I shove the remaining piece in her face.

She licks her lips and laughs, then wipes some cake back on me.

"Food fight!" Charlie screams.

And that's all it takes for the kids to engage in a full-on armadillo cake war. Morgan joins us, then Easton. I hug Brooke close, shielding her from flying sugar. We laugh until my throat hurts.

This is not what I planned on happening. But I've learned that life is more fun when we can't predict it. I've already gotten the only thing I ever really wanted: life with Brooke.

Whatever else happens is just icing on the cake.

Want to know what Elijah said to Morgan at the ballpark? Sign up for Kaci Lane's newsletter and get a free bonus epilogue from Morgan's POV.

ACKNOWLEDGMENTS

First, I'd like to thank God for giving me creative ideas and placing the right people in my path to help see them to fruition.

My husband, Blake, gets credit next for always supporting my writing endeavors, even if he finds my stories a little too "girly and Hallmarkish." Of course, this book kind of broke the mold when it comes to that.

My husband and son also get credit on this particular book for helping me with random baseball questions and terminology.

I also want to thank my readers and ARC team for their support. It means the world to me that busy people would give of their time to read early, post reviews, and share the news of my books with their friends. I couldn't do this without y'all!

As always, I'd like to thank my editor, Joanne, and my proofreader, Charity. Both of these ladies are huge help to making my books shine! They get an extra shoutout this month: Joanne went above and beyond with the baseball research, and Charity helped me beat a tight deadline. I love and appreciate you both more than you will know!

BOOKS BY KACI LANE

For exclusive deals, check out kacilanebooks.com.

Single Southern Mamas Series*

Mom Squad

Mom Ball (Coming Summer 2024)

Mom Bod (Pub date TBD)

Bama Boys Series*

Hunting for Love

Chicken about Love

Hammered by Love

Cutting out Love

Geared for Love

Guilty of Love (Pub date TBD)

Apple Cart County Christmas*

Christmas in Dixie

Crazy Rich Rednecks

Queen of My Double-Wide Trailer

*New Christmas Novella coming soon

Schooled on Love Series

Taco Truck Takedown

Side Hustle

Buggy List

Off-Season

Books in Shared Series with Other Authors

The Coffee Loft

No Time for Traditions

A Perfect Match in Silver Leaf Falls

*If you enjoyed spending time in Apple Cart County, revisit your favorite Southern community with these series. Check them out on my website.

www.ingramcontent.com/pod-product-compliance
Lightning Source LLC
LaVergne TN
LVHW041748060526
838201LV00046B/949